THE MURDER OF MRS CHADWICK

This book is entirely a work of fiction. The names, characters, and incidents portrayed in it are entirely a work of fiction. Any resemblance to actual persons, living or dead, is entirely coincidental.

Copyright© 2025 Caroline Blake

All Rights Reserved
No part of this book may be reproduced in any form,
by photocopying or by any
electronic or mechanical means,
including information storage or retrieval systems,
without permission in writing from both the copyright owner
and the publisher of this book.

First published April 2025

Instagram @caroline.blake.author

www.carolinemelodyblake.co.uk

"There is nothing I wouldn't do for those who are really my friends. I've no notion of loving people by halves, it isn't my nature."

— **Jane Austen**

Other Books by Caroline Blake

Just Breathe

Forever Hold Your Peace

Unexpected Storm

The Brief

An Unfortunate Situation

Thursday, 7th October 1976

Jack

Jack Chadwick has been in the police station interview room for more than an hour. He watches the hands on the wall clock count down the passing minutes unbearably slowly. He asks Detective Inspector Holt when he will be able to go home. He needs some air. He needs some sleep.

Call me Elena, she says with a smile. He has never met a woman policeman before. She seems kind and Jack wonders whether she has been trained on when to show compassion, or does it come naturally to her? So far, her smile has never faltered, even on the journey from the house to the police station, when she twisted around in the front seat of the car and told him he would have to stay somewhere else tonight, she continued to smile. She felt sorry for him, he could tell. As he peered out of the back passenger window of the blue and white Ford Cortina, his breath steaming the glass, he wanted to ask her to stop the car. He needed to run back into the house and tell them to be careful. His train set is delicate; some of the pieces are quite expensive. They shouldn't knock the table, otherwise the signal office will dismantle. He hadn't had time to glue it properly this afternoon, and the house was so busy. There were people everywhere. But Detective Inspector Holt had interrupted his thoughts. It's unlikely that the forensic team will be finished this side of midnight, she had said. She could arrange a hotel room, or he could stay at a relative's house? She posed it as a question, although she knew Jack didn't have any other family. He had already told her that.

Now, Elena assures him that they are almost finished. Just a few more questions. Jack sighs and leans back in the vinyl armchair, the colour of rust and decay, resting his head on the back cushion.

Elena tells him that his tiredness is probably caused by the trauma. It's his body's natural response. But if he wouldn't mind answering a few more questions, it will help them to catch his mother's killer. Jack flinches at her choice of language. *Killer.* His eyebrows come together in a frown. He wants to tell her he can't take much more. It is almost ten o'clock. He is always in bed by now, and he hasn't eaten for hours, since he made himself a snack this afternoon, a couple of cream crackers and a slice of cheese. It's important that he eats regularly, otherwise he has trouble thinking properly.

He tells the inspector he has never seen a dead body before. His mother's is the first, and she agrees that would be a traumatic experience for any person.

Elena is particularly interested in Jack's relationship with his mother. Did he love her? Did she love him? Didn't he find it difficult still living at home when he was, how old? Twenty-nine years? Jack can't fathom why these questions are important. What relevance do they have? But he assures the inspector that yes, he was very happy, and, no, the thought of leaving home had never occurred to him. They looked after each other, him and his mother. Why would he want to live anywhere else?

Until now. Now, she is gone, and now he doesn't have anyone to look after, or to look after him.

Jack tells the inspector that he can't believe she has

gone, as he sobs into his hands. She tells him to take his time, and Jack sips more stewed tea from a tired brown mug. He runs his fingers over the chip on the rim and the crack that meanders from the handle down to the bottom. He wants to point it out to the inspector and warn her of the dangers of hot tea. The mug could break at any moment and scald him.

His mother would have told her. His mother would never drink tea from a chipped mug, and she wouldn't have put up with stewed tea, either. She would have asked for a fresh one. She would have pushed it back across the table with derision and refused to speak until a 'proper brew' was made. She liked things to be 'just so'. Each night, as she dragged her tired feet along the path to their front door, Jack would dash into the kitchen and put the kettle back on the stove. By the time his mother had shrugged off her coat, kicked off her shoes, and hung her handbag on the hook at the bottom of the stairs, the pot of tea was waiting for her, fresh and perfectly brewed. A silent gesture of her son's enduring devotion.

'You're not stewing my tea, are you?' she would inevitably complain.

'No, Mum,' Jack would answer, as she inspected the tea, peering into the pot as though it contained the secret to life itself. 'It's just how you like it.'

Elena asks Jack where he was all afternoon. Jack tells her he was at home, as usual, except for the time he went to the corner shop. He has already explained this to the officer who attended at the house, how he had returned from the shop and dropped the cigarettes his mother had asked him to buy on the floor when he fell to his knees to check whether his mother was still breathing. He is pretty sure that she wasn't. She was a strange colour and very still. He admits he had moved her, in order to check. He apologises, saying he knows he shouldn't have done. The police officer, the one in uniform who came to the house, told him that you shouldn't disturb a crime scene. But at the time, he didn't know, and he wasn't thinking straight. It was such a shock, he says, to find his mother on the floor like that.

Jack watches Elena whisper something into the ear of her colleague, who promptly leaves the room. No doubt they will be checking his story about the corner shop. Jack is sure the woman behind the counter can vouch for the fact that he has been in there. Less than two hours ago. It feels like a lifetime ago.

'She's off to Spain in a couple of weeks, Angela and that live-in boyfriend of hers,' his mother had told him earlier. They were in the kitchen, standing near the stove. She had taken her cup of tea from Jack with one hand and picked up the saucepan lid with the other. 'What's in there?'

'It's potato hash,' he replied. 'We had some corned beef that needed using up.'

Mrs Chadwick dropped the lid onto the saucepan. 'You stupid boy. I was going to have that on my sandwich tomorrow. What am I going to have now?' Without waiting for a response, she marched into the living room, tea splashing from her cup onto the saucer with each pound of her heavy feet. 'You've over-filled it again, stupid boy. Here.' Jack followed her into the living room, taking the tea from her outstretched hand. 'Tip a bit down the sink.'

Jack did as he was told, while wondering how many times a day she called him a stupid boy. He returned the cup to her when she was settled on the sofa, and pushed the footstool towards her legs. He lifted one of her legs, and then the other leg, onto the footstool. He plumped a cushion and placed it under the arm holding the cup, and then stood back waiting for her to tell him that she was comfortable.

'Whereabouts in Spain?' he asked. Knowing that his mother loved to talk about the people she cleaned for, he thought a chat about Angela Bennett's future travels would snap her out of this grouchy mood.

Last week, his mother had arrived home with tales of the exciting and exotic food Angela had bought from the new grocers in Wellington – they called it a delicatessen - avocado pears all the way from Mexico, kiwi fruit, prawns, and oil made from olives in Italy that his mother had the pleasure of putting away for her, as Angela had chatted excitedly about what meal she was planning to make for her dinner party, and the show she was going to watch at the theatre next month in Manchester. His mother had enjoyed listening, stealing away little snippets as though they were golden coins to pay for future opportunities to gossip.

But Angela now seems to be out of favour and her planned trip had touched a nerve, for some reason, and had made her angry.

'I didn't ask,' she said. 'She wanted me to, but I told myself, no, I'm not pandering to her.'

'Quite right,' agreed Jack. He hoped that he was saying the right thing. Agreeing with his mother was his usual appeasing course of action.

'She stood leaning against the worktop, getting in my way when she could see me trying to clean the kitchen, flicking through her magazine, pointing out this, that, and the bloody other that she wants to buy. Her wardrobe is already fit to bursting. I thought to myself, you don't need a new outfit for every day, do you? I don't care how many stars the hotel has got. You're just showing off, telling me you want to buy all them things just to make a point. She was doing it to annoy me. As per usual.'

His mother continued to complain about Angela. Jack tried to keep listening. He didn't think Angela was a particularly annoying person, but maybe she was sometimes. He simply agreed with his mother. The sooner he could pacify her, the sooner they could begin to enjoy their evening together.

'You know where she was off to yesterday afternoon?' his mother had asked. Jack shook his head. 'Having lunch in Wellington, again. There's something going on there. She's probably got another man stashed away somewhere, you mark my words. She had painted her nails bright red. You know that kind of woman has red nails, don't you?' His mother held out her hand and inspected her own short nails, at the end of dry, cracked fingers. 'What are you looking at?' she shouted.

'Nothing, Mum,' said Jack.

'We can't all be born a princess, you know. Some of us can't afford to put nail varnish on, just for it to chip the next day. We have to work for a living.'

'We can go to Spain,' Jack had said to his mother. He wanted to distract her attention away from her fingernails, to calm the storm of anger. 'One day, when I get a job, we can go away. You'd like Spain, wouldn't you?'

'Who's going to employ you? Look at the state of you. When was the last time you put on a clean shirt?' said his mother.

Jack, perched on the edge of the sofa next to his mother,

looked down at his shirt. 'This was clean on this morning,' he said, pulling it away from his body and inspecting it.

'Liar! Stop lying to me!' his mother shrieked. She pushed him away from her and lifted the cushion under her arm. 'And where did you put my library book?'

'I don't know, Mum,' said Jack. He jumped up, lifting the rest of the cushions in turn. 'It's not here. I don't…'

'I'll find it myself, you stupid boy,' she shouted. 'Get out of my way.' She batted him away with the back of her hand.

'I can't think when you shout, Mum.' Jack put his hands over his ears and scrunched his eyes closed.

'I'm not shouting,' she had said. She was. 'Now, go and check on that potato hash. You're not burning it, are you?'

'No, Mum,' said Jack. He lowered his arms and trundled off to the kitchen. Why did his mum have to ruin his mood? Every day was the same. Every day she grumbled and moaned and picked at him, as though it was his fault that she was miserable. All he did was try to make her life as comfortable as possible. He cleaned the house, cooked her food, and washed all the clothes. The only thing he didn't do was work. But one day he would. One day he would get a job that would pay enough to take them on holiday. Maybe to Spain. Maybe somewhere else. Anywhere she wanted to go.

The inspector is still looking at him. She asks him again to recount his afternoon. She tells him to take his time. She has already asked him so many questions, one after the other. How many more can there be? He wants to go home. The walls of the police station interview room, the colour of weathered bricks, are giving him a headache.

He doesn't want to admit that he and his mother had a falling out. It doesn't seem right now, besmirching her memory. Not now she isn't here to tell her side of the story. He bites his bottom lip. He doesn't want to tell the police that his mother was grumpy every day and that her face wore a persistent deep frown. Jack can't remember the last time he saw her smile.

Elena asks Jack if he is ready to continue. Jack's eyes flick once more to the wall clock. Is this almost over?

Angela

Angela Bennett's blood-red Porsche 911 skids around the corner into Southgate Drive and comes to a sudden stop under the shelter of a large oak tree. The old roots push their way through the concrete flags of the narrow residential pavement where two of the Porsche's wheels now rest. The last of the autumn leaves, bending under the pressure of the recent rainfall, plummet down onto the roof of the car.

Through the windscreen, Angela watches the police activity at number eight, Miriam Chadwick's house. Blue flashes from the parked police car at the bottom of the footpath spin around the dimly lit cul-de-sac, mixing with the amber light from the open front door as it spills out onto the front step. An officious-looking uniformed policeman, chin held high, back straight, stands guard, feet hip distance apart, ready to glare at any inquisitive neighbour who dares to peer out from behind half-drawn curtains.

A sharp siren wail introduces another police vehicle as it pulls into the cul-de-sac and stops across the road from the first one. She watches two police officers jump out and hurry to Mrs Chadwick's house. A middle-aged plain-clothes policeman appears at the front door, hands thrust into the pocket of his trousers. He steps onto the path, where he waits for his colleagues to approach him. Angela recognises Detective Sergeant Miller. She would know his bald head and protruding stomach anywhere. She knows all of the detectives from Wellington Police Station. There isn't a single one who hasn't given her house or shop a visit at one time or another. Angela watches them talk. Presumably, DS Miller is giving the newcomers a synopsis of the events, as far as they know. The new arrivals nod as they listen, their heads bobbing up and down. Eventually, they follow the detective to the front door, before wading into the house.

Angela reverses her car out of the cul-de-sac and drives off. If she was religious, she would pray that DS Miller has not spotted her car.

Jack

Elena tells Jack that the next-door neighbour thought she heard shouting. Was there any shouting? Were he and his mother arguing? Every day, he thinks. Every single day. But Jack explains that they were having a discussion, him and his mother, that's all. It may have seemed loud because he was in the kitchen, checking on the potato hash, and his mother was in the living room, and her hearing isn't what it used to be. He has told her on countless occasions that she should get it checked.

She gets tired after her day at work, he tells the inspector. He couldn't have expected her to follow him into the kitchen, not when she has been on her feet all day. That wouldn't be fair, would it? The inspector shakes her head and tells him to carry on. What happened next?

Jack wonders exactly what the neighbour has heard. He knows it is Eve from next door, although Elena doesn't tell him her name. She is always listening to them. Jack can tell when she has heard something because she smiles at him with pity and concern the next time she sees him. Had she heard the tirade from his mother about how she had to spend all day scrubbing other people's houses, only to come home and have to do more work because of her bone-idle, good-for-nothing, stupid-as-dog-shit son? He doesn't want to ask.

As Elena gets ready to scribble in her notebook with a chewed pencil, Jack bends forward and rests his head on his folded arms. He is going to be sick. He manages to mumble that he is all right, he just needs a minute, but Elena opens the door of the interview room and dispatches someone to the police station kitchen in any event, with instructions to get him a glass of water. As though a cold drink can erase the memory that will be indelibly etched in his mind. The picture of his dead mother lying on the kitchen floor, a puddle of congealed blood around her head, is something that cannot be unseen.

He has to be careful now, to pause before he says anything else. He doesn't want to be unkind to his poor mother's memory. He remembers her testing the potato hash, leaning over the steaming pan with a spoon in her hand and a distasteful look on her face.

'It's a bit thick, that. Put some more stock in.' His

mother had thrown the spoon towards the sink, but it had missed and landed on the floor. Thick splodges of gravy littered the floor tiles.

'I think it's all right, Mum,' he had said.

'You what?'

Jack realised too late what he had said. His mother punched him on the arm with her fist. It didn't hurt, but he instinctively took a step back, clutching his arm.

So, tell me again what time you got home from the shop? Elena is smiling at him, waiting with seemingly endless patience for him to reply. Jack says that he can't remember exactly. A minute or so before he ran rang 999. The telephone box is just down the road and across the square. He ran to it as quickly as he could. It was probably around six o'clock.

Jack has already told her that his mother had arrived home from her job just before four, as she always did. Nevertheless, Elena asks him to confirm that this incident must have occurred in the two-hour period between four and six. That's right, isn't it? Jack nods. He links his fingers together and wraps them around his left knee, to stop himself from fidgeting.

You went to Robertson's grocers, a ten-minute walk away? Yes, that's right, approximately, maybe less. Jack waits for the inspector to do her mental calculations. Before she asks him another question, he tells her that he didn't go home immediately. He fancied a walk around the village. He hadn't been out all day, and he knew his mother wouldn't mind. They can't see the pond and the village green from their house and he wanted to see the ducks.

He dabs at his tears with the sleeve of his shirt. It is obvious that the killer was watching the house, he suggests.

Maybe he pounced the minute he saw me leave.

Elena agrees it is a possibility. But the question is, who would want to do that? In her whole career, there has never been a murder in Eldenbridge, it is such a quiet and peaceful village, and being murdered by a stranger, well it doesn't bear thinking about.

Jack had thought about nothing else on the ride from his house to the police station. He is well aware from what he has read in the newspaper that a large percentage of murders are committed by people known to the victim. Wives are murdered by their husbands. Children are murdered by their parents. Mothers are murdered by their sons. He had an inkling that he would be at the top of the police's Most Wanted list. As he peered out of the window at the back of the police car, the thought had sent a shiver of excitement down his spine.

He tells Elena that he doesn't want to do her job for her, but she will no doubt discover that his mother has no enemies. Nor does she have any friends. She isn't even a member of a book group or a member of the Women's Institute. No, his mother's murder had to be a result of a burglary gone wrong. An opportune crime carried out by some crazy individual intent on stealing a couple of bob. It must have been a burglar, he tells the inspector, what other explanation can there be? A random passer-by who maybe saw him leave the house and took the opportunity to sneak in. You hear of gangs of boys coming in from Wellington, don't you? They get the bus and then walk into the village, usually at night when it's dark, peeping into windows and trying door handles to see whether any of them have been left unlocked. Skinheads, they call them.

Elena stares at him for longer than is comfortable. He

wonders whether she has already considered his suggested hypothesis. She flicks through her notepad, lifting the pages with the sharp end of her pencil. He is tempted to fill the silence but doesn't. Eventually, she asks him again whether anything was stolen.

Well, as far as he could tell, nothing was stolen, he tells her. He didn't go upstairs and search his mother's jewellry box. He was too busy trying to see if she was breathing. Then he ran outside immediately to ring the police. When did she think he had time to search for missing stuff? Nobody had asked him to check. Why didn't they ask him?

Please try and stay calm, the inspector says, holding up her hands as though in surrender. She tells him she can appreciate that he finds himself in an extremely stressful situation, but shouting won't make it any easier.

He knows he is failing to control his agitation. He presses down on his bouncing leg with one hand and clasps the other over his mouth to stop more unwanted words from escaping. Stay calm, stay calm, he repeats to himself. Although, that is easier said than done. He is beginning to realise that being on the top of the Most Wanted list isn't particularly appealing. He wants to come off it.

Elena is eyeing him warily, one eyebrow raised. He wipes a sweaty palm on his jeans. He tells her he wouldn't have chosen this pair, given the choice. They are old and a little big around the waist, but the alternative was his Sunday best suit and it felt odd wearing that on a Thursday. The young police constable who arrived first had felt sorry for him and had fetched him some clothes from his wardrobe when he had been asked to take off the ones he had been wearing. He was a nice lad, only young, probably new to the job. He had seen his eyes glistening with tears as he poked his head into the kitchen and took in the devastating scene. Probably his first murder case.

There was blood everywhere, he tells Elena. Before the police arrived, he had thrown himself onto his mother and hugged her lifeless body. He had also thrown his arms around the unsuspecting police constable as he opened the front door and had cried onto his shoulder. Despite everything, he is going to miss his mother. He can't imagine what his life will be like without her.

There is a knock on the door and the other detective returns to the interview room. Elena looks noticeably relieved that they are no longer alone, and Jack admonishes himself for losing his cool. He wonders whether to apologise but decides not to.

DC Harry Beckford, a big bear of a man, sits next to the inspector, across the table from Jack. He is wearing a cream suit, complete with a matching waistcoat. He smiles at Jack in the way a cartoon fox would smile at a frightened hen, moments before he pounces on it and tears it to pieces. He tells Elena that the woman working at the shop on Croft Street has been spoken to by a uniformed officer. She knows Jack and she remembers him going in there tonight at approximately four-forty, and purchasing a packet of twenty cigarettes.

Neither of the officers speak for a moment. Elena shows her colleague the scribbled notes in her notepad. DC Beckford sits back in his chair. He places the ankle of his right leg onto his left knee. Jack studies the detective's bright red and yellow tartan socks, at odds with his plain suit and white wide-collared shirt. What is puzzling, Jack, says DC Beckford, as he strokes what looks like an expensive silk tie, is the fact that there doesn't seem to be a sign of a break-in. Jack tells them that the front door wasn't locked. It very rarely is. Until bedtime, of course.

DC Beckford confirms that uniformed officers are still carrying out house-to-house enquiries, but from what they gathered so far, none of the neighbours have reported anything suspicious. Jack shrugs. What can he say?

Elena wants to know about his mother's work.

Jack is glad she is back asking the questions. He doesn't like the other detective. Not one bit. She's a cleaner, he tells her. Well, she *was* a cleaner. He can feel tears pricking the back of his eyes again and he wonders whether to blink them away or let them fall. He doesn't want to appear weak in front of DC Beckford's machismo. But it is all too much. The whole thing is too much. Unwanted images flash through his mind. His mother's outstretched arm as she lay on the floor. And the blood. So much blood.

Elena passes him a tissue from the box in the middle of the table. Clearly, this is a room where people are expected to cry. The Victim Suite, they call it.

Jack takes the tissue and wipes his eyes. He tells the detective that his mother had worked for three different people; the vicar of St. Mary's Church; a lady called Claire, and a woman called Angela. He has never met Angela or Claire, he tells her earnestly, but of course, he knows the vicar.

Every Tuesday and Friday his mother cleaned St. Mary's Church and the vicarage, he says. It's an old Victorian property with threadbare carpets, feather-filled leather sofas, and dark wooden furniture. Reverend Adam Hargreaves lives with his wife and two young sons. Jack has been there a number of times when the vicar and his wife have hosted summer barbeques and harvest festival get-togethers for the small church congregation. His mother had told him that she loved that house. It smells of furniture polish, old books, and broccoli soup.

On Thursdays, she cleaned at Claire Simons' place. She lives in one of those tall terraced houses, the row next to the new Larchwood Estate. His mother had been there today.

The biggest of them all is the huge detached house, the one near the river, behind ten-foot tall wrought-iron gates owned by Angela Bennett, where she worked Mondays and Wednesdays. There's a lot to do there, says Jack. It's a big place, marble worktops, white leather sofas with tiger-print cushions, and thick shag-pile carpets. Super fashionable, his mother had said. They have a colour television in the living room and another one in the bedroom.

The detectives look at each other. Elena slaps her notepad closed, and declares that will be all for now. Jack breathes a sigh of relief.

Friday, 8th October 1976

Claire

Claire takes a bowlful of porridge from the worktop in the kitchen and sprinkles a teaspoon of sugar into it. 'I wish Helen would wait for me to come down to breakfast before she takes the porridge off the heat,' she grumbles.

Her sister, Sophia, is only half-listening. A large textbook about the Titanic is flattened out on the kitchen table in front of her. Her twenty-month-old daughter, Wendy, is sitting next to her in a high chair, clutching a plastic spoon that she intermittently drums against her bowl.

'I can't think of anything worse than cold porridge,' says Claire.

'Drowning in an icy sea would be worse,' says Sophia. She taps a fingernail on the book, pointing to a photograph of a huge iceberg.

Claire frowns at her as she sits at the square oak table next to the French window looking out into the back garden. 'Don't take me so literally, Sophia. I thought you were on my side about this porridge. When are we going to mention it to her?'

'When we have nothing else to worry about,' says Sophia. 'You know Helen is employed as a nanny, not a housekeeper? She's here to look after Wendy, not to make breakfast. She does it to help, as a favour to us. So be grateful.' Sophia watches her young daughter as she teases another spoonful of porridge into her mouth. Wendy grins at her Auntie Claire across the table. 'Wendy seems to like it,' says Sophia.

'Does she? Or is she just being polite? Don't you remember her first words? Get that disgusting porridge away from me, she said, didn't you, my darling?' Claire leans across the table and blows her niece a kiss. Wendy giggles in return. Sophia smiles at the two of them; her sister and best friend, and her fatherless daughter. Her world.

As soon as Sophia discovered she was pregnant, she broke the news to her boyfriend, hoping he might pop the question. But he told her that, unfortunately, he would have to bring their short relationship to an end. It was a mistake, and he never expected her to get pregnant. He was already married, he told her in a matter-of-fact tone with no consideration for her feelings, and he didn't have any intention of leaving his wife. But he is now forgotten. In the past. Wendy, a delightful, mischievous girl, a whirlwind of toddling steps and uncontrollable curls, is thankfully nothing like him.

'I would have liked to have gone on The Titanic, if I'd been alive then,' says Sophia.

'What do you mean? So you could have perished and died in the Atlantic Ocean? There are other ways to be remembered,' says Claire.

'No, no, of course not,' says Sophia. 'Some passengers survived. But can you imagine setting off on an adventure to the land of the free, back in those days? Starting a new life in another country, without the stupid class system we had here, where poor people were respected for their hard work and paid well.'

'I'm not sure that was the case. Didn't immigrants have a pretty hard time in New York?'

'Now then, good morning to my favourite ladies.' It is Trevor, their lodger. 'And good morning to you, too, Claire.'

He laughs and Sophia and Claire laugh alongside him politely, despite having heard the same joke almost every day since he moved in with them six months ago. They are both fond of him. He's an elderly gentleman, in his late seventies, a widower who moved from Manchester to Lancashire to escape painful memories. His wife was around every corner in his home town, he told them when he applied to be their lodger. She was in every shop, in the church, and in every room of their house. Initially, friends had told him that it was a comfort to be surrounded by his wife's things, her favourite teapot that she refused to use except on Sundays and Christmas Day; the pot dog that sat by the fireplace, its eyes following him around the room; and the half used bottle of perfume on the dressing table in the bedroom that reminded him of her delicious smell. But he didn't find them a comfort at all. Far from it. His grief seemed to be dragged out, the objects shackling it to him, keeping it in place until it seemed like he might never be free of it. And so, he told Sophia and Claire that summer evening over the dining room table, he sold his house and made the decision to move, and when his wife's cousin had told him they were looking for a lodger in Eldenbridge, it seemed perfect.

Sophia and Claire's house was meant to be a temporary measure for Trevor; a stopgap until he found a more suitable residence. Scotland was his final destination. He liked the idea of buying a little cottage in the Highlands, somewhere remote, where he could live with a small dog, a border terrier perhaps, and go for long walks and fill his lungs with fresh mountain air. But he fell in love with Lancashire, and with Eldenbridge in particular, and try as he might, he couldn't find a single reason to leave.

Trevor occupies the two large rooms at the top of the three-storey house. On the right-hand side of the upper staircase is his bedroom and a small bathroom, and on the left, another room is used as a sitting room. His rent includes meals, which Helen makes for all of them five days a week, Monday to Friday.

Initially, Helen was employed simply just to look after Wendy to allow Sophia to return to her writing. With one book sent off to the publishers just a month before Wendy was born, and with the deadline for the next one looming six months later, Sophia needed help. At first, she told herself she could easily write during the times that Wendy slept. Newborn babies slept all day, didn't they? She would have tonnes of time on her hands. But nobody told her about the sleepless nights, the endless washing, the colic-induced crying. After eight weeks of not writing a single word, Sophia cried out for help and Helen arrived, her Guardian Angel, with her soothing voice and calm demeanour.

On her first day, Sophia handed Wendy to Helen gratefully, and as Helen's eyes lit up and she took baby Wendy into her warm, welcoming arms, Sophia took herself back to bed for a snooze. She awoke two hours later to the smell of something delicious wafting up the stairs. What was it? Roasting meat? Sophia jumped out of bed and was met in the kitchen by a smiling Helen, holding a large spoon over their never-before-used roasting dish. Wendy was fast asleep in her pram in the corner of the room.

'I've made you a lamb roast. It just needs a couple more hours on low and the meat will be tender as a baby's bottom,' she said. 'There are potatoes and carrots in this saucepan. They just need half an hour to simmer while your meat rests.' She put the lid back on the saucepan and returned the roasting dish to the oven. 'I noticed you didn't have much in the fridge and I was wondering what you would have for your tea, so I popped down to the butchers and got this bit of lamb for you.'

'We have been eating a lot of toast-based meals recently,' said Sophia, with tears in her eyes. 'Soup and toast, beans and toast, cheese and toast. The variety is endless.'

'Yes, well, you're a working mum now. You need to look after yourself.'

'Thank you so much, how much…'

'Nothing at all,' said Helen. 'It's my pleasure.'

After that, they came to an agreement that Helen would make something for her and Claire every night. Something that could easily be kept warm in the oven, or in a casserole dish, as Claire often worked late and was always hungry when she got home. Sophia made an effort to make sure there were ingredients in the fridge and Helen somehow worked her magic.

Although Sophia couldn't manage without her, nannies don't work for free, so she and Claire decided to decorate the unused rooms at the top of the house so they could take in a lodger, to help pay the bills.

The house is tall and slim like an elegant aristocrat. Sophia and Claire both fell in love with it on the first viewing. As the estate agent pointed out the original features, the ceiling roses, the black and white tiled hallway floor, the sash windows, and Edwardian fireplaces in every room, they had already decided they wanted to buy it. Their wealthy grandmother had recently left them a sizeable inheritance and she would have been over the moon that they chose to spend it on such a beautiful old house. The damp walls, the threadbare carpets, and the roof which would invariably need replacing within the not-too-distant future, did not faze them. They put in an offer and within months, the house was theirs. They continued to live with their parents until the renovations were complete.

On the night they moved in, the two sisters lit the fire and settled into their warm and inviting sitting room, tastefully decorated with Edwardian style dark green wallpaper, with amber and gold sumptuous cushions on two soft brown, leather Chesterfield sofas, and made a toast as they clinked their glasses of orange squash together - Claire refused to drink alcohol if Sophia couldn't have any, that wouldn't be fair.

'To the future,' said Claire.

'Good riddance to married idiots,' said Sophia.

'We were just talking about the Titanic,' Sophia says now to Trevor as he takes a seat at the kitchen table next to Claire.

'What a dreadful tragedy,' he says. 'All those people who lost a loved one.' He shakes his head as he stares at a photograph in Sophia's book. 'Their journey through grief must have been extra hard because it could have been avoided if only they had more lifeboats.'

Sophia reaches across the table and grasps his hand. He gives her a melancholy smile, as he remembers his much-loved wife.

'Sophia said she wishes she had been on the Titanic,' says Claire. 'In a previous life.' She forces her spoon through the nearly-cold porridge, lifts it to her mouth, but then lowers it again and pushes the bowl into the centre of the table. She can't stomach it. Not today.

'Oh, my dear girl,' says Trevor. 'That would have been a very sad state of affairs if you had been. What would have been the reason for you going to America, do you think?'

'I'm not sure exactly,' she says. 'I think I might have been a singer, or some kind of struggling artist, off to make my fortune. Wouldn't it have been wonderful to have an adventure?'

'We began an adventure when we bought this house,' says Claire. 'There aren't many people who get a chance to have two adventures in their lives.'

Sophia can't decide whether she has said something to upset Claire, or whether she got out of the wrong side of her bed this morning. Her mood certainly seemed to have been fixed before she came downstairs.

'I disagree, Claire,' says Trevor. 'One should have as many adventures as one can manage. Life is a wonderful gift, is it not?' He pours tea from the huge blue and white striped teapot into his cup, a gift from Claire and Sophia's mother when they moved in. He adds a splash of milk, stirs it three times, as he always does, taps the spoon on the side of his cup, and winks at Wendy as he takes a sip. 'Where would you like your next adventure to be, Miss Wendy?' he asks.

'The zoo!' she shouts. 'With the lions, raaaa.'

'That's a great choice,' he says. 'Although America sounds like a wonderful place from what I've heard.'

'Well, I like it here,' says Claire. 'Adventures are overrated.'

'I love it here, too,' says Sophia. 'But a girl can have a daydream, can't she?'

Claire shrugs. 'I need to go to work. You can daydream all you like.' She pushes back her chair and leaves the room.

'What is the matter with her this morning?' asks Trevor.

'I have absolutely no idea,' says Sophia.

Elena

'Good morning team.' Detective Inspector Elena Holt enters the investigation room at Wellington Police Station, followed by a cloud of her familiar perfume. It has become her signature. It follows her around like a puppy, persistent and demanding attention. Everyone has seen the bottle of Shalimar by Guerlain which stands on the corner of her desk and is sprayed liberally throughout the day. Anyone who doesn't know the inspector would assume that the blue bottle and sweet floral fragrance were indicative of her femininity. Those who know the truth are aware that the spray is more to cover up the smell of cigarettes than to compliment her personality. The inspector wears flat shoes, black or navy blue wide-legged trousers, and button-down shirts in pale blue or cream, and never wears make-up. Her red hair is cropped short; the once-fiery hues of a setting Mediterranean sun are now somewhat softened and interwoven with streaks of grey. Ordinarily, she wouldn't have been classed as the perfume's target market. More than likely it had been an unwanted Christmas gift, which is now being used as a very expensive room spray.

Her small team consists of DC Rahul Sharma and DC Harry Beckford, who are perched on the edge of a table munching digestive biscuits and drinking tea, ignoring the crumbs littering the floor around their feet.

Standing next to them, WPC Imogen Winters is eagerly awaiting her first case in the Criminal Investigation Department. She has been a uniformed police constable for three years. At her last performance review, she made it known to her sergeant that she would eventually like to join the CID, and the fortunate death of Miriam Chadwick has given her the opportunity she has been waiting for. When Elena asked the patrol sergeant to send the best constable he had over to the CID team, as they needed an extra pair of hands and an enquiring mind, he had no hesitation in recommending Imogen. Her notepad is ready and she jumps up as Elena enters the room, almost standing to attention. She catches Harry's eye and forces herself to soften, as she stares at the blackboard in front of the wall in front of them.

'Gather round everyone,' says Elena. 'Let's summarise the basics. This investigation has been given the name Operation Bulldog.' She grabs a piece of chalk and writes the name of the operation at the top of the blackboard in scrawly capital letters before turning back to her team. 'The death of Miriam Chadwick was reported by telephone by her son, Jack Chadwick, at seven minutes to six yesterday evening. He reported that he had been to the local shop for some cigarettes and had come home to find his mother's body on the floor in the kitchen, surrounded by the contents of a pan of hot potato stew, which seems to have been knocked off the oven in the struggle.'

'Tata ash,' says Harry.

'I beg your pardon?' says Elena.

'Potato hash, boss,' he replies. 'Boiled potatoes, onions, and corned beef in gravy. My mum used to make it with a pastry top when we were kids. Don't tell me you've never had it.'

'It's what poor people eat,' says Imogen, grinning at Harry.

'How utterly disgusting,' says Elena. 'I've never heard of such a thing.' She puts on a false upper-class voice, disguising her strong Lancashire accent. Laughter trickles through the room. 'Now then, gang, back to it. Early indications are that Mrs Chadwick suffered blunt trauma to the head. No murder weapon has yet been found.'

'Was nothing else discovered as a result of the fingertip searches, boss?' asks Harry.

'No, nothing. The dog was out doing his thing for a number of hours and apart from a couple of used condoms and an empty can of lager, nothing of interest was found in the surrounding area.' Detective Inspector Holt waits for her team to digest this information and for the mutterings to die down before she continues. 'The search is continuing this morning. Extra staff have been brought in to help out. They have been out since daybreak. As soon as I hear anything, I'll let you know, of course. Rahul, you have been looking at the timings, haven't you? What can you tell us?'

She holds out the chalk, which Rahul takes from her as he approaches the blackboard. Rahul writes *5.53pm* in the middle of the board. 'This time is not contentious. We know that Jack Chadwick made the 999 call at this time.' He writes *4.40pm* above. 'This is the time that the staff member at Robertsons confirms Jack left the shop. The female member of staff was spoken to last night by uniform, and has confirmed that Chadwick was only in there a minute or so. He walked straight up to the counter, asked for the cigarettes, and left immediately.'

'How can she be so sure of the time?' asks Elena. 'Imogen, do you have her statement over there?'

'Give me a second, ma'am,' says Imogen. She flicks through the pile of papers at the side of her desk. 'Here it is. I've got a witness statement from her and also one from Police Constable Gary Thornton, the officer who spoke to her.' Imogen runs her forefinger down the page. 'This is what she said, "It had been an extremely quiet day, and by late afternoon, I was bored. Only a handful of customers had been in since lunchtime. When Jack Chadwick walked in, I thought he might stay for a chat, as he usually does, but he made it obvious that he did not want to talk. After buying a packet of cigarettes, he left the shop immediately."'

'So we have Jack Chadwick showing unusual behaviour,' says Elena. 'Interesting. Anything useful from the house-to-house enquiries yet? Rahul, have you managed to read through the statements?'

'Yes, boss,' says Rahul. 'The occupants of seven out of the eight houses in the cul-de-sac have been spoken to. Nobody reported seeing anyone either enter or leave number eight, not even Jack Chadwick. Most people were not yet home from work at the time of the murder, but those who were, couldn't help.'

'What about the house that hasn't been spoken to yet?'

'That's number five, the home of Mr and Mrs Gregson, a well-to-do couple. They are away on holiday. They have been gone a week, according to the next-door neighbour, and they have another week left. Costa Blanca.'

'All of the neighbours need to be spoken to again,' says Elena. 'See if anyone remembers seeing any visitors in the days prior to yesterday. Harry, can you and Imogen cover that?'

'Yes, boss,' says Harry.

'So, myself and Harry spoke to Jack Chadwick last night,' says Elena. She takes her notepad from her jacket pocket and opens it with the end of her pencil. 'He seemed genuinely upset, I've got to say. He said that he went to the shop for cigarettes. It's a ten-minute walk away, but he didn't go straight home afterwards. He went for a walk to get some fresh air. He said he found his mother on the floor when he got back and he was of the view that she was already dead, but he checked to see. He said he hugged her and held her body in his arms for a few minutes, and then he ran outside to make the 999 call from the nearest phone box. Police Constable Adebayo was first on the scene.'

'We've got PC Adebayo's statement here, ma'am,' says Imogen, waving a sheet of paper and then returning it to the pile on the desk.

'And what does he say? What were Jack's first words to him?' asks Elena.

'He said that he cried a lot,' says Imogen. She reads through the statement again until she reaches the relevant paragraph. "He threw his arms around me and said 'My mother's dead. I think my mother's dead.' I looked into the kitchen and it was clear that the victim was deceased. I preserved the scene by keeping Jack Chadwick away from the kitchen. I led him to the sofa in the living room while I went upstairs to get him some clean clothes to change into.

I left the clothes he was wearing in the hallway for senior officers to deal with." The clothes have now been sent to the lab, ma'am.'

'So Jack Chadwick was at the shop at four forty. Where did he go after that? What was he doing for more than an hour?' asks Elena. 'Did he really go for a walk after he left the shop, or is he lying to us? If he went straight home from the shop, he would have arrived home at four fifty, which gives him plenty of opportunity to commit a murder. If he went for a walk, where did he go? You can walk around the whole village in less than half an hour.'

'Shall I speak to him again, boss?' asks Harry. He is quietly confident that he can secure a confession. Not that he's a bully. If Jack Chadwick gets intimidated, that's not his fault, is it? As long as the truth comes out, that's the important thing.

'No, it's okay. I've asked him to come in this morning to collect his house keys,' says Elena. 'I'll speak to him. At the moment, we don't have any evidence to arrest him, so he's just a witness and he needs to be treated as such.'

'But boss, didn't you say that, from what you could see last night at the scene, there didn't seem to be any trace of any other footsteps in the house, either going in or coming out?' asks Harry.

'Well, I'm not a forensic expert, but the victim's hallway has a linoleum floor, and the only footprints I could clearly see belonged to PC Adebayo. Jack Chadwick's shoes were lined up very neatly at the bottom of the stairs, with the toes facing the skirting boards, and he doesn't appear to be the type to wear his shoes indoors.'

'Well, bearing in mind the amount of rain we had yesterday and the amount of blood in the kitchen, it leads me to think only one thing. We have already spoken to the guilty man.' Harry nods at Imogen, confirming that, in his view, Jack is guilty, and he has laid out the evidence for all to see. 'Watch and learn, young Imogen, watch and learn,' he says. 'There was no sign of a break-in, and the window of opportunity was extremely small, which points to the murderer being someone close to home.'

'What are your thoughts on Angela Bennett, boss? The victim cleaned for her, didn't she?' says Rahul.

Nobody in the police station likes Angela Bennett. She likes to give the impression that she's an above-board businesswoman, but everyone knows she is shady as Hell and up to her neck in something, although, as yet, nobody has been able to pin anything on her.

'Yes, we'll need to speak to her,' says Elena. 'Just as we will need to speak to everyone Mrs Chadwick knew and had contact with.'

'Angela Bennett is many things, but I don't think she's a murderer,' says Harry. 'I'm telling you, it's him. The son. He is the only one with the means. He tried to suggest that some gang came into the village and that somehow it was a burglary gone wrong.'

'But what about the motive?' asks Rahul. 'Why would he kill his own mother?'

'I don't know, maybe she was a bitch and he hated her. My mother-in-law is a right cow, and if I got the chance…'

Rahul shakes his head. 'I don't think so. Didn't you say he was visibly upset in the interview, and that he sobbed on the constable's shoulder when he first arrived at the scene?'

Harry shrugs. 'Means nothing.'

The door to the Incident Room is thrown open. Detective Sergeant Geoff Miller saunters in, carrying a bag of jam doughnuts. 'Supplies for the troops,' he says. 'Sorry I'm late, boss. I had a trip over to the forensics lab with Jack Chadwick's clothes.'

'Via the cake shop, I see,' says Elena. She peers into the paper bag, takes out a doughnut, and bites into it. Jam oozes from the bottom. She stops the flow with her finger. 'You haven't missed much, we were just talking about the timings from last night. So, what have you got from the forensic team?' She hands DS Miller another stick of chalk and he makes his way over to the blackboard, dropping the bag of doughnuts on the desk behind Rahul and Harry.

'The forensics team arrived at number eight Southgate Drive at six-twenty-one.' He writes the number *6.21pm* on the board. 'When they arrived, I spotted a red Porsche 911 parked on the other side of the road. The headlights were still on, which attracted my attention. I know the car, boss. It's registered to Angela Bennett. As I went inside the house, the car reversed out of the cul-de-sac and drove away.' DS Miller writes the words *Angela Bennett Porsche* on the board next to the time 6.21pm.

'According to Jack Chadwick, Mrs Chadwick worked for Angela Bennett as a cleaner and housekeeper every Monday and Wednesday,' says Elena.

'Why would she be outside Miriam Chadwick's house on a day when she wasn't working for her, on a day which happened to be the day she was murdered?' asked Geoff.

'Well, that's what we need to find out,' says Elena. 'Geoff, go and have words, will you? Bring her in, if necessary.'

'Yes, boss.'

'Harry, I know you suspect Jack Chadwick, but give me your thoughts on his interview. Why do you think he might be guilty of murdering his mother?' asks Elena.

'It just didn't add up, the things he was saying. According to him, she isn't the type of woman to have any enemies, but nor did she seem to have any friends. I find that odd in a village such as Eldenbridge,' says Harry.

'What do you mean, Harry?' asks Elena. 'Tell us what you're thinking.'

'I'm not sure yet, boss' says Harry. 'Call it a gut instinct, but I don't think the son is telling the truth. I can't believe that in such a small community a woman like her didn't have any friends. I don't live there now, but I was born and brought up there and you couldn't fart without someone finding out. It's the kind of place where people say hello to each other in the street, even to strangers. People chat while queuing in the shop, you know the type of place. My parents still lived there until recently. Nobody is lonely.'

'He didn't say she was lonely,' says Elena. 'He just said she didn't have any friends. She worked hard, cleaning five days a week. At her age, she was probably settled in her ways, she had her work, she had her son, and that was it. He said she was happy.'

'Was she happy though?' asks Harry. 'Didn't the next-door neighbour say they were always arguing, her and her son? She heard raised voices on a number of occasions, didn't she?'

'Yes, she did. Okay, well when you speak to her, get as much detail as you can about what she heard through that party wall.'

'Yes, boss,' says Harry.

'Geoff, when you go to speak to Angela Bennett, I want you to call into the Robertson's shop and see what you can get from anyone else who works there. Jack Chadwick told us that his mother used to work for the vicar of St. Mary's Church, a man called Adam Hargreaves, and also Claire Simons. Rahul and Imogen, as you're new to the team you won't know her, but Claire is an ex-policewoman and used to work on this team.'

'And she was a very good detective,' says Geoff, 'for a woman.' Geoff winks at Elena, a small gesture of confirmation that he is joking.

'Yes, she was a very good detective,' says Elena. 'So what she can tell us about the victim will be gold. She still lives in Eldenbridge. I'll go and speak to her and then I'll call in at the vicarage and see Reverend Hargreaves. We will meet here again at five o'clock. Off you go.'

Adam

Reverend Adam Hargreaves likes to have peace and quiet in the mornings, which isn't easy, given the fact that he shares his house with a wife and twin seven-year-old boys who like to begin their day with loud contemporary music. By now, he should have become used to the high energy levels of his young family, but he never has. He has long ago given up trying to convince his wife that a silent breakfast gives the mind the time and space to think, to connect with God, and to prepare for the day. Her attitude is that there will be plenty of time for that when they get old. While they still have the energy to dance and sing, she insists the music should be loud.

He should give thanks for his spirited boys, he knows that. Their love of music, singing, and dancing is a gift, isn't it? Sometimes, when he is feeling generous, he likes to think of his boys as his beautiful little hummingbirds. They have the ability to hover around the fridge, waiting to be fed, then they zip around the house with remarkable speed and agility, from one room to the next. A colourful blur. Their high energy expenditure means they need to be fed frequently.

But today, they are more like young chimpanzees. Argumentative and competitive. Their loud screeches grate on his nerves and no matter how many times he asks them to keep the noise down please - show kindness to one another, brothers should love each other, shouldn't they, especially at the breakfast table - his pleas are ignored. His wife pours milk onto the boys' cereal and raises the volume of her singing as she watches her angels tucking in.

She asks Adam if he wants anything to eat, but today he has no appetite, not after what happened yesterday. His stomach is knotted with anxiety, which he is desperately trying to hide.

He puts his coffee cup into the sink and grabs his coat from the row of hooks in the hall. He shouts that he has a busy day, lots of paperwork to do, and leaves the house without breakfast, to travel the two hundred metres to St. Mary's Church.

Angela

Angela places a mug of black coffee on the bedside table next to Kamal and climbs back into bed with him. She leans over and kisses him on the lips. 'I've brought you a coffee.

It's almost seven thirty.'

'What have I done to deserve this treatment?' he asks.

'I'm in a good mood,' she says. 'Make the most of it while it lasts.'

'I will,' he says. 'It will make a pleasant change.' Angela laughs and smacks him hard on the leg through the sheets. He rolls on top of her and pins both arms on either side of her head. 'Much as I would love to continue the fight with you, because you know I will win, I do have to get to work today.'

'Feeble excuse,' says Angela. 'You're just too frightened to try. You're all smoke and mirrors.'

He laughs and kisses her again. A long passionate kiss that could lead to them staying in bed all morning if Angela doesn't drag herself away from him. She knows Kamal can't resist her, and she loves the power that gives her. Reluctantly, he moves back to his side of the bed, sits up, and rests his back against the grey faux-leather padded headboard. He picks up his coffee cup.

He told her when they first got together that he had never felt this playful passion with his soon-to-be ex-wife. She had been passionate, sure, but her longing for him and her obvious devotion was a turn-off. Angela felt slightly sorry for her when she heard that. You can never win with men. If you are frosty towards them, they label you an ice queen. If you show them too much love and passion, they feel suffocated. Over the years, Angela has perfected the craft of keeping a man interested. There's something about the way she dismisses Kamal with a wave of her hand when she's too busy to give him any attention, and the way her life doesn't revolve around his which keeps him begging for more. He has told her he finds her a refreshing change, and quite frankly, a huge turn-on.

'Are you confident the work will be finished today?' asks Angela.

'Yes, I don't doubt it will be,' says Kamal. 'The men do as they are told, otherwise they know they won't get any more work. Simple as.'

Kamal is Angela's employee, her project manager, although he likes to think of himself as Second-in-Command. Angela has to regularly remind him that, just because they now live together, she is the one who makes the decisions. He simply follows them. She decides which properties to buy, what renovations need to be done, and with what budget. Kamal's job is to stick to the budget and get the job finished on time.

Following the death of Angela's husband twelve months ago, she relocated from Liverpool to the north Lancashire village of Eldenbridge, where she opened a florist and gift shop. Prior to that, the only shops in the village were a Post Office selling newspapers and sweets, a cake shop and bakery, and the corner shop, Robertsons, which all overlook the village green and pond. So Angela's flower shop was warmly welcomed and has thrived.

She hired Kamal, who had previously done jobs for her husband, to fit a new state-of-the-art kitchen and bathroom in her new house. What was meant to be a two-week job was stretched out to four. Kamal was reluctant to leave at the end of each day, and Angela was happy for him to hang around and keep her company. She began to ask him to stay for dinner. She turned a blind eye the first time when he said he had a phone call to make, and he nipped outside to use the phone box rather than Angela's telephone. She didn't ask whether he had anyone to go home to. She didn't need to know. Neither of them were looking for a relationship. Just some company, some attention from the opposite sex. The uncomplicated transaction suited them both. Until the day Angela asked him for more. She wanted Kamal to become part of her business. Not the property renovation business, or the pretty florists in the village. They were just a front. She wanted him to become involved in her real business. The one that made her money.

One night after dinner, settled on Angela's vast sofa in her living room, Kamal had sipped fifteen-year-old whiskey from a crystal glass as he listened to her proposal. Suddenly, his comfortable lifestyle and average earnings didn't seem enough. Angela was offering him much more. Easy money that would propel him from the lifestyle of the comfortably well-off to that of the super-rich. All he had to do, with a little assistance from some of Angela's regular builders, was to shift some cocaine. Small bundles. Just pass them from one person to the other. It wasn't really dealing. No, he wouldn't be at risk at all, she told him. There are no police in Eldenbridge, and the ones who are on duty are as useless as a knitted teapot, as her mother used to say.

The whiskey burned the back of Kamal's mouth and slipped down his throat. He could feel his heart beating with excitement and, as he smiled and asked for more details, Angela topped up his glass and told him to make himself comfortable. Kamal had the perfect view of Angela's new and very shiny Porsche 911 parked outside the living room window on her curved stone driveway. He would like one of those, he thought. He would like it very much.

The job is certainly not without risks, she told him, but it pays extremely well.

Kamal has not looked back. He left his wife within a month and moved in with Angela. Now the cocaine no longer needs to pass through Angela's house or the beautifully fragranced flower shop in the village. Kamal takes care of everything for her. Every Friday morning, he collects the assignment and hands it to one of Angela's most trusted builders, who makes the sales for her. Every Monday morning, the profits are collected from him. The builder is happy, Kamal is happy and Angela is happy.

'Shall I tell you why I'm in such a good mood?' asks Angela now. Kamal nods, as he sips his hot coffee. 'It's Miriam. She's dead.'

'Miriam? Your cleaner?'

'Yes.'

'Dead? How?'

'She was murdered yesterday. I put the radio on in the kitchen just now and it was on the local news.'

'Bloody hell. Did they say what happened to her?'

'Apparently, her son, Jack, nipped out to the corner shop, and when he got back, she was dead as a dodo on the kitchen floor. Whacked over the head with a blunt instrument. They worded it slightly better than that, obviously.' Angela laughs.

'That's awful,' says Kamal. 'The poor woman.'

'Oh come on, it isn't awful at all, admit it,' says Angela.

Kamal shrugs. 'I didn't know her like you did,' he says. 'But nobody deserves a violent death, do they?'

Angela frowns at him. 'Are you getting soft in your old age?'

'No, but, come on, she was an old woman, wasn't she?'

'Not that old. Fifty-something, I don't know. She looked seventy on some days.'

'What kind of blunt instrument? Have the police found anything?'

'No, I don't think so.' Angela laughs. 'Serves her right, the witch.'

Kamal stares at her. What does he know about this woman? She's intelligent, she's a brilliant business woman and she's sexy as hell, with her wavy shoulder-length blonde hair and blue eyes. But she's also devious and adept at breaking the rules with a chilling precision that blurs the line between ambition and criminality. Surely, Angela doesn't have anything to do with this, does she? He wants to ask her about her movements yesterday, but he can't. That's talk for 'I know you did it, now prove to me you didn't.' He watches her as she sips her coffee. No, she wouldn't harm a fly. Just because one of her businesses is illegal doesn't mean that Angela is a killer. What on earth is he thinking?

'I wonder who did it,' he says.

'I don't know, but it saved me the job.'

Kamal watches as Angela picks up the morning newspaper, and becomes immersed in national news.

'It will be on the local television news tonight, I would imagine,' says Kamal.

Angela shrugs. 'I don't care one way or the other. I will have forgotten all about her by then. Good riddance to her, that's what I say.'

Jack

Jack pushes the bed cover off and sits on the edge of the

bed. He likes to be up and dressed by seven-thirty and has been in bed for long enough. This particular hotel brand prides itself on offering a good night's sleep. He wonders what the reception staff would say if he demanded a refund on account of the fact that his mother was murdered yesterday and he had too much going on in his head to sleep, despite their soft mattress, duck-down pillows, and their *Relaxation Guarantee*.

He had listened to the bin men at the back of the hotel clattering the steel bins about just before dawn, followed by the frantic barking of a disturbed dog. Just as he was closing his eyes, a young baby in the room next door had woken and had cried for at least twenty minutes. He lay staring at the ceiling, illuminated by the orange glow of the street lamp outside, wondering what the parents were doing and why it had taken them so long to warm the baby's milk. He was about to hammer on the party wall when the crying stopped. The baby was finally soothed.

The frantic bell of the telephone next to his bed breaks the heavy silence. Good morning, I have Detective Inspector Holt on the line for you, says the bored-sounding receptionist, as though detective inspectors call people in hotel rooms every day. He waits a moment for the call to be put through. The inspector delivers news he has been dreading. He will be able to go home today. The forensic team has finished examining the house. Jack is about to tell her he doesn't want to go home, when she says she wouldn't recommend it yet until the place has been cleaned properly, as he might find it traumatic. She asks him to call into the police station 'at his earliest convenience' to collect his door keys. She will then be able to give him the phone numbers of some specialist cleaning companies that he might like to use. They will return the house back to normal, she tells him. He wants to say that nothing will ever be normal again. He thanks her and returns the phone to its cradle.

He doesn't want to go to the police station today. He wants to stay here, in the warmth and security of this hotel room. He wants to crawl back into bed and sleep for hours and hours. He wants to forget the events of yesterday. He wants to pretend that they never happened.

He picks up the kettle from the shelf at the side of the television and fills it with water from the bathroom tap. He takes it back to the shelf, flicks the switch on, and sits on the edge of the bed again waiting for it to boil. He stares at the space in the corner of the room where a small armchair would fit perfectly. He should suggest it when he speaks to the reception staff.

*

Jack made his way to Wellington by bus. He waited in the hotel until after nine o'clock, until he was sure public transport would be free of gregarious teenagers on their way to school. Any jostling, swearing, or indeed just general liveliness was likely to be met with hostility on his part. Now, as he waits at the front counter of the police station for the bell to be answered, his hostility hasn't waned.

He can see the uniformed constable behind the front desk chatting to a colleague, although he can't hear what they are saying. He wonders whether they are talking about police business and decides that, unless they are completely without the slightest trace of compassion, they can't possibly be. Their raucous laughter suggests they are discussing lighter subjects than those regularly dealt with by police officers. He wants to ring the bell again, but he knows that he doesn't need to. The constable heard him the first time. Jack had watched him glance over his shoulder. He didn't quite manage to look amenable. His features told Jack he was being a nuisance, interrupting something of greater importance. Jack has seen that look on his mother's face a thousand times.

Excuse me, he wants to say, can you stop talking and do your job? I'm here on important business. My mother died yesterday and I have been *asked* to come in. I'm not here simply because I have nothing better to do.

But yet, he doesn't have anything better to do. What is he to do now? The day looms long and lonely ahead of him and he has no idea how he is going to fill the hours and hours before bedtime. He has heard that there is a mountain of paperwork to fill in when someone dies. But he doesn't know where, or what, or when. Maybe the lady detective can help him with that.

When the constable finally frees himself from the hilarious anecdote being told by his colleague and lumbers over to the desk, Jack tries not to stare at the yellow stain on his tie. Egg? Probably. At the sight of it, Jack's stomach grumbles and he remembers that he hasn't yet eaten breakfast. He looks at the man's chin, searching for more breakfast stains, but can't find any. He wonders whether to tell him about the egg on his tie or whether that would be impertinent. His mother was always telling him off for being *impertinent*. She liked to use long words, especially when she was reminding him how stupid he was.

'You should have listened more at school,' she would say. 'Then things would be different. You wouldn't be wasting your time lolling about the house all day. You'd be out there in the world, making money like a real man.'

A real man? Jack never knew what she meant by that. Was this specimen in front of him a real man? As opposed to what, someone who wasn't real? A pretend man or an invisible man? Jack didn't question what his mother said. He took the insults from her, collected them, and piled them up around himself like bricks in a wall. The more she threw at him, the more he was ready for them and the less they hurt. His defence grew stronger and stronger with each passing day, with each passing insult. One day, he was hoping that they would mean nothing to him. But it is too late for that now.

The constable asks Jack if he can help him, although it seems that helping is the last thing on his mind. He wonders what his mother would say to this man if he were standing in front of her in his egg-stained tie, with an obvious reluctance to help.

Jack explains that a lady policeman by the name of Elena has asked to see him. No, he can't remember her second name, but surely there can't be more than one Elena in the building. The police station isn't that big. Even if there are two, ask them both to come out and he will then choose the one he wants to speak to. The constable goes red in the face and looks very cross. Jack turns his back on him and goes to sit on one of the plastic chairs along the wall underneath a notice board where posters of various sizes have been pinned. The reader is reminded to 'Clunk Click Every Trip' and 'Save Water Now'. The picture of a dripping tap has been defaced by a black felt tip pen. The amateur artist has drawn a sad face on the bottom of the tap, with the drip being a giant tear. Jack wonders who is in charge of keeping the notice board up-to-date, as the long summer drought ended weeks ago. He wants to ask the constable whether updating the notices is his responsibility, but he wants to keep the transaction between them as short as possible. He ignores the constable's mumbles about only trying to help, needing to make sure the right person gets called to come down.

Jack rests his chin in his hands and examines his shoes. They could do with a clean. His mum wouldn't be pleased if she saw the state of them. Not one little bit. As the words 'no need for that attitude,' drift over from the counter, Jack closes his eyes and lets the tears fall.

He can't tell how much time has passed, but the lady detective is now in front of him, asking him how he is and pressing his door keys into his hand. She thanks Brian behind the counter for his help, as she guides Jack into a side room. It isn't the Victim Suite, where he was interviewed yesterday, but a much smaller room, dominated by a grey table. There is hardly room on either side to squeeze in, and there are no windows, which makes it appear even smaller. Elena asks him to sit down and he notices that the chairs here are identical to the ones outside in the waiting area. He wonders what kind of company manufactures chairs like this. They always seem to be red or blue, like the ones they had at school, and always seem to be extremely flimsy. The company director clearly doesn't take much pride in his product. He wants to ask Elena how much they are, to assess whether the police force is being ripped off, but he suspects she wouldn't know.

How did you sleep, Elena asks him. Not well, he replies. The hotel is on a main road, and there is a bright streetlamp right outside his window. The curtains are not thick enough to block out the light. He is used to the dark skies and the quiet of Eldenbridge. He never knew that so many people were awake during the night. There wasn't a time when the road was empty. All night cars and lorries trundled past the hotel, their headlights sweeping a beam of light into the room before they moved on. Where were they going at that hour?

Lots of deliveries are made during the night, says Elena. You'd be surprised how busy the main roads can be.

No, I wouldn't, thought Jack. Not anymore. Not now that I know.

Elena says she wants to ask him a couple more questions if he doesn't mind. No, he isn't under arrest, she says. Why would he ask that? Jack sees a flash of something he can't read on the detective's face. He isn't very good at facial expressions, he never has been. His mother was. She used to tell him that she always knew when he was telling lies.

'It's written all over your face, you bag-of-shite, useless animal.'

A different day, a different insult. His mother was full of them. Quite clever really, how she could come up with them so quickly. Maybe she lay in bed at night thinking of all the different and hurtful things she could say, so she could hurl them at him at a moment's notice. She could have done that, she had such a good memory. She never forgot a time when Jack had let her down/ done something wrong/ shown her up in public/ generally been useless. Past demeanours would be used against him at a future date, to be added to the present-day ones.

Jack tells the detective that he has watched plenty of

murder mysteries on the television, and he knows that close family members are always the Number One Suspect. He wonders whether he is a suspect. He blinks and fresh tears drop onto his hands which he is clenching as he leans forward onto the table. Elena reaches across and pats his hand, apologising that she doesn't have any tissues. She tells him that, right now, he isn't a suspect, but having said that, everyone is a suspect until they have more evidence to go off. Jack understands that. He wipes his wet cheeks with the sleeve of his shirt.

Elena asks him where he went when he left the shop after buying his mother's cigarettes. Jack reminds her what he said yesterday. He went for a walk before he went home. Elena assures him she hasn't forgotten what he said, but she wants to know where exactly he walked to. Jack can't remember. Just around the village. He stopped at the green and watched the ducks for a bit. Yes, he knows it was dark, but he likes to watch them sleeping, all huddled together at the edge of the water. He wanted to be outside. He feels claustrophobic sometimes, after spending all day in the house.

Elena wants to know if he knows the neighbours at number five, the ones who have gone on holiday. Jack shakes his head and tells her that they seem to be very busy people. The only time he sees them is at the weekend. They both work long hours. The woman tends to rush out of the house early on a Saturday morning, dressed in black shorts and a running vest. He assumes she is going running. She wears bright green running shoes, he tells Elena, with three yellow stripes down the sides. That's why he notices her. He isn't one to stand at the window and twitch the curtains. He's not a nosy parker. He just notices the bright colours on her shoes, that's all.

Elena asks him about the man, Mr Gregson, is that his name? Jack shrugs. He knows his name, but he doesn't want to tell her anything else. She will think he's a stalker. He isn't, of course, but the Gregsons' house is directly across the street, so when there is any activity, he can't help but see it. On a Sunday afternoon, he watches as the man zips up and down his square lawn with the lawnmower, and then carries it back to his immaculate garage that has never housed his car. He emerges a minute later with clippers and walks down the borders, clipping any stray blades of grass that don't align with the others.

Don't worry, Elena says now. She was just wondering if he knew when they would be back from their holiday. Jack doesn't reply. He asks whether he can go now. He needs some breakfast. He would really like to go.

Elena tells him that the forensic team has finished in the house and, although he can go home, she would advise him to ring these people and have the place cleaned first. They are very good. They might be able to go and do it this afternoon, or tomorrow. She passes him a card and he reads the name Ultimate Clean and the words *crime scene*. He folds the card in half and buries it in his fist. He doesn't want to read any more of those distressing words. He doesn't want his house to be a crime scene.

He asks the detective how he will be able to ring the cleaning company. He doesn't have much money left, and he needs some bus fare to get back to Eldenbridge. Elena says that's a good point and gives a small laugh, as though he has just made a joke. Cleaning his dead mother's blood off the kitchen floor isn't a laughing matter, he wants to say. But he needs to be polite. He doesn't want her to think he is aggressive, even though he can feel the anger rising inside. The more time he spends in the police station, the more agitated he becomes. He needs to get out. There is no air in this room. He pulls at the collar of his shirt and opens the top button. He pulls his tie down an inch.

Elena tells him that she will ask the constable at the front desk to call the cleaning company for him. One less job for him to worry about. It doesn't matter, he says, he will phone them from the hotel.

Keep us informed about where you'll be staying, Elena says, as he leaves the room. We will need to contact you.

Claire

The location of Claire's office is known to only a select few people. Only Sophia, their parents, Trevor, Helen, and the occasional visitor who has made an appointment to speak to her know that her office is located through the discreet door positioned between the florist and the Post Office. The unmarked gloss door, black as night, hides away at the back of a dark porch. The office can be found up the steep flight of stairs.

Claire likes the anonymity. Whenever she needs to see a client face-to-face, she prefers to visit their house, or meet them on neutral ground, such as the pub, a café, or a park bench. She isn't a particularly tidy person and having to empty the waste paper basket, wash the coffee cups, and squirt some furniture polish over her desk for the benefit of visitors isn't something she has time to worry about. The less visitors, the better.

So when she hears the gentle knock on the glass of the internal door, her first reaction is to pretend she isn't there and hope the inopportune visitor will go away. She peers at the outline of the figure through the frosted glass. The feeble glow of the light bulb at the top of the stairs casts a shadow of a tall slim person in dark clothes. She waits to see if they knock again. They do.

'Claire, are you there?' says a mumbled voice.

Claire doesn't reply. She scans the room to see whether it is suitable to accept visitors. It isn't. She hasn't opened the window for weeks, allowing the gas heater's dizzying odour to linger. She jumps up from her desk, pulls the cord to open the Venetian blind, and throws open the sash window. The cool blast rattles the blind and shakes the papers on her desk. She covers the papers with her overflowing wire in-tray.

'Claire, I know you're in there. I can see you moving about. For goodness sake, let me in.'

She hasn't heard that voice for almost nine months. She would love to ignore the visitor, but it's too late now. She has no choice but to let her in.

Elena

'The door is open,' says Claire.

Elena hears her faint voice through the door. She turns the handle and lets herself into the office. A cold breeze is blowing from the open window. Claire is standing in front of an old-fashioned mahogany desk, which looks like something she might have picked up from the tip. The varnish has long since been polished off and various circular cup rings litter the cluttered surface. Claire is grasping tightly onto the handles of three large white cups with one hand. One of the cups has a picture of a cat playing with a ball of pink wool on the side, one is decorated with bright yellow flowers and the other one has *The World's Best Detective* scrawled in black joined-up writing.

'This one's got the beginnings of mould inside it,' she says, waving the cat cup in the air. 'I guess this is the one that has been dirty the longest.' She drops it into a waste paper basket at the side of the desk. 'It wasn't one of my favourites,' she says, 'as you know, I'm more of a dog person, and really, I only need two. I don't get that many visitors.'

Elena follows her into a tiny kitchen located through an archway to the right of the office. 'Your kitchen doesn't have a door,' she says.

'Well spotted. Now that's why you're a detective,' says Claire.

Elena laughs. 'I didn't mean to state the obvious.'

'The landlord told me that arches are the latest trend. All the new houses have them. Like being open plan but a bit cosier, he said. I wanted to tell him that heat can escape through the tiniest of gaps, so a six-foot-tall archway can hardly be called cosy, and to be honest, I didn't relish the idea of visitors to the office being able to see whether I had washed the pots or not, but what can you do? It was the only available place in the village, so I took it.' She drops an unwashed bowl with the now-dried remnants of tomato soup into the sink, together with the two dirty cups, squirts washing-up liquid over them, and turns on the hot tap.

'I can understand that,' says Elena. 'It's a nice office though, and you have a great view of the village.' She looks out of the kitchen window as Elena swishes water around the sink. The window looks out onto the edge of the village green at the front of the building and she can see St. Mary's Church from here, at the other side of the pond. It looks pretty at the moment. Golden leaves blanket the winding path from the road to the arch of the main door. Tips of ancient gravestones peek through the neat grass on either side of the path.

'Yes, it's a beautiful view, isn't it?' says Claire. She pushes the sleeves of her blouse up her arms, turns off the tap, picks up a dishcloth, and begins to wash the pots.

Claire is right, the church is beautiful, but Elena isn't looking forward to going in. She hasn't stepped foot inside it for almost a year, not since the morning of her brother's wedding day. The day he should have married Claire. The day he died.

She picks up a tea towel from the draining board, ignoring the smattering of various stains, and begins to dry one of the cups. 'How are you, Claire?' she says.

'I'm fine really, considering. The business is growing. I can't complain.' Claire scrubs vigorously at the dried-on soup in the bowl with the edge of the dishcloth.

'I've been thinking about you lately, wondering how you are,' says Elena.

'Thank you,' says Claire, not looking up.

Elena sighs. 'I miss Stephen, too, you know, especially this week, coming up to his anniversary.'

Claire stops what she is doing and faces her now. 'Sorry, I know you loved him too. I suppose you think what I did was extremely selfish,' she says.

Elena gives an imperceptible nod. 'Grief makes us selfish, doesn't it?' she says. 'You don't need to apologise. It's hard to see someone else's suffering when you are struggling with your own. I get it. I am sorry you left though.'

'If you've come to ask me to go back into the police, the answer's still no. I think I made the right decision when I left.'

'That's not why I'm here,' says Elena.

'Well, if you're here to talk about Stephen, I don't…'

Elena shakes her head. 'I'm not.' An uncomfortable silence settles between them. Elena wants to tell Claire how selfish she has been, and how much she hurt her by cutting her off. She wants to ask her how she could have dropped her the way she did, if they were true friends. After Stephen's death, all Claire thought about was herself. She didn't seem to care about the rest of his family, the other people who loved him and lost him that day. 'You know people say that one of the hardest things in the world is to lose a husband or a wife, or a child. But nobody talks about how difficult it is to lose a brother. I loved Stephen, not like you did, obviously. But I loved him. He had been my brother my whole life. And now there's just -'

'I'm sorry,' says Claire.

Elena can see from the tears about to fall down Claire's cheeks that the apology is heartfelt and genuine. 'Stop saying you're sorry,' she says. Claire smiles at her and wipes her tears with soapy fingers. Elena dabs at her face with the tea towel.

'It's nice to see you, anyway,' says Claire.

'Is it?' says Elena. 'I wasn't sure how you would react

when you saw me. I know you wanted a complete break from me and our family.'

Claire shrugs. 'It's easier to deal with such a tragedy when you don't have to face it every day, isn't it?'

'I suppose so.'

'But time's a healer, as they say. Anyway, how's the team? Geoff okay?'

Elena laughs. 'Yes, still the same male chauvinist pig that he's always been, but he's all right. I'm used to him now. He wasn't happy when I got the promotion. I'm an inspector now, did you know?'

Claire gives her a sudden and unexpected hug. 'No, I didn't. Wow, congratulations. That's wonderful, you deserve it. No, he wouldn't have liked that at all. A woman boss.' She shakes her head. 'Now that I would like to see.'

'He got a promotion, too. He's a sergeant. You can come back, you know. The force is crying out for good officers like you. We worked well together didn't we?'

'I'd rather you came to join me here. Maybe bring Geoff with you. We can be the English version of Charlie's Angels. Simons, Holt and Miller. Doesn't exactly roll off the tongue, does it?'

Elena laughs. She has missed Claire. She wants to shout at her for not keeping in touch after Stephen died. She wants to tell her how angry that made her feel, that she had lost her brother and her best friend within months of each other, but the words are lost in too much emotion at the back of her throat.

After the funeral, when Claire went back to work at Wellington Police Station, Elena told her it was a blessing that were able to work together. They could comfort one another. They knew what each other was going through.

They never needed to be alone with their grief. But Claire wanted to be alone. She told Elena she couldn't bear the weight of someone else's heartbreak as well as her own.

Elena found working in a male-dominated environment such as the police station was good for her. She worked with men who wouldn't recognise emotion if it walked up to them and introduced itself. Keeping busy at work helped her to forget her pain. She hoped that Claire, too, would get through each day on a wave of dark police humour, bury herself in her work and before they knew it, the worst of the grief would be over and she would be out the other side. Out of the darkness and into the light. But it didn't work like that for Claire. Elena watched her battle with her anger day after day, unable to defeat it, and whenever one of her stupid colleagues made a joke, whatever the subject matter, she fired aggression at him like bullets from a machine gun, unable to help herself.

Elena, her sergeant at the time, had to tell Claire that she was acting inappropriately. She couldn't shout at her work colleagues like that, even if they are insensitive arseholes. Claire nodded silently and allowed tears to run down her face while she listened to the admonishment. Eventually, she said Elena was right. She shouldn't shout at her colleagues and wouldn't shout at them ever again. In fact, she wouldn't speak to any of them ever again, because she was leaving. She threw her police ID badge on Elena's desk, grabbed her handbag from the back of her chair, and walked out.

Elena didn't follow her. She wanted to, but Geoff told her to give Claire some space. Women can be like that at certain times of the month, he had said. His wife was a crazy nightmare. Like Jekyll and Hyde, she was. Elena told him to get out of her office, mind his own business, and get on with his work. As he closed her door, she could hear him telling the other lads that the sergeant was having her time of the month, too, by the sounds of it. Steer clear.

The following day, Claire's resignation letter was hand-delivered by Sophia to the front desk of the police station, together with a sick note from the doctor. Claire wouldn't be working her notice period. She was suffering from grief-induced depression. Sophia told Elena that Claire was struggling, and the best thing she could do was to leave her alone for a bit. Losing your fiancé was bad enough, but losing him in a car accident on the morning of your wedding was the worst possible thing, Sophia had said as she was leaving, as though Elena needed to be told. She had better rush back as poor Claire was inconsolable, and she needed looking after. Elena wanted to say that *she* needed looking after too. Yes, Claire was suffering, but losing a brother was horrendous too. Giving up your career in the police force wasn't the answer. But she kept her thoughts to herself as she watched Sophia push baby Wendy out of the station.

'Shall I put the kettle on?' she says now. 'It seems that you're not going to ask me if I want a coffee, so I'll make my own.'

'Sure, help yourself,' says Claire. 'You might be able to find a stale biscuit in the tin.'

When the coffee is made, Elena carries the cups into Claire's office and, unable to find any coasters, places them on the desk. Claire sits in a black leather chair on one side and Elena sits in an identical chair on the other side.

'How did you find me?' asks Claire.

'I went to your house and Sophia told me where your

office is. Looks like you're busy.' Elena nods towards the disorganised pile of papers on the corner of the desk.

'Thankfully, I am,' says Claire. 'Who would have guessed that so many people around here need a private investigator? It's women mainly. I think they'd rather come to me to spy on their husbands than to ask another man to do it, and being an ex-policewoman is a bonus. They seem to trust me.'

'That's great,' says Elena. 'I'm glad things have worked out for you. I was worried about you when you left the force. You never took my calls.'

The accusation is clear. Claire is guilty as charged. For weeks after she left the police force, Elena phoned the house asking to speak to her, but was told she was either asleep, busy working, or she was out. Gradually, she stopped calling.

'I wasn't myself for a long time,' says Claire. 'I can't explain it. I felt as though my whole world - not just my present, but my future too - had imploded. I just couldn't - ' She stops and takes a gulp of her coffee. The hot liquid burns the back of her throat, but she ignores the pain.

'I'm not here to berate you for what you did,' says Elena. 'I would never do that.' Her warm smile offers an olive branch of friendship. 'Especially not coming up to the anniversary of his death. I'm actually here on police business, in relation to the murder of Miriam Chadwick.'

Adam

'Hello, who's there?' shouts Adam from the vestry in St.

Mary's Church. He is working at his desk. He can feel the torn sheet of paper from yesterday, a fragment ripped from the notepad on his desk, burning with a quiet intensity in the pocket of his cassock. A message undelivered. He needs to get rid of it before someone reads it.

'It's me.' It is Carol, the churchwarden. 'Have you heard about Miriam?'

She marches into the vestry, like a soldier with a special assignment. She is wrapped up for winter in a grey woollen bobble hat, matching scarf, and a long brown sheepskin coat. He can't see her feet from where he is sitting behind his huge pine desk, but he would bet his next week's wages that she is wearing boots and thick socks. It irritates him more than it should. Last winter she complained daily about how cold it was in church, telling him that he shouldn't expect the vulnerable and the elderly to shiver as they connected with God. They like to be warm, she told him. Churches should be warm and welcoming places. 'The wind comes right off the hills,' she said. 'Down through the village, blasts through the open doors and right round my ankles. I can't bear it. It isn't healthy. It's going to make me ill.'

Adam bit his tongue. He wanted to tell her to spend more time at home. He could manage the church very well on his own, thank you very much.

'You need to ask for more money in the collection,' Carol went on. 'Tell them we don't want coins anymore. Just pound notes. That should help.'

He told her there was a financial crisis going on, families were struggling with the rising cost of heating and food, and many people were unemployed. He didn't want them to stop coming to church because it was too expensive. People would be happy to sit in their coats, he told her. Nobody expected churches to be as warm as houses. Carol disagreed. Of course, she did. She disagreed with everything he said. She told him she would bring it up at the church council meeting. Thankfully, the other, more reasonable, members of the council were on his side and they voted to leave the heating off, except on Sundays for the morning service, and on Monday mornings when they ran the Mums and Toddlers playgroup. Carol wore her protest in the form of winter clothes fit for an Arctic expedition for the rest of the season. And now they're back. Despite having just experienced the warmest summer on record, and before all the trees have lost their leaves and weeks before any expected frost, Carol is bundled up again.

'Miriam is dead.' Carol whispers the word 'dead' dramatically. 'Haven't you heard?'

'No, no, I haven't heard,' says Adam. 'Poor woman. What on earth happened? Was it a heart attack?'

'No. She was murdered, Adam. I can't believe you haven't heard. Killed stone dead right there in her own kitchen.'

'Goodness, are you sure? I mean, how do you know?'

'I've just been in Robertsons for some bread. Everyone's talking about it. A blunt instrument, that's all they can say right now. Blunt trauma to the head, I don't know, something like that. They have a way of wording it, don't they, the news people?'

'Yes, yes, I suppose they do,' says Adam. He chews on his thumbnail. A vision of Miriam's bloodied head and the sound of her ear-piercing screams flash through his mind and he blinks rapidly to clear it.

'Don't you have the morning radio on at your house?'

asks Carol.

Adam thinks of his loud, raucous children and the music that blasted around the kitchen this morning. Mindless banal chatter from the Radio One DJ, followed by a pop song that he didn't know, but which his wife apparently knew every word of. She sang quite happily as she made the children's breakfast, oblivious to Adam's longing for peace.

'Yes, we do,' he says. 'But not the local one, just Radio One. I didn't hear the local news.' He shoves his hand into his cassock pocket and plays with the corner of the note he wrote for Miriam yesterday afternoon, the redundant note that she will never read.

'I'll go and make you a strong cup of tea,' says Carol. 'I'll put you a drop of sugar in it, too. You look like you need it.'

Carol wanders off down the aisle towards the kitchen. Adam can hear her mumbling about it being a shock to everyone in the village, she has known nothing like it in all the years she has been alive, and she hopes the police catch whoever did it soon, otherwise she won't get a wink of sleep, worrying that she might be murdered in her bed. Adam wants to tell her that she will be perfectly safe. Nobody would dare cross her.

He waits until she is out of earshot before he picks up the phone. He dials the number he knows by heart. 'Hello, it's only me. It's over. She's dead. We have nothing to worry about now,' he says.

Angela

Angela is wrapping a bouquet, a selection of vibrant orange dahlias, chrysanthemums the colour of soft apricots, and delicate white anemones, for a young female customer when DS Miller bursts into the florist. As she pulls a section of sticky tape off the roll, sticks the tissue paper around the bunch of flowers, and hands it to the woman who immediately buries her nose in the flowers, she watches the detective stroll around her small shop. He goes to the wooden shelves along the back wall. He picks up a bottle of bath salts, smells it, scrunches up his nose, and puts it back down. On the shelf below, he picks up a small glass vase, turns it upside down, and raises his eyebrows in mock astonishment as he reads the price tag. He blows air out of his mouth and shakes his head, in the way that plumbers do when asked for a cheap quote to fix an annoying dripping tap.

Angela tries to ignore him. 'Are these for anyone special?' she asks the customer. She turns her back on the detective. She doesn't want to watch him. It is clear he wants her to, but his immature acting skills do not amuse her, not one little bit.

'They're for my mum,' says the customer. 'She's in hospital, so I'm on my way to see her now.'

'That's lovely,' says Angela, forcing a wide smile. 'I hope she loves them, and I hope she gets well soon.'

The customer thanks her and leaves the shop. DS Miller, in an act of forced chivalry, holds the door for her and then closes it behind her. He slides the bolt across.

'You might as well turn the sign around too,' says

Angela. 'If you want people to think we're closed.'

'Just for your own good, Mrs Bennett,' he says. 'I'm sure you don't want all and sundry listening to private police matters.' DS Miller turns the *Open* sign so that it now says *Closed*.

'I've got nothing to hide,' says Angela. She folds her arms and waits for the detective to tell her why he is there. If he has wind of the cocaine business, he's too late. He won't find anything incriminating here. She is careful not to leave drug paraphernalia lying around in the shop or at home. Kamal is on his way to collect it right now. In fact, he should already be there. Do the police think she is so stupid as to run the cocaine through the shop? She doesn't even do that with the weed. Kamal collects it from Wellington Motorway Services on the M6. A quick transaction, in a far corner of the car park away from the beedy-eyed general public. The suppliers use a different car every time, more often than not on false plates. It is as low risk as it can be. Angela is confident that nothing can be traced back to her. But if it is, she already has a get-out plan. If Kamal is ever arrested, she will simply deny that she knows anything about it. She has rehearsed her speech – either to the police or, God forbid, to a jury - many times in her head. She has her rental properties and she has a very successful florist and gift shop in the village, why would she need to get involved in anything dodgy? Her late husband's generous life insurance policy ensures she is well cared for. Kamal, on the other hand, well, he is out of work and a man's ego won't allow him to be kept by a woman. It is obvious he has been doing something illegal. How else would he be able to afford that BMW he drives? Have you seen how much they are? It is criminal what they charge for new cars these days.

For years, Angela has been scrupulous with her bank accounts. Only legitimate business expenses have been paid for using the florist cheque book. She has been careful to pay herself a reasonable wage each month through the books, and she pays her taxes on time. She should get a certificate from the Inland Revenue for her bookkeeping skills. Let them try and pin something on her. They'll have a job.

Kamal, on the other hand, won't be so lucky. She pays him in cash. He will have a lot of explaining to do when - no, she shouldn't say that - *if* he is ever arrested. If he can afford to pay for a brand new car worth over three thousand pounds, and his clothes are the type worn by successful company directors and pop stars, yet, on paper at least, he isn't in employment, well he will have an uphill battle on his hands trying to explain where his money comes from.

DS Miller walks over to the counter and stands in front of her, his hands in the pockets of his leather jacket. It isn't fastened. He would probably struggle to do it up, she thinks. Each time she sees him, his beer belly seems to have expanded a little. On close inspection, she can see the beginnings of a drinker's nose. She wonders whether he spends his evenings alone in the pub, or does he have a special someone waiting for him at home? She has never seen him in the Dog and Duck in the village, but then again, he doesn't live around here.

'I've come to ask you some questions about Miriam Chadwick,' says DS Miller. 'She worked for you, didn't she?'

'Yes, she was my cleaner. I know she has been killed. I

heard about it on the radio this morning. Terrible news.' Angela keeps a neutral face. She can't be bothered to pretend to be grieving for someone she didn't like and didn't respect.

'When did you last see her?'

'Yesterday morning, just outside the shop. She was on her way to work, and she stopped for a chat, said hello, not much more, and went on her way.'

'Are you sure about that?'

Angela laughs. 'No, what I really meant to say was that I saw her last night, just before I killed her with a blunt instrument. It wasn't me, if that's what you're thinking.'

'There's no need for sarcasm. This is a serious police investigation, and if you don't stop wasting my time, I'll take you in.' DS Miller pulls his notebook from his jacket pocket and takes his time writing in it. Angela knows what he is doing. She has met police provocation before; a weak and useless adversary who never manages to unsettle her.

'How well do you know Jack Chadwick?' he says eventually.

Angela shrugs. 'I know him, he's Miriam's son, and he lives in the village. Everyone knows everyone around here.'

'What's he like?' asks DS Miller.

'What do you mean, what's he like?' asks Angela. 'I presume you've met him yourself, why are you asking me what he's like?'

'Well, at his age, a man still living at home with his mother. Bit odd, don't you think?'

'I lived at home until I was nearly thirty,' says Angela. 'Would you say it was a bit odd if he was female? Although, it's different for girls, isn't it?'

'Don't give me that, Angela. You know it's odd, as well

as I do. Although, I've got to say, I'm surprised you stayed at home so long. A strong independent woman like yourself. A Women's Libber, no doubt.' He laughs, but there's no humour. She wonders whether he secretly admires her business acumen, or loaths her for it. She can't tell. What she does know is that she wants to pick up the glass paperweight sitting inches from her hand and smash it into his ugly face. She would take great pleasure in that. Instead, she takes a deep breath.

'I have found Jack to be a very pleasant man, on the odd occasion I have met him. He lacks confidence, that's all. Maybe now his mother isn't around, he will come out of his shell a bit.'

'He'll bloody well have to, won't he?' says DS Miller. He fingers the petals on a deep purple hydrangea sitting in a bucket of water next to the counter. 'These real?' he says.

'Yes, ten pence a stem,' she says.

He whistles. 'You've got to sell a lot of stems to make a few bob then, don't you?'

'I am generally quite busy on a Friday,' she says. 'Apart from Saturday, it's my busiest day of the week. When I'm open, of course. So if you wouldn't mind…' She nods to the door.

'Not so fast,' he says. 'What were you doing in Southgate Drive last night?' He holds up his right hand, palm facing her as though he is taking an oath in court. 'Don't deny it. I saw your car.'

'I'm sure you did,' she says. 'It's a bright red sports car, so not exactly subtle, is it? I saw you on Miriam's path. It was obvious that something terrible had happened. They only send that many coppers when there has been a serious crime don't they?'

DS Miller narrows his eyes and frowns at her. 'You didn't think to come over and check whether she was all right?'

'Oh, come on,' says Angela. 'Is that a serious question?'

DS Miller shrugs. The silence drops between them like a judge's gavel, neither of them wanting to be the first one to capitulate. A knock on the door breaks their eye contact, as DS Miller turns around to see who it is.

'Tell her you're closed,' he says.

Angela goes to the door, pulls back the bolt, and opens it a fraction. 'Hi, Helen,' she says. 'The police are here at the moment, just asking a few questions about Miriam Chadwick.' She turns back to him. 'How long are you going to be, officer?' She knows that calling him officer, rather than detective, will rankle him.

'Who knows, another ten minutes maybe,' he says.

'They'll be speaking to everyone in the village, I expect,' says Angela to Helen. 'Do you want to come back in a few minutes? I'll put the kettle on and make us both a nice cup of coffee.' She isn't a fan of Helen, but she's a good customer. She buys fresh flowers every week for Claire and Sophia Simons' house, and she's much more tolerable to talk to when she has little Wendy with her. That child is the cutest thing! But more importantly, Angela needs to show DS Miller that she is a well-respected and friendly businesswoman, who has loyal customers.

Angela closes the door again. She is beginning to lose patience now and struggles to stop it from showing. 'What were you saying?' she asks.

'Why were you in Southgate Drive last night?'

'I wanted to speak to Miriam, obviously. Why else

would I be there? I was going to ask her to run a few errands for me next week.'

'And you couldn't have asked her that over the phone?'

'She doesn't have a phone in the house,' says Angela. 'You must know that.'

'Where were you yesterday afternoon between the hours of four and six pm?'

'I was here, in the shop,' she says.

'What time does the shop close?' As he asks the question, DS Miller walks to the door and looks at the opening and closing times stencilled onto the glass in gold cursive writing. 'It says here that the shop closes at four-thirty on a Thursday. But of course, you're the boss and you can close whenever you like, can't you?' Angela doesn't answer. 'Was anyone here with you who would be able to verify your alibi?'

'It's not an alibi, because I haven't done anything wrong. Look, this whole conversation is starting to annoy me. I get that everyone has to be spoken to, but not everyone has to be accused of murder, so I'd appreciate a little respect until you can prove that I have done something wrong.'

'No need to get your knickers in a twist.' DS Miller laughs.

'I'd be interested to know, when you go into Robertsons, and the pub, and the cafe are you going to insist that they close the doors in the same way you've done here? I don't think so.' Angela marches over to the door and flings it open. 'I'm open for business. You can ask me whatever you need to ask me while customers are browsing. If you don't like it, arrest me.' She puts her wrists together and holds them out in front of the detective.

He slaps them away. 'Don't push it, Angela,' he says,

leaning close to her. 'We're watching you.'

'You need a mint,' she says.

DS Miller marches to the door. 'By the way,' he says, 'Jack Chadwick told us that he has never met you before. I'll ask him why he said that, and then I'll be back.'

Let him come back, thinks Angela. He won't get any more information. The fact that Miriam told her something very interesting yesterday morning is a little nugget she will be keeping to herself. Knowledge is power and DS Miller has far too much power already. He doesn't need any more handing to him on a plate.

Jack

Jack is trying his best to control his anxiety. The sparsely furnished hotel room offers no home comforts. He closes his eyes and tries to conjure the feeling of his mother's love. He would give anything to be able to sit with her now and feel safe and protected. On the rare days when his mother felt like being kind to him, she would stroke his hair as he sat on the floor by her feet, and tell him he was her *special boy*. She never went as far as to say she loved him, but on these days, Jack felt a modicum of love through her fingers, without the need for words. There is no love for him now.

He slides from the bed onto the floor and rests his head on the edge of the bed, imagining his mother is with him right now. He tries to feel her warm fingers in his hair. But it doesn't work. The hotel bed is too high for him to be comfortable. His head doesn't rest comfortably on his mother's imaginary lap. When he hears the knock on the door, he is thankful for a distraction. He clambers up and asks who it is, as he walks to the door. He can't hear a response, so he opens the door an inch.

The young lady from the hotel reception is standing in the corridor, smiling at him. She informs him that the cleaning company telephoned a moment ago. His house is ready and he can go back home. They have left the front door key with the next-door neighbour, someone called Mrs Eve Hardy.

It's the first time the receptionist has shown any interest in him. This morning when he passed the room key to her across the counter, on the way to the police station, she didn't look up from her magazine. She simply mumbled thanks - at least that's what he thought she said - through her pink-lipglossed, gum-chewing mouth. She reached across the counter, slid the key towards her, and deposited it next to her magazine. Jack wanted to remind her to do her job properly and hang the key on the hook behind her, underneath the number 5, so it wouldn't get lost. But part of him wanted her to lose the key. He wanted to return to the hotel in the afternoon, ask for his room key, and take great pleasure in watching as she fumbled around, shuffling papers and searching underneath the desk on her hands and knees for the missing key. She deserves to be sacked for her lack of customer care, he thinks to himself. If he had that job, he would do better. He would be friendly. He would tell guests to have a nice day and enjoy their stay at the hotel, and he would smile at everyone, even the children and those irritating guests who demanded extra pillows.

She is still smiling at him, as though she is waiting for some kind of response from him. Jack frowns. That's annoying, he tells her. What's annoying? she wants to know.

She holds her head on one side, as though trying to empty one of her ears of water after a long swim. Jack wonders what she would do if he tapped her on the side of her head. Would that help to get the water out? He can't explain to her that he is angry because the house has been cleaned too quickly, which means he can now go home. She wouldn't understand that he isn't ready to go home. He is getting used to the hotel and was planning to stay another night.

Jack doesn't reply. He looks her up and down. The hotel would do much better if their staff had a uniform, he thinks. It might drag them from being a three-star hotel to a four-star. Really, white leather knee-high boots, a denim skirt that is much too short for the workplace, and a pink t-shirt so snug it looks as though it has shrunk in the wash do not give off a professional appearance. Not one little bit. And her makeup is just too much. Aqua blue eyeshadow and jet black liner should only be worn in the evening, in his opinion. It is inappropriate to be so brightly coloured during the day.

She's the type of woman his mother would have called a tramp. His mother liked to have names for people. She very rarely called them by their actual names, preferring Busybody or Gossip, Scarlet Woman or Floozy, Slacker or Lazy Bastard. He wonders what name she would choose for the hotel receptionist.

Jack looks at the young lady's chest. The only clue that she works here is a cheap name badge pinned to the front of her t-shirt. Alison. He wonders whether people call her Ali. There used to be someone in his class at school called Alison. Jack tried calling her Ali once, in the hope that it sounded friendly and familiar. Alison had scowled at him and asked him who did he think he was. When he replied he was Jack Chadwick of number eight Southgate Drive, Alison had burst out laughing and called him a weirdo. Then she had skipped away from him with her gang of friends, their ponytails swishing behind them as though beating away annoying flies.

The young lady has taken a step back from the door and is looking up and down the corridor as if searching for someone. I'm going to go now, she is saying. I need to get back to reception. I think I can hear the telephone ringing. Then she is gone, scuttling down the corridor on her high heels.

Jack closes the door. He paces up and down the room, counting his steps. Doctor McCarthy told him once that if he begins to feel upset or anxious about something, he should count something. Count the plates in the cupboard if he is at home, or count the leaves on the trees if he is outside. What should I do in the winter? Jack had asked him. The trees won't have any leaves in the winter. Count in your head, the doctor had said. Walk up and down and count your footsteps. One, two, three, four, five, six. He reaches the opposite wall now, spins around, and counts again as he walks back to the door. One, two, three, four, five, six. It isn't working. The room is too small and it is impossible to reach ten. He can hear his heartbeat and his anger is growing inside like a drumbeat, relentless and impossible to ignore. He quickens his steps, counting faster and faster as he paces the room. But each time he passes the full-length mirror on the wardrobe door, he doesn't see himself reflected, but flashes of his mother, laughing at him, mocking him, shouting at him. He stops, wanting to confront her, to tell her to leave him alone, but his mother's blood-soaked body and wide, frightened eyes stare back at him, forcing him to turn away.

It's not real, it's not real, he tells himself. With his eyes clamped shut, he opens the wardrobe door so he can no longer see the mirror. Maybe a cup of tea will help. People always make tea in a crisis. He has a couple of teabags left. He flicks the switch on the tiny kettle and watches over it until he begins to hear the slow build of the bubbles and steam inside. When it has boiled, he pours water over a teabag, adds a splash of milk and two sachets of sugar. The motion of stirring, watching the pale brown liquid slosh around the cup, calms him.

He reminds himself that things could be worse. He is lucky he is in a hotel room right now, rather than a police station cell. After all, close family members of murder victims tend to get arrested, don't they? He needs to keep his cool and keep a lid on his anger. He can't allow mundane things to set him off. He doesn't want to be like his mother. He doesn't want to frighten people and make them wish they weren't alone with him. It isn't nice to be like that. As he drinks his hot tea, he tells himself that he must apologise to the young lady on his way out.

Claire

Claire watches Elena as she crosses the road, walks across the village green, and strides up the path to the door of the church. It was nice to see her. Maybe she should rebuild their friendship. She should never have lost touch with her. They used to be close. If it wasn't for Elena, she would never have met Stephen. She has her to thank for that. But for now, she needs to work. She closes the window, pulls the string to close the Venetian blind, to keep the draft from snaking its way around her neck, and sits at her desk. She shuffles through the papers, making two piles, one of urgent and one not-so-urgent work. She begins to type a report to one of her clients, but her focus is as scattered as dandelion seeds on the wind. She has no control over her thoughts, and after fifteen minutes of staring at the blank sheet of paper in her typewriter, she admits defeat, locks up the office, and goes home.

The warm, familiar smell of vegetable soup greets her at the door and she can hear Helen, Sophia, and Trevor chatting in the kitchen.

Sophia rushes over as soon as she sees her, pulling her into a hug. 'I'm so sorry about this morning,' she says.

'What do you mean? What do you have to be sorry about?' asks Claire.

'I was wondering why you were so quiet, you just weren't yourself, and then I remembered that it's coming up to Stephen's anniversary. I'm so sorry.'

'It's fine,' says Claire, with a small smile. 'I know you have no idea whether it's Wednesday or December most of the time.'

'Exactly,' says Sophia.

Claire settles at the kitchen table next to Trevor. Helen ladles soup into four bowls, setting an extra bowl on the worktop for Wendy when she wakes up from her nap.

'Did you speak to Elena?' asks Sophia. 'She came here looking for you.'

'Yes, she came to the office,' says Claire. 'That's why I'm home. I can't think straight anymore today. I've had two shocks, one seeing Elena after all this time, and the other with her coming with the news about Miriam. I had no idea that she was dead. Elena said she had been killed.'

'It is shocking, isn't it?' says Helen. 'I gather the police will be speaking to everyone in the village, trying to build up a picture of who she was.'

'What did Elena tell you?' asks Sophia.

'She said she was found in the kitchen by Jack around six o'clock. He had gone to the shop for some cigarettes, so it must have happened sometime between four and six.'

'Well, it's a good job we were all here then, isn't it?' says Trevor, dipping a chunk of bread into his soup. At their stunned expressions, he shrugs. 'What? Well, it's got to be someone she knows, hasn't it? All I'm saying is, it's good that we can rule each other out.'

'I wasn't here,' says Claire. 'I worked late, remember?'

'Ah, well, I'm afraid you are still considered to be a suspect, unless you can prove your whereabouts,' says Trevor.

Claire laughs. 'I suppose I'm not in the clear just yet, but why are you so sure it was someone she knows?'

'Just statistics. Consider how many people are murdered by strangers and how many are murdered by people they know. The odds are, especially in a village like this where the crime rate is next to zero, that the perpetrator is someone close to Miriam.'

'Who would that be then?' says Helen. 'She wasn't one for going out, except when she went to church, and the only family I'm aware she had was Jack.'

'There you go then - it's him.' Trevor slathers butter onto another slice of bread, oblivious to the stunned silence around him.

Helen's voice is sharp. 'It's *not* Jack, never in a month of

Sundays. I know him well. We all do. My sister lives next door to him and his mother and I've spent many hours chatting to him over the fence. He wouldn't hurt a fly. He's a lovely boy.'

'You mark my words, the murderer is someone Miriam knew well,' says Trevor. 'If it isn't him, it must be someone she worked with.'

Elena

Elena goes straight to St. Mary's Church from Claire's office, leaving the news of Miriam's shocking death to sink in. Claire told her that Miriam had been cleaning her house yesterday. Alive and well. Claire was at the office all day, so she didn't know what time Miriam left the house, but it was usually no later than four o'clock. Claire picked up the phone to check with Sophia, but there was no reply at home. Elena told her not to worry, she would be able to call and see Sophia another time.

At the church door, Elena turns around and looks up at Claire's office window across the road. She wants to wave, but can't tell whether Claire is watching or not. She turns back, pushes at the heavy oak door, and walks into the darkness of the church.

A middle-aged woman is on her knees polishing the brass handle of an umbrella stand at the end of one of the pews. Her sheepskin coat is thrown like a blanket over the backs of her legs and feet, and her head is covered by a cream-coloured Arran wool hat, pulled down low over her ears. She throws Elena a look that would kill the devil and hugs the chunky collar of her coat into her neck with her free hand. Elena closes the church door behind her and the woman relaxes the grip on her collar.

'Good morning,' says Elena. 'Is the vicar available to speak to, please?'

The woman nods towards a mahogany-stained door at the top of the church. Elena can see a rectangular wooden sign with the word *Vestry* engraved in swirly letters. 'He's in there, but I doubt he'll see you without an appointment. He's a very busy man. Would you like to make an appointment?'

Elena wants to ask what he is busy with. She always wondered what vicars actually do. Apart from the Sunday services and the occasional wedding and funeral, how do they fill their time in a village as small as Eldenbridge? She imagines him sitting behind a huge desk, sipping strong tea from a china cup and pondering an ecclesiastical jigsaw whilst listening to the morning news, and later An Afternoon Theatre on Radio 4 while he wrestles with The Times crossword.

'My name is Detective Inspector Elena Holt,' she says. She takes her warrant card from her jacket pocket and shows it to the self-appointed gatekeeper.

'Oh, why didn't you say so?' says the woman. She leans on the back of the pew and pushes herself to her feet. 'These brasses will be the death of me one day,' she says. 'I'm Carol, the churchwarden. Follow me.' She scuttles off with an air of great importance down the aisle and, without knocking, opens the door to the vestry.

'Adam, someone from the police is here to see you. A detective inspector.' Carol holds the door open and allows Elena to enter the office. 'I expect it's about Miriam, is it?'

she says, nodding at Elena for confirmation.

'Yes, indeed,' says Elena. 'We're speaking to everyone who knew Miriam Chadwick.'

'I knew her very well,' says Carol. 'Here take a seat, Inspector.' Carol pulls a heavy ladder-back chair away from the desk and indicates that Elena should sit on the faded tapestry seat.

The bewildered-looking vicar stands and holds out his right hand. 'Adam Hargreaves,' he says. 'Pleased to meet you.'

Elena shakes his hand and introduces herself, showing her warrant card again, despite the fact she has already met Adam Hargreaves. On Saturday 11th October 1975, almost twelve months ago, she was here in this church, forced into wearing a floor-length bridesmaid's dress, the colour of Advocaat, eagerly awaiting the wedding between her brother and her best friend, Claire. Adam had shaken hands with the waiting family on either side of the church, remarking on what a beautiful day it was, now that the rain had stopped. Her grandparents had laughed and told him how the Heavens had opened on the day they were married, so the omen wasn't true - you could still have a long and happy marriage if it rained on your wedding day. Elena had watched as the vicar floated down the aisle towards the open door of the church in his immaculately ironed cassock and white and gold embroidered stole, where she and Sophia were waiting, each nervously grasping their floral bouquets.

Adam informed her and Sophia that the groom hadn't yet arrived and when they caught sight of the wedding car, could they please ask the driver to go around the block until the coast was clear? They all stood there, watching the road and listening for the sound of an approaching car. They engaged in small talk for a few minutes, as the vicar checked his wristwatch for the third time, and remarked that it was unusual for a groom to be late. Brides, yes, but grooms were expected to be early. Sophia's mother and Elena's parents followed him to the door, each of them wearing their worried expressions like shadows creeping across the sunlit churchyard. Elena's mother checked her watch and asked where on earth Stephen might be. He wasn't one to be late, not for anything. Her father grasped her hand and told her not to worry, he would be there soon. Maybe their car had broken down, her mother had said. He should never have agreed to be driven in Gary's old rust-heap. It was always breaking down. They should have splashed out on another wedding car. Her father had said that Stephen wasn't daft and that if Gary's car had broken down, he would call the taxi company. He would be here any minute, he said, just wait and see.

Then the bridal wedding car appeared containing Claire and her father. Elena waved it on, but after two trips around the village, Claire ordered the driver to stop and dashed up the path in her billowing wedding dress, closely followed by her father. As she lingered outside the door, the cool autumn wind forcing her carefully curled hair from its clips, Elena was the one to tell her that Stephen was late and they were beginning to worry about him.

Adam suggested they should wait inside the church foyer. He then closed the door. The bride was beginning to shiver. The weak October sunshine had been replaced by a darkening sky, heavy with the threat of a downpour. He laughed then and said he was sure the groom would be here soon. There was nothing to be concerned about.

But Stephen never arrived. A uniformed officer was the one to tentatively knock on the church door and deliver the devastating news that there had been a tragic accident. A bend taken too quickly, excess rainwater on the road, and worn tyres had all contributed to the collision between Gary's old car and an oak tree. Gary walked away from the wreck with cuts and bruises. Stephen wasn't so lucky. The passenger side of the vehicle had taken the brunt of the impact. He died later that day in hospital, with his family and his bride-to-be by his side.

If Reverend Hargreaves remembers the name of Holt, or recognises Elena in any way, he doesn't show it. Elena's hair had been covered by an Alice band of flowers the last time they met. Today her clothes are very different and not half as colourful. She isn't surprised he doesn't recognise her.

'Carol, would you mind if I chat to Reverend Hargreaves alone for a moment?' says Elena. 'I'd like to speak to you too though, so if you wouldn't mind waiting in the church, that would be great.'

'Of course, of course,' says Carol. 'I'll carry on with the brasses.' She closes the door behind her.

'Call me Adam, please,' says Adam. 'Reverend Hargreaves is something the bishop calls me when I'm in trouble.'

'I can't imagine what kind of trouble a vicar would be in,' says Elena. They both laugh politely.

As they settle in their chairs, Elena watches Adam closely. When she became a detective, her interview training wasn't extensive, she learned more about bullying tactics than clever questioning, but over the years she has taken an interest in the body language of a suspect and she watches Adam for the tell-tale signs of a guilty man. Someone who shifts in their seat, or struggles to maintain eye contact, or blinks rapidly and clenches their hands usually has something to hide. But at first glance, Adam seems to be relaxed. He smiles, showing white straight teeth and small crinkles around his deep brown eyes. He would be an attractive man, Elena supposes, in normal clothes. He can't be more than forty and still has a full head of dark hair, which brushes his collar at the back. He rests his hands on the desk in front of him, fingers intertwined. Elena wonders whether that is his normal position or whether he is forcing himself not to fidget. She pictures him standing at the top of the church, his clenched hands resting on the top of the pulpit about to give his weekly sermon, and concludes that he must feel comfortable like this.

'As Carol guessed, I'm here to talk to you about Miriam Chadwick,' she says. 'She worked for you, I believe?'

'Yes, she did,' says Adam. 'She was due here today, as a matter of fact. It's shocking, isn't it?'

'How did you find out about her death?' asks Elena, although she can guess the answer. Village life doesn't allow secrets for long.

'Carol told me this morning,' he says. 'She heard it from someone in the shop on her way to church.'

'When was the last time you saw Mrs Chadwick?'

Adam gazes out of the window to his right. 'Let me think.' Elena watches his fingers clench slightly until the knuckles turn white. 'Tuesday.' He nods and faces Elena again. 'Yes, Tuesday. She cleans here and at the vicarage every Tuesday and Friday.'

'And did you see her here or at the vicarage on

Tuesday?'

He pauses for a second longer than Elena expects. 'At the vicarage,' he says. 'She arrived just as I was leaving for church.'

'Can you remember what time that would have been?'

'I usually leave the house around the time the boys leave for school, so around eight-thirty. I remember she arrived just after they left. I had to wait to let her in.'

'Doesn't she have her own key?'

'No, there's no need. I'm so close to the church, if she's a minute or two late, it doesn't adversely impact my day at all.'

Elena opens her notebook and scribbles down what Adam has told her so far. 'Did you see her after that?'

Adam shakes his head vigorously. 'No, I let her in the house, said good morning, and left her to it. My wife deals with whatever jobs she wants Miriam to do, so I didn't need to chat to her about anything. Like I said, I left her to it.'

'What was Mrs Chadwick like?' asks Elena. 'I mean as a person, not as a worker? Did people generally like her?'

There's a sharp knock on the door and Carol pushes the door open with one hand, while the other holds tightly to a small wooden tray. 'Excuse the interruption,' she says. 'I've made you both some tea and there's a couple of biscuits.' She slides the tray containing two small cups of milky tea and two custard creams onto the desk. 'Sugar?'

'No, thank you,' says Elena.

'Like me, watching your figure, are you? Although there's no need.' Carol pats her stomach. 'Wait until you're my age. That's when it piles on.'

'Carol, if you don't mind…' says Adam, nodding

towards the open door.

'Right, yes, well take your time. I'll busy myself with the polishing until you're ready, Inspector, although I do need to get my grandsons from school at half past three. I'll let Adam be the one to tell you about Miriam. Sorry, sorry, but I couldn't help hearing you ask as I came to the door. God rest her soul, you shouldn't speak ill of the dead, I know, but she could argue with her own shadow, that woman. Not a kind word to say about anyone. It will be interesting to see how many people turn up to her funeral. Not many, I would imagine.'

Saturday, 9th October 1976

Adam

Adam is in his study, pretending to be working. He hates Saturdays. It's a day tinged with expectation. He is expected to play with his children, be patient when they begin to quarrel and bicker, and then give father-son talks about how to be kind to each other. He is expected to play the part of a happily married man, hold hands with his wife when they go for a walk, and later show her the kind of attention he wants to reserve for his girlfriend. He knows he shouldn't be in a position where he has a wife and a girlfriend. No man who took his marriage vows seriously should be in that position, especially a vicar. If the bishop found out, he would lose his job and his home along with it. But most importantly, he would lose his reputation; in the words of Iago, that idle and most false imposition, oft got without merit and lost without deserving. Except, unlike Othello, he would deserve it, wouldn't he? In all truth and honesty, he deserves to lose everything; his reputation and his family.

He should end it before anyone gets hurt. Every day he tells himself he will. But every day, he doesn't. He can't.

Does that mean he is in love? Lust, definitely. He isn't sure about love yet, but whatever it is, he is enjoying it and doesn't want it to stop. Now that Miriam is dead, there is no need for it to stop.

He runs a hand through his hair.

Except that, how can he stand in the pulpit tomorrow and pontificate to his parishioners about the virtues of living a Christian life? They would be appalled and disappointed if they knew he was having a sordid affair. But when he is with her, it doesn't feel sordid. It feels right.

He tugs at his dog collar. He decides he won't be going back to church this afternoon, so he can take his cassock off. He hangs it on the hook at the back of the study door. The note is still in his pocket. The one he wrote for Miriam, but didn't give her. He needs to get rid of it before someone sees it. He decides to put it on the fire. He can sneak into the living room and do it now while his wife, Cheryl, is busy in the kitchen. It's coming up to twelve-thirty, so she will be in the kitchen preparing lunch for the boys. He grabs the note and scrunches it tightly into his fist.

The sharp knock on the door makes him jump, just as he is about to open it.

'I need to go shopping, are you okay with the boys?' Cheryl pops her head around the study door.

'I'm working on my sermon,' he says.

'It doesn't look like it,' she says.

'I was just taking a break, about to make myself a coffee.'

'Come here.' She holds her arms out wide like Jesus welcoming his disciples. 'You look like you need a hug.'

Adam surreptitiously shoves the note back into the pocket of his cassock behind the door and wraps his arms around his wife. Her hair smells of coconut shampoo. Familiar. Comforting. He kisses the top of her head.

'I was pegging the washing out just now, and you were

staring into space. I could see you through the window. How many words have you actually put down on paper?' She pushes him away and wanders over to his desk. 'As I thought. None,' she says, as she peers at the blank sheet of paper on his desk. She walks back to him and stands in front of him. She runs a finger down the side of his face, gazing with love into his eyes. So much love. Sometimes it suffocates him. 'Why don't I make us something delicious for dinner tonight?' she says. 'I'll get a bottle of that nice red you like, and if you take some time away from your desk now, you might get some inspiration later. You can finish your sermon while I put the boys in bed, and then afterwards, it is just you and me.'

He smiles at her. 'That sounds like a plan.' Although, he doesn't need inspiration. The sermon was written on Wednesday, but she doesn't need to know that. He just wanted some time to himself, locked away in his study, away from the noise of the house. He never gets time to think these days. 'I feel bad spending more time in here tonight,' he says. 'Are you sure you don't mind?'

'How can I mind? That's my job, isn't it? To support you.' She kisses him tenderly on his cheek. 'Take your time getting it finished, and then when it's done, we can open the wine.'

He nods. That sounds appealing. He can close the door while she deals with the children. He can read one of his books, and have some peace. Anything is better than watching The Generation Game. All that shouting and false bonne amie. He can't stand Bruce Forsyth and those stupid contestants who can never remember what has just passed them, literally seconds ago, on the conveyor belt.

'That's a plan then,' says Cheryl. 'I won't be long. I've

left the boys at the kitchen table with some crayons. They have already had a sandwich for their lunch. Yours is on a plate in the fridge.' She stands close to him, resting her hand on his back.

'Thank you,' says Adam. Why does she do this? Why does she do nice things that just add to his guilt? She would have been devastated if Miriam had told her about his affair with Claire. He needs to be more careful in future, and make sure nobody sees them together.

'If the boys argue too much, shove them into the garden. The football is in the garage.'

'I know where the football is, Cheryl.' He brushes her hand away and pushes past her out of the room.

'Oi, no need to be so snappy.' She follows him down the hallway and into the kitchen. 'It isn't my fault you can't think of what to write in your sermon. Have a word with Him upstairs.' She lifts her eyes to the ceiling and laughs. 'He's meant to help you with stuff like this, isn't He?'

Adam ignores her. He fills the kettle with water and throws a teabag into a mug.

'Boys, your daddy needs some help with his sermon. What should he talk about tomorrow that would stop his congregation from falling asleep?'

'Pirates!'

'No, aliens!'

'There you go,' says Cheryl. 'Two perfectly good subjects.' She presses her body into his back and wraps her arms around his stomach. 'Don't worry, darling. The words will come. They always do.' She stands on her tiptoes and kisses the back of his head. The gesture tugs at his heart. He shouldn't be bad-tempered with her. She doesn't deserve it. She's a good wife and an excellent mother. She doesn't deserve what he is doing to her.

What he has already done.

Angela

Angela spots DS Miller before he sees her. He is knocking on the door of the flower shop; his face shielded by his giant hands as he peers through the frosted glass of the front door.

'The shop's not open yet,' she says when she gets to him.

DS Miller makes a show of looking at his wristwatch. 'On the busiest day of the week? That boyfriend of yours keeping you in bed too long, is he? You'll never make money if you don't open your shop. That is how you make your money, isn't it?'

Angela takes a deep breath. How can one man be so irritating? She can't stand him. Just the sight of his face sends angry adrenalin rushing through her veins. Punching him squarely in the jaw would release some of it, she's sure. She looks at his left hand and is surprised to see a wide gold wedding band. So he does have a special someone, after all? What kind of idiot woman would marry a man like that?

'I've had something to attend to,' she says. 'Not that it is any of your business.'

'Really? And what kind of something would that be?' DS Miller stands with his legs wide apart and his hands in the pockets of his trousers.

'Women's issues actually, if you must know.' That will

shut him up. 'What do you want?' she asks.

'Aren't you going to open up, so we can talk inside? Or do you want a discussion on the street?'

For a moment she considers staying right where she is. She doesn't want him to make himself comfortable in her shop. She wants him to say his piece and get gone as soon as possible. But, she's freezing cold, so she reluctantly unlocks the door and he follows her inside.

'I'll get straight to the point,' he says. 'Our enquiries suggest that Miriam Chadwick was murdered between the hours of 4pm and 6pm on Thursday night. I'm not convinced that you were where you said you were.'

'Am I a suspect?' asks Angela.

'Tell me where you were between those times on Thursday night.'

'I was right here in the shop, like I said the last time you asked me.' Angela leaves the door open, despite the cold, and begins to pull at the string to open the window blinds. She flicks the switch on the wall and light bursts into the shop.

'I know that's what you *said,* but your door sign says you close at four-thirty, so why would you still be here at six o'clock?'

'I was doing paperwork,' she says. She carries a bucket of pink roses outside and deposits them on the pavement underneath the window. DS Miller waits for her inside the shop.

'Was anyone else with you?' he asks as she returns. He is leaning with his back to the counter, arms folded.

'No, just me.'

'Not that young lover of yours, what's his name, Shamal

something or other?' DS Miller grins at her.

'Kamal,' says Angela. You know damn well what his name is, you scumbag, she thinks. She keeps her thoughts to herself. She knows DS Miller will do anything to see her behind bars. It is clear he is trying to antagonise her until she loses her temper. She refuses to give him any ammunition. She picks up a bucket of dahlias. 'These are my favourite flowers, you know. Aren't they beautiful? Look at those petals. They remind me of stage curtains in a theatre, you know, that luscious velvet red.'

'What are you talking about, woman?'

'Not a theatre-goer?' She looks him up and down, taking in his drab black trouser suit, cream shirt, wide brown tie the colour of damp soil, and his black leather jacket which remains unfastened over his round stomach. 'No, I don't suppose you are.' She takes the bucket of dahlias outside, placing it next to the roses. 'Anything else you wanted to ask me, sergeant?' she says. She turns the sign on the door to indicate that the shop is now open.

'What paperwork did you do on Thursday night?'

'Oh, I don't know. Accounts, that kind of thing.'

'Can you prove it?'

'I don't have to prove it,' says Angela.

DS Miller slams his hand onto the counter. 'Stop wasting my time,' he shouts.

'All right, all right, keep your hair on,' she says. She looks up at his bald head and smirks. She walks into a small room at the back of the shop and returns carrying a large notebook, which she places on the counter. She opens it to a page marked *Thursday 7th October*. 'Here, look.' She turns the book to face him and points to the column marked *Sales*. 'This shows how much I took that day. This column next to it shows how much the variable outgoings are. There was nothing on that particular day.' She flicks the page to the previous day. 'You can see here that I had a delivery the day before, so that figure goes in that column' She snaps the book closed.

'That shows jack-shit,' says DS Miller. 'You could have filled that in last night.'

'I could have done, but I didn't,' says Angela.

'What about that boyfriend of yours? Will he attest to your whereabouts? I suppose he will say you were at home, nice and cosy on the sofa by six o'clock?'

Angela shakes her head. 'He won't actually. He was playing football until after eight o'clock. You can check with the landlord of the Bull's Head on the main road. He's on their five-a-side team.'

DS Miller scribbles in his notebook, not attempting to hide his disdain. He clearly thinks she is lying, but there is nothing she can do about it.

'What do you want me to do?' she says. 'Don't you think that if I'd killed a person, I would make sure my alibi was nice and water-tight? I would have at least killed her on another night, a night when Kamal was at home, don't you think?'

He ignores the question. 'What's your relationship with Jack Chadwick?'

'I don't have a relationship with Jack Chadwick?' she says. 'I know him as Miriam's son.'

DS Miller stares at her for a moment. Angela waits for his next question. 'When was the last time you spoke to him, prior to his mother being killed?'

'I've got no idea. You know what this place is like, like any village, you bump into people all the time. I could have seen him the day before. I could have seen him the week before. To be honest, I can't remember.'

'There's nothing honest about you, Angela Bennett, and one day I'll prove that. You mark my words.' DS Miller storms out of the shop and slams the door behind him.

Jack

Jack hasn't yet apologised to the young lady, the receptionist at the hotel. He wants to. If his mother was here, she might tell him to try harder.

Last night, after pacing the bedroom for an hour, he felt calmer. His heart rate gradually returned to normal and his thoughts weren't as frantic. He closed the mirrored wardrobe door and was relieved to see that his mother was no longer there. He wandered down the corridor to the hotel reception but the young lady, Alison, wasn't there. An older man with a short crew cut and a grey beard asked him if he needed any help. Jack said he would like to have the room for another night if that was okay. Sure, the man had answered. Jack felt irritated that he was trying to sound American. Nobody he knows says *sure*. He mumbled his thanks, turned his back on the wannabe American, and returned to his room.

This morning, the young lady is back at work. Jack puts his suitcase on the floor next to the reception desk and hands her the room key, together with the carefully folded pound notes to settle his bill. But she seems too busy to talk. She doesn't count the money, although Jack isn't bothered about that; he knows it is all present and correct.

He is about to ask her if she wants to count it, but she pushes it into a drawer and picks up the telephone on her desk. Good morning, this is the Eldenbridge Hotel, how can I help you? She speaks in a sing-song voice. Jack hasn't heard the telephone ring. He hovers for a moment, waiting for the call to finish, but when the young lady glances up at him, she frowns and turns her back on him, clasping the phone receiver tightly to her ear.

Jack decides to leave when it becomes apparent the call will be a long one. The customer on the other end seems to have a lot of questions and Jack only has a few moments before the bus is due. He is anxious not to miss it. He pushes open the door and stands on the pavement outside while he fastens his coat. He glances back through the glass door and sees that the receptionist has finished her call now. Never mind. He needs to catch the bus back to Eldenbridge. It seems like she won't be getting her apology after all.

Claire

Saturday mornings at Claire and Sophia's house are usually leisurely affairs. Helen doesn't work at the weekends, so the sisters have fallen into a pattern of eating a cooked breakfast together at the kitchen table, followed by an hour or so of reading the paper and chatting while Wendy potters about with her toys. Trevor is always welcome to join them. Sometimes he chooses to take a walk around the village or get the bus into Wellington to visit his wife's cousin. But today he has no plans and is busy frying bacon and making toast for everyone.

'Aren't you going out today?' Sophia asks him.

'I don't think so. I'm feeling lazy. It's a beautiful day though, so if you girls want to go anywhere, I don't mind looking after the little one for you. She's no trouble.'

'Thanks, Trevor,' says Sophia. 'What do you think Claire? There's a new boutique opened in Wellington, we could go and have a look at that?'

'Yes, if you'd like to,' says Claire.

'Great,' says Sophia. 'Let's go this afternoon then, shall we, while Wendy has her nap? I could do with a new pair of jeans.'

'Yes, okay,' says Claire. She is still wearing her pyjamas and her long brown hair is tied up into a bun on top of her head. She gets up from the table and sits on the floor next to Wendy, who immediately toddles over to show her auntie the various Stickle Bricks from her toy box, which are now scattered across the kitchen rug. Claire takes hold of one of Wendy's hands and pulls her onto her knee. As Trevor splashes oil over the bacon in the frying pan and turns the rashers over with a fork, and Sophia fills the teapot with water, neither of them notices the exact moment when Claire begins to sing. It has been so long since either of them heard it, they have been unaccustomed to the sound. It begins with Claire softly humming to her niece as she rocks her on her knee. When Wendy begins to giggle at the tickles of warm breath on her neck, and wriggles out of Claire's arms, Claire gets to her knees and, holding each of Wendy's small hands in hers, she sways from side to side, softly singing the lyrics to *Dancing Queen*. Wendy giggles even more and jumps up and down. Sophia is desperate to join in. She loves Abba, but she doesn't want to spoil the moment between her beloved sister - the sister who has lived under a cloak of grief for twelve months - and her daughter.

After a while, Claire gets to her feet and sits at the table. 'What?' she says, still laughing.

'Nothing,' says Sophia. 'It is just so lovely to hear you sing again.'

Claire bats the remark away with her hand. 'Oh, it's that song, it sticks in your head, doesn't it?' 'Yes, it does,' Sophia agrees. 'It's on the radio all the time, but nevertheless, it's good to see you happy again.'

'I agree with Sophia. Stephen wouldn't want you to mourn for him forever,' says Trevor. He butters three thick slices of toast, lays them in the middle of the plates, and tips two rashers of the perfectly cooked bacon onto each slice. 'I know you loved him deeply,' he says as he carries the food to the table, 'as I loved my wife, but if either of them could talk to us now, they would tell us to be happy. Don't you agree? Life is so short not to be.'

Claire loves the way that Trevor talks about his wife. Not every day, but often. He reminisces with more fondness than sadness, to the extent that Claire feels as though she knows her. She loves to hear the stories of their lives together. How they met at the dance hall and Trevor swept her off her feet, literally, to the sounds of the jazz band's saxophone. They quickly fell in love, married at the Manchester Register Office in the summer of 1923, and honeymooned in Blackpool for three nights before returning to Manchester, to the semi-detached house that they continued to live in until she died. They weren't blessed with children, but Trevor said they made up for that by making sure they saw other members of both sides of the family regularly. As they got older and had more money, they took holidays in Cornwall and the Gower Peninsula, and then later in Spain, where his wife laughed at Trevor's initial reluctance to try the local delicacy, paella packed with prawns and spicy meat. But after a couple of mouthfuls, Trevor loved it and washed it down with delicious Sangria served in bright yellow and green ceramic jugs.

By contrast, Claire has found her life with Stephen too difficult to remember, never mind talk about. She keeps his memory safely locked away in a part of her heart she doesn't want to access. In the early days, she imagined that leaving the police force behind, including Elena, would help her to grieve. Out of sight is out of mind. It wasn't until yesterday, when Elena had visited her at her office, that it occurred to her how wrong she had been. She had so many wonderful times with Stephen, it is a sin not to look back on them and share them with friends and family.

This morning, she definitely feels brighter. She has finally put down the burden she has been carrying for so long. Maybe now is the perfect time to pick up her friendship with Elena. She must ring her and see if she would like to go to the pub for a drink some time.

As she begins to eat her breakfast, she remembers the night Stephen asked her to marry him. They had been dating for less than three months, so the proposal was all the more special for it being completely unexpected. Afterwards, Stephen told her he couldn't let Valentine's Day pass without doing something special. Claire knew he was a hopeless romantic, but had only expected a bunch of roses or a box of chocolates, not a diamond ring.

It was February 1974. Candles up and down the country

were lit, not for romantic dinners for two across decadently set tables in expensive restaurants, but in ordinary houses, providing light for ordinary families. The three-day week was underway, power cuts were prevalent, and candle sales were soaring. Families huddled together in the half-light. Mums forced their children into coats and hats indoors, and grannies were wrapped in blankets. Although, on the whole, children loved the blackouts and dashed around the house, ignoring pleas to be careful, don't trip, don't leave the candle unattended. They played at dressing up, pretending to be Victorians forced to live by candlelight every day. Upstairs, they made dens from their coats, tucking the hems into the space between the mattress and the bed frame and draping the other end over the back of a chair. Downstairs, parents clustered around dining room tables, shifting Monopoly pieces across the board until the fading light made the cards too difficult to read, whilst their children told each other ghost stories and shivered with self-inflicted fear. In the almost pitch-black, adult conversations were mainly focused on politics, the miners' strikes, and workers' pay.

But nothing could dampen Claire's spirit back then. She loved Stephen. She loved candlelight. She loved firelight. She was happy and in love.

As she admired her new ring, Stephen struggled with the bottle of Champagne, tugging at the cork, trying desperately to keep hold of it before it flew from the bottle and damaged Claire's mother's precious lamp. They were in her parents' library at the back of the house. Stephen had already asked her father for permission for his daughter's hand in marriage, and, unbeknown to Claire, the couple were being given privacy. Claire's mother was counting down the minutes until her daughter announced the good news. It was a magical time. As soon as Claire shouted for them to come in, her mum, dad, and Sophia bounded into the room and wrapped the happy couple in their arms.

Claire was already looking forward to a long and happy marriage with Stephen.

But now he is gone and someone else has her heart.

Whether she is ready to give it completely, well, that's another question, but for now, she is enjoying his company. She knows it might not lead anywhere, but focusing on someone else is helping her to heal. One day at a time. She doesn't want to be miserable forever. Yesterday was a turning point. Seeing Elena was so much nicer than she thought it was going to be.

She smiles at Trevor, as she watches him stir his tea, tapping the side of the cup three times with his teaspoon, as he always does. 'This is delicious, Trevor, thank you.'

'You're welcome,' he says. 'It's lovely to see you smile again.'

Claire wants to tell Sophia and Trevor that she has another reason to smile, other than her beautiful niece and the catchy Abba tune. She wants to tell them about the handsome man in her life, the one she has been seeing for months now but has been keeping secret. The one who has helped her heal. But she knows she can't. Right now, she can't tell anyone. She knows that having a relationship with a married man comes with sacrifices, such as not being able to giggle with her sister about how wonderful he is, not being able to see him at the weekend when his wife is around, and having to be content with snatches of time here and there in private places where they won't be seen. Right now, she doesn't know whether the relationship has longevity, or whether it's just a bit of fun. She is taking it day by day. But when, or if, they tell people, it has to be at the right time and on their terms.

So far, they have been careful and only one person has found out about their affair - Miriam Chadwick - but now she will no longer be able to share their secret before they are ready. Miriam walked into the vestry on Thursday morning, just as Claire and Adam were in the middle of a passionate kiss. Claire had never seen Adam so panicked. He practically knocked her over in his rush to push her away from him, as though touching her scorched his fingers.

'Shit,' he said, as he shot to the vestry door. 'Miriam! Miriam, come back!'

But Miriam was halfway down the aisle, on her way out, calling Adam a dirty cheating bastard. She slammed the church door closed behind her. Claire ran after Adam and grabbed onto his arm, as she tried to persuade him not to chase after her. Someone might see the altercation between them, and more questions would be asked. She told him not to worry, to let her go. Miriam was known for her temper and her foul language, but she would calm down. Claire promised she would speak to her later at home.

'What is she doing here anyway?' said Adam. He paced up and down the aisle, impervious to Claire's pleas for him to sit down. 'She's meant to be cleaning your house today, isn't she? What did she want me for?'

'I don't know, but it doesn't matter. I told you not to worry,' Claire said. 'I'll speak to her. Look, I've got to go now, I've got a meeting with a new client in ten minutes, but I can finish early and have a word with her before she leaves our house. I'll ask her not to say anything.'

'It will be too late by then,' said Adam. 'You know what a blather mouth she is. Can't you talk to her now, before she has a chance to pick the phone up and start spreading malicious gossip?'

But it isn't malicious gossip, is it? It's the truth. 'She doesn't have a phone, and she wouldn't use ours, not with Sophia in the house. I've got to go.' Adam's attitude annoyed her. Who cared whether Miriam blabbed or not? Would it be such a hardship if their secret was revealed? It would be good if they didn't have to scuttle about. They could go on normal dates like normal people. They could have meals in restaurants and walk by the river holding hands, rather than stealing a quick snog whenever they thought nobody was looking. After all these months, she was getting a little tired of being the bit on the side.

'Can you go home after your meeting?' said Adam.

'Adam, calm down. Miriam has a busy day ahead of her, she won't see anyone other than Sophia and Helen, and if she gossips to them, they won't say anything. They will want to protect me. I said I'll speak to her later this afternoon.'

'What will you say?' asked Adam.

Claire shrugged. She had no idea. How could you stop the village gossip from engaging in her favourite activity? All she could do was appeal to Miriam's better side, to make her see that people would be hurt if she told anyone. Adam's wife and children didn't deserve to find out from anyone other than him. She would ask Miriam to keep her counsel and assure her that it was a one-off and it would never happen again. She would blame herself. She would tell Miriam that Adam hadn't given her any indication that he was interested in her, but she had thrown herself at him. She could blame grief. Tell Miriam about Stephen's anniversary coming up and tell her she was deranged and wasn't thinking straight. That would do it, until they decided it was time to tell Adam's wife themselves.

She told Adam she would think of something.

But as the day went on, Claire's phone never seemed to stop ringing and the post delivery only added to the ever-growing piles of paperwork on her desk. The plan to chat with Miriam escaped her mind. By the time Claire finished work and arrived home, exhausted and hungry after a very long day, Miriam had already been and gone.

Now their secret is safe and she doesn't need to speak to her.

Now Miriam is dead.

Elena

As Elena walks up the narrow path to the vicarage, she can hear screams coming from inside the house. Not the sounds of an assault, or a murder taking place, but the ear-piercing sounds of two small boys having temper tantrums. Another reminder to Elena that she has made the right decision in choosing not to have children. As she reaches the front door, she can hear a man's low mumbled voice coming from the room at the front of the house, followed by another scream. His placatory manner doesn't seem to be working. She waits for a hiatus in the noise before she knocks on the door.

'Oh, good morning, Detective Inspector,' says Adam, as

he opens the door.

'Good morning, Reverend Hargreaves,' says Elena. 'I'm sorry to arrive unannounced but I was in the area. I've just got a couple of questions for you, if you don't mind giving me a few moments of your time. I won't keep you long.'

He holds the door open and invites her inside. 'Sorry about the mess. Watch your legs on those bikes. Those pedals can be lethal to the ankle bones.' He laughs, but it isn't the easy-going laugh of a man relaxing at home on his day off. It is the forced laugh of someone at the edge of their tether. She gets the impression that he isn't often left alone with his children and that maybe he doesn't find parenting quite as easy as his wife does. 'Come through to the kitchen.'

As they walk down the narrow, cluttered hall, they pass a closed door to the right. 'The boys are in there,' says Adam. He cracks open the door, revealing a room packed with furniture and toys. Two small boys are kneeling on a rug in front of the fireplace, surrounded by a selection of toy cars, lined up as though in a miniature traffic jam. Boxes of games and jigsaws are piled onto the sofa and half a dozen picture books are discarded onto one of the chairs. Adam tells the boys to put the television on and be quiet while he speaks to the police detective about something very, very important. She hears little voices telling him yes Daddy, they will. He closes the door and shakes his head. 'I don't know how my wife copes with them all day, I really don't. Roll on Monday when they're back in school.'

'I had a brother, so I know what young boys can be like,' says Elena when they reach the kitchen.

'You *had* a brother?'

'Stephen Holt. He died on the morning of his wedding

to Claire Simons.'

Two pink circles appear on Adam's cheeks and the tips of his ears turn red. 'You're Stephen's sister? I'm so sorry, I didn't recognise you. Please forgive me.' Adam indicates for Elena to sit at the kitchen table, and hurriedly pushes a pile of folded washing to the other end.

'Don't worry about it,' says Elena. She runs a hand over her short hair. 'My hair was a little longer and covered in flowers on that day, and of course, I don't tend to wear yellow satin dresses to the office.' She is wearing a black two-piece suit with a white shirt, and flat black lace-up shoes. Her uniform. Adam looks her over. Elena feels a flash of irritation. She wants to remind him that he is a married man and shouldn't be looking at her in any kind of way. Would he look a man up and down and judge him in the same way? Maybe he would, she thinks, deciding to give him the benefit of the doubt. The way Harry Beckford dresses invites comments. He loves it when his up-to-the-minute three-piece suits and two-tone platform shoes are noticed by someone, whereas Elena prefers to blend into the background.

'Do you smoke, Inspector?' asks Adam. He opens one of the kitchen drawers and takes out a packet of Benson and Hedges, which he holds out to her.

'I do,' she says. 'It's a guilty habit which I'm trying to shake, so I'm going to decline, thank you.' She watches as he takes a cigarette from the packet, places it in his mouth, and lights it with a silver lighter. He takes a deep breath in, closes his eyes for a second, and blows a plume of smoke up to the kitchen ceiling.

'Daddy, Daddy!' A small boy dashes into the kitchen, holding a naked Action Man in front of him. 'I can't find his clothes, Daddy.' The boy's bare feet skid to a halt and he stares at Elena. He is wearing denim jeans and a Batman t-shirt. His dark brown hair, the same colour as his father's, sticks up in various places at the back of his head. He pushes a long fringe from his eyes. 'Hello,' he says.

Elena smiles at him, before the boy is ushered out of the kitchen with orders to search for Action Man's clothes in the toy box. Adam leans with his back to the kitchen door, a barrier between the parent and the recalcitrant children he is doing his utmost to ignore. The cigarette dangling from his mouth causes him to scrunch his eyes closed. He looks different today. More handsome than yesterday, when he was wearing his cassock. Today he is dressed in a pale blue, well-fitted button-down shirt and dark jeans. The sleeves of his shirt are casually rolled up, revealing strong forearms and a watch that is more functional than flashy. His hair is neatly combed but the slightly too-long length gives him just a touch of rebellious charm. He smiles at her. There's a twinkle in his brown eyes that hints at flirtation. If Elena didn't prefer women, she might be attracted to him. She could see why some women would be.

'I think I can keep them at bay,' he says. 'We have ten minutes, maybe eight.' He shrugs. 'They get their attention span from me, I'm afraid. It's short.' He pushes himself away from the door and sits down opposite her at the table. He flicks ash from his cigarette into the ashtray in the centre of the table. 'So, how can I help you?'

'I'm just double-checking when Miriam Chadwick was last seen,' says Elena. She wants to appear casual. Backing someone into a corner doesn't usually get the best results. She gives Adam a wide smile. 'If I can track her movements on Thursday, and perhaps in the days running up to

Thursday, then we can get a clearer picture of what she did and who she spoke to.'

'Yes, yes, absolutely,' says Adam.

Elena takes her notebook from her jacket pocket and makes a pretence of searching her various pockets for a pen while she studies Adam across the table. Silence tends to make people nervous, but she can't decide whether this man is nervous or not. A little bit frazzled, yes. But who wouldn't be when dealing with two young boys? He watches her and makes good eye contact when she looks at him. He is either an innocent man, waiting patiently to assist the police with enquiries, or he is a cold-blooded murderer, an emotionless psychopath, confident that he has covered all his tracks and amused at the police's attempts to catch him. She wavers to the former. After all, how many times has a vicar been arrested for murder? She has never known it to happen.

So why did he lie to her about when he saw Miriam last? Carol, the churchwarden, has confirmed that Miriam and Adam were both in church on Thursday morning, but Adam claims he hasn't seen Miriam since Tuesday. It doesn't make sense. She needs to give him another chance to tell her the truth. Maybe when she first asked him, he simply forgot. After all, he does have a lot on his plate.

'We know that Miriam cleaned for Claire and Sophia Simons on Thursday until around four o'clock,' she says, 'and she then made her way home. What I'm trying to do is piece together her movements earlier in the day. I'd like to speak to anyone who may have seen her around the village.' Adam nods and takes another drag of his cigarette. 'Did you see her at all on Thursday?'

'No,' he says, a little too quickly. 'Like I told you

yesterday, I last saw her on Tuesday.' He flicks ash into the ashtray again and watches the end of the cigarette as it burns, seemingly avoiding eye contact.

So, twice he has told her the same thing. Elena knows this is a lie and wonders why Adam won't admit that Miriam was in church on Thursday morning. What is he hiding? Twice she has asked him when he last saw her, and twice he has said Tuesday. Unless Carol is mistaken. That's a possibility, of course. Elena can clarify that with her later. Yesterday, Carol had to dash off to collect her grandchildren from school, so they didn't have much time to talk. The only question Elena managed to ask her was when she had last seen Miriam. 'She was in church on Thursday morning,' Carol had said. 'I presumed she was here to see Adam about something. She didn't speak, we just passed on the path outside. We said hello and she went on her way.'

'Can you tell me what you did on Thursday?' says Elena. Adam hesitates. 'I'm asking everyone, I hope you don't mind,' she says. She flashes him a smile as though to say, you may be under investigation and I know you have just lied to me, but it's nothing personal, I'm asking the same question of everyone in the village.

'I was in church most of the day, preparing for the upcoming council meeting and writing some letters. I came home at lunchtime and had a sandwich with my wife, then I went back to church for a couple of hours.'

'Until what time?'

'Three o'clock, something like that. I was home when

the boys came home from school.'

'And you stayed at home the rest of the evening?'

'Yes, that's right.'

The kitchen door creaks open, blown open by a blast of fresh air from the open front door. Elena peers down the hallway and can see Adam's wife struggling with two bulging carrier bags of groceries. 'I'm back,' she shouts. Mrs Hargreaves kicks off her shoes and makes her way to the kitchen. 'Oh, sorry, I didn't realise there was someone here,' she says. 'Where are the boys?'

'Watching television,' says Adam. 'Cheryl, this is Detective Inspector Holt. She is leading the investigation into the murder of Miriam.'

Cheryl drops the shopping onto the floor and holds out her hand to Elena. 'Pleased to meet you,' she says. 'Anything we can do to help you, anything at all…'

'I was just checking with your husband where he was on Thursday,' says Elena. 'Don't look so alarmed, I'm asking the same of everyone, just so I can figure out who saw Miriam in the hours leading up to her death.'

Cheryl nods and takes a seat in the chair next to her husband, facing Elena. This isn't ideal. Elena would have preferred to speak to Adam alone. He might not be so willing to open up in front of his wife. Vicar or no vicar, he's a man, and in Elena's experience one of the main reasons men lie about their whereabouts to the police is because they have already lied to their wife.

'Now that you're here, can you tell me when you last saw Miriam and what you did on Thursday?'

'I didn't see her at all on Thursday,' says Cheryl. 'She cleaned here on Tuesday, so I saw her then, in the afternoon. On Thursday I was at home, apart from taking the boys to school and collecting them again, but I walked straight there and back. It was raining, if you remember, so I didn't loiter at the school gates like I usually do, you know, chatting to the other mums. As soon as the boys came out of school, we rushed home.'

'And then all of you stayed in for the rest of the evening?'

Adam says yes as his wife says no. Cheryl laughs nervously. Elena can see unspoken questions flitting between the couple as they glance at each other. Cheryl frowns.

'Mrs Hargreaves?' says Elena, inviting her to clarify.

'That's the night you went to see that young couple, isn't it?' Cheryl says to her husband.

'I don't think so.' The pink has returned to Adam's cheeks. 'I was at home Thursday night.'

'Yes, yes. I remember because I'd made sausage and mash for dinner, but by the time you got home I had gone to bed and turned off the oven. The potatoes were all dried and horrible.' She faces Elena. 'It isn't easy to keep a meal like that warm for very long.'

'Wasn't that the day before?' says Adam. He stabs the end of the cigarette into the ashtray. Stab. Stab. Stab.

'No, you didn't go out on Wednesday. That's my aerobics night, remember? In the village hall?' She smiles at Adam, like you smile at an elderly confused relative. 'You were here with the boys on Wednesday. It was definitely Thursday when you went out.' Cheryl turns to Elena and explains that the couple he went to see live at the other side of Wellington, but they want to be married at St. Mary's because it's such a pretty little church, so Adam went to see them to speak to them about becoming members of the congregation. They kept him talking for hours. Very interesting couple, Adam had told her. 'You talked about lots of different things, music, politics, foreign holidays, until quite late, didn't you, darling? Then that terrible rain made driving conditions difficult, so it took ages for Adam to get home.'

'What time did you get home?' asks Elena.

Adam is still focused on the remains of his cigarette in the ashtray. 'I don't know,' he says softly.

'It was quite late,' says Cheryl. 'I wasn't asleep, but I was in bed reading my book when he got in.' She smiles at Elena as she tells the story, completely oblivious to the fact she has just lit a fuse and blown her husband's alibi into a hundred tiny pieces.

Adam

Adam can tell the detective inspector doesn't believe him. He tries to tell her he made a mistake about which evening he was out, but it is obvious she thinks he's lying. He can see it in her face. She's how old? Late thirties, forty maybe? It's hard to tell a woman's age when she dresses like a man and doesn't wear makeup, but she's probably been doing her job for a million years and she will know a liar when she meets one. Adam tries his best to appear nonchalant. He smiles a lot and forces himself to look the detective in the eye as she chats to him and Cheryl, but his ears are burning. Giving him away, like a lighthouse guiding lost sailors. Here he is! Here is the man you're looking for! The guilty one!

'Thank you so much for your time,' says the detective

eventually. 'You've both been very helpful.' She puts her notebook into her jacket pocket. 'If there's anything else you can think of…'

'Oh, we won't hesitate to ring you,' says Cheryl. She is loving this, Adam can tell. She is desperate to be a helpful citizen, to be the one who finds the missing piece of the jigsaw and hands the completed puzzle to the police. As she closes the front door behind the detective, she skips into the kitchen. She can't wait to tell her boys how their mummy has done her good deed for the day.

Adam closes the door to the study and rings Claire's home number. He knows he shouldn't. They have an agreement that he will only contact her at the office, but he needs to speak to her. Thankfully, she is the one who answers the phone and not her sister. He hasn't bothered thinking of an excuse as to why he called.

'Hi,' she says. Just the sound of her voice makes him feel instantly calmer. 'How are you?'

'Not good,' he says. 'Not good at all.' He keeps his voice to a whisper so Cheryl doesn't hear him and start asking questions.

'What's wrong?' asks Claire.

'The police have just been here, asking me where I was on Thursday night.'

'I spoke to them, too,' she says. 'They will be asking everyone in the village. Routine procedure. Was it Elena, Stephen's sister?'

'Yes, that's her. Well, Cheryl has well and truly dropped me in it. I told Elena I was at home on Thursday with the children, then Cheryl came home and told her I was out until late, having drinks with a young couple who want to get married in St. Mary's. She said she was in bed when I got home.'

Claire pauses for a second too long. 'And is that true?' she asks.

'Is what true?'

'That you were out until late on Thursday?'

'Yes.'

'Well, you have nothing to worry about then. If necessary, just ask that couple to confirm they were with you. I can do that, if you want me to. Give me their address and I'll go and see them.'

'No, keep out of it,' says Adam. His tone is sharp and dismissive. He can sense Claire's hurt. In his mind's eye, he can see her beautiful face frowning. 'I'm sorry, sorry,' he says quickly.

'It's okay,' she says. He knows it isn't okay.

He takes a deep breath. 'The issue is, I lied.'

'What do you mean?'

'I lied to Cheryl and I lied to the police. I didn't meet anyone. I was alone. Now Elena is waiting for me to produce the names and addresses of this couple, and I can't, because they don't exist.'

Jack

As Jack turns into Southgate Drive, he can see Eve Hardy, his next-door neighbour, in her front garden. She is busy brushing crisp brown leaves into a pile against the privet hedge. Every time she adds to the pile, more of the leaves float away like untethered rowing boats. She chases after them, using her brush to steer them back into position.

Ordinarily, Jack would prefer to avoid any chatter with the neighbours - tell them nowt, his mother used to say, then they have nowt to use against you - but today, he has no choice. He needs his front door key.

Eve spots him and smiles. She rests her brush against the hedge and walks over to their short boundary fence. Jack wants to tell her that the leaves are making a dash for it behind her back but decides against it, as he isn't sure how she will take it. If he dared say anything of the sort to his mother, it would have resulted in an argument. Jack would have been accused of criticising her and the brush would have been thrown at him, for him to do a better job, if he felt like he could. Although he never felt like he could. Nothing he did was ever as good as his mother could have done. She reminded him of that at every opportunity.

Jack, how are you? Eve looks concerned. She doesn't give him time to reply before she begins talking again. Silly question, I know, she says. You must be traumatised, poor thing. But the cleaners assured me they have done a good job. There's no trace of, well, you know, everything is as it should be. I haven't been in myself, but they looked like trustworthy chaps. She dashes inside to get the key, telling Jack to stay right there and don't move. Where does she expect him to go?

Within a moment, she is back with the key in one hand and an envelope in the other. She holds them both out like an offering at an altar. Jack doesn't know which to take first, so he takes them both at the same time, which results in him dropping the envelope. It flutters across Eve's lawn towards the mound of leaves. Eve tells him not to worry. It's just a card to say how sorry she is for his loss, she tells him. She rescues it and hands it back to him. Go and get yourself inside before you catch your death, she says. I'm sorry, I'm so sorry, she says. Her hands shoot to her mouth.

Jack's mother always told him that he wasn't the brightest button in the box, but even he, with no qualifications, no job, and no prospects, knows when a blunder has been made. On another day, at another time, he would forgive Eve for her tactless remark, but not today. He doesn't feel like forgiving anyone for anything today.

He drops the door key into his coat pocket, holds the envelope high in the air, and rips it in half. I don't want your sympathy! I don't want it!

He can't help shouting. The words leave his mouth before he has a chance to modify their volume. He takes one of the halves and rips it again. He does the same with the other half. He drops the pieces onto the garden path and stamps on them with both feet.

I don't want anything from you. He leans close to Eve's face over the fence, so there can be no misunderstanding.

Eve begins to cry and tells him she is just trying to help, and that there is no need to shout at her. She is being neighbourly.

No, no, you're not helping, Jack screams. Telling the police you could hear arguments through the wall is not helping. Now they think my mother was bad-tempered. She wasn't a monster. She wasn't. He holds his hands over his ears. He doesn't want to hear Eve's reply. He closes his eyes so he doesn't have to look at her. She doesn't have the right to cry. He is the one who is upset.

He can hear a car engine and waits with his eyes closed until it passes. It will be one of the neighbours. A few of them have cars now. Posh Rich Bastards, his mother used to call them, especially that couple across the road, the

Gregsons. Although, they're in Spain, so it must be someone else. Then the engine stops, and a car door slams. Footsteps are marching up his garden path, getting closer and closer. A hand on his arm. Come on Jack, let's get you inside. He opens his eyes. It's Angela Bennett.

Eve has gone. Her brush lies abandoned; the leaves are flying around completely out of control.

What are you doing, Jack, making a show of yourself like that? You need to keep your head down. I told you that, didn't I? Give me your key. She has one hand on his arm and the other takes the key from his hand.

Jack allows himself to be ushered into the house, down the hall, and into the kitchen at the back. There is a nasty smell that makes his eyes water and the back of his throat sting. He assumes it is cleaning liquid.

The floor has never looked so clean, says Angela. She laughs. Your mother would have a fit. She wouldn't be happy that someone could get a shine as good as that when she never could. Lighten up, Jack, she says. It could be worse. You could be in a police station right now, facing a long stretch.

A stretch of what?

Angela laughs again and begins to fill the kettle with water. She opens the fridge, takes out a bottle of milk, and sniffs it. She wants to know if he has got any coffee. Jack points to the cupboard above the fridge and watches as Angela takes out two cups and spoons granules of Nescafé into each one. She tells him about the policeman who asked her questions at the shop. Useless piece of shite, she calls him. He wouldn't be able to detect a bad smell if it was right there under his nose. She laughs at her own joke and smacks Jack on the arm. He laughs with her, but he isn't sure why.

When the coffee is ready, Angela carries the two cups into the living room, where she tells Jack to make himself comfortable and tell her everything the police asked him. She wants all the gory details.

He doesn't want to relive everything, but as they sit side by side on the sofa, she leans closer to him, puts her hand on his knee, and tells him she is his friend and if he needs someone to talk to, she is here for him. I'm a friend, aren't I? I won't gossip about you, you know. I'm not your mother. Jack should feel angry. He should jump to his mother's defence and tell Angela not to talk about her like that, but he knows Angela will laugh at him and tell him to stop defending the dead. He doesn't like to be laughed at, so he keeps quiet and drinks his coffee.

Angela is right, it is nice to have friends, but as it turns out, she is as bad as his mother. As soon as he tells her about the conversation with the detective lady and that horrible man with the brightly coloured socks, she gets cross and tells him he was stupid. Why would you deny that we know each other? We live in the same village. I own the flower shop. Everyone knows me. I'm Angela Bennett.

Yes, knowing Angela Bennett and knowing you, the person, are two different things, he tries to explain.

No! She is shouting now. He doesn't like it. He wants to tell her to leave him alone. He didn't ask her to come into the house. He sinks into the chair.

She takes hold of his hand and tells him everything will be okay. She is talking softly now. You can lie to the police, yes, but not about something as silly as that. That will get their radar twitching. Angela explains how the police love lies. They collect them and keep them safely stored and use them as weapons against you later. She knows what she's talking about.

He understands now. But now it's too late. He has already said it and can't take it back.

It's not too late, says Angela. Don't worry. Things will be fine.

She gets up then. She has to go home. She just wanted to pop in and check on him. She asks him whether he has any food in the house. A flash of the potato hash strewn across the kitchen floor, the gravy mixed with his mother's blood running in rivulets between the floor tiles makes him feel sick. He tells her he will make himself a sandwich, but he doubts whether he will be able to eat anything. He doesn't feel like it. The smell in the kitchen has turned his stomach.

Jack closes the front door behind her and listens to Angela's Porsche burst into life as she drives away. She likes to rev the engine. She likes people to know she's around. Probably because she was one of eight children and didn't get much attention from her mother. He told her that's what he thought when she first bought the car and had raced around the corner into the cul-de-sac showing it off. Angela had laughed and punched Jack playfully on his arm. Not like you, eh? You get all your mother's attention. He didn't tell her that he hadn't wanted *all* his mother's attention. Some of it, yes. But all of it was too much. You really can have too much of a good thing, despite what everyone says. Living with Miriam Chadwick was like living under a microscope. His every move was under scrutiny, like a scientist searching for rogue cancer cells, desperate to find something bad. She searched out the bad in him and revelled in pointing it out. Nothing he did was ever good enough for his mother.

But he didn't tell Angela that. He didn't need to. Angela knew what his mother was like. She had tolerated her – in fact, they had tolerated each other, but he could tell Angela hadn't liked his mother. Not many people in the village had, truth be told.

The house is quiet now. Jack takes the dirty coffee cups from the living room and rinses them under the tap in the kitchen. If his mother were around, she would be shouting at him to use the washing-up liquid. Do it properly, you dirty little sod. He can hear her voice reverberating around the kitchen. He knows she isn't here, but glances over his shoulder just to be sure. Then he stares at the floor, the spot where his mother's body lay, surrounded by the potato hash they were meant to be having for tea. What an undignified way to go.

He dries the cups on a tea towel and puts them back on the shelf in the wall cupboard. The kitchen clock ticks slowly to remind him that the rest of the day is spread before him. Empty and alone.

It was good of Angela to visit. She said she was checking how he was, making sure he had everything he needed. Everything except my mother, he had wanted to say.

He was glad she arrived when she did. Who knows what would have happened if he had been left in the front garden for a moment longer with Eve. Angela told him that he shouldn't blame Eve, not really. She thought she was being a good citizen, and she wasn't telling the police anything that people in the village didn't already know. Everyone knew that Miriam had a temper. She couldn't help it. That's the way God made her. Angela had looked earnest then. She nodded at him as they walked hand in hand back down the narrow hallway to the front door, where she gave him a kiss on his cheek and told him to take care. He had never seen Angela in church. He didn't know she believed in God. But he didn't mind either way. She was a good friend, and he needed one of those more than ever right now.

Elena

Elena leaves the vicarage with more questions than answers and makes her way to the church to speak to Carol Turner, the churchwarden.

'I'm always in church on a Saturday, keeping the place open so that anyone can call in and light a candle, say a prayer, or just have a look around,' Carol had told her yesterday. 'I like to make sure the vicar gets his Saturdays off,' she said, 'you know, with him being a family man.' Elena wonders how much of a family man the vicar is. He is clearly lying to his wife about something. He is either a murderer or an adulterer. Right now, she isn't sure which.

'Good morning, Mrs Turner,' says Elena, as she pushes the church door open. She spots Carol lighting a candle on the candle stand in the square foyer just inside the door. She is wearing the same knee-length pale brown sheepskin coat she wore yesterday, this time with a bright red woollen scarf, wrapped tightly around her neck. Her legs are covered in thick tights and she is wearing sensible brown shoes.

'Good morning, detective,' says Carol. 'I light a candle so other people can use it to light the other candles. You don't want them messing about with matches, not in a place as old as this.' She nods sagely and looks up towards the ceiling which is criss-crossed with ancient wooden beams. Elena can tell she takes her role as the churchwarden extremely seriously. She imagines that someone like her would be difficult to work with. She probably likes things done a particular way and deviation from the norm would not be accepted. But from a detective's perspective, she is pure gold. She misses nothing and hears everything. When you want some witnesses, people like Carol are the ones to seek out. The eyes and ears of the village. The centre of everything.

'Don't let me stop you doing whatever you need to do,' says Elena. 'I'm happy to have a look around until you've completed your jobs.'

'Thank you,' says Carol. 'I won't be a moment. I just need to put these matches back in the drawer in the vestry and change the water in the flower vase, then I'm all yours.'

Elena tells her to take her time. Of course, the tiny box of matches will be perfectly safe in Carol's coat pocket and the flowers certainly don't need to be tended to right now, but Elena wants her to be relaxed, with all her jobs done before she begins questioning her. In any case, it gives Elena time to look around the church. Not that the murder weapon will be here. The church, in fact, all the public buildings in the village, have already been searched. But another look is never a waste of time.

The tiny church has just ten rows of wooden pews on either side of the centre aisle. The stone floor is carpeted from the door to the altar by a narrow threadbare carpet, which Elena can tell was once the colour of sapphires, but is now worn to a muted grey/blue, like the sky before a storm. She hardly noticed it on the day of Claire and

Stephen's wedding - on the day that *should* have been their wedding. There were so many people jostling about, happily chatting, shaking hands, and laughing, all looking forward to the meal and the party afterwards in the Wellington House Hotel. Most of them, including herself, aren't religious and only step foot into churches for weddings and funerals. But Claire had wanted a church wedding and Stephen, who generally wanted what Claire wanted, was happy to agree.

As Elena strolls down the aisle, trying to shake the memories from twelve months ago, she takes in the three stained-glass windows overlooking the altar, illustrating various stories from the Bible. She recognises Noah and the Ark in one of the windows, a man covered in sheep's clothing - she can't remember his name - in another one, and, of course, Jesus carrying his cross in the window in the middle.

'They're beautiful, aren't they?' Carol joins Elena at the altar. 'It's over a hundred years old, you know, this place. Built in 1863 when the village began to grow with mill workers. Amazing, isn't it?'

'Yes, it's a beautiful church. My friend planned to marry my brother here but…'

'Oh no, split up, did they? Happens such a lot these days,' says Carol. 'Suppose it's better before the wedding than after.'

'No, he died.' Elena keeps looking forward, focusing on Jesus's thorned crown, as she blinks tears away. 'On the morning of the wedding, he was killed in a road accident.'

'Oh my goodness, not Claire and Stephen's wedding?' Carol grasps Elena's right hand in both of hers. 'I'm so sorry. What a tragedy that was. Stephen was your brother, was he?'

'Yes, my younger brother by a couple of years. Did you know him?' Elena pretends to search in her jacket pocket for a tissue to release her hand. Too much empathy will make her cry and right now, she is just about managing not to.

'Not him, no, but I know Claire. She lives in the village, just down the road there.' Carol nods towards the back door. 'But of course, you know that.'

'Yes, she's a good friend,' says Elena. At least, she *was* a good friend. The best. But now isn't the time to discuss the ins and outs of her complicated relationship with Claire. 'Anyway, that's enough of me.' She smiles. 'Churches have a way of making people emotional, I'd imagine?'

'You're not wrong there,' says Carol. 'Tissues and tea are always in high demand in places like this. Come on, follow me, I'll make us a cup of tea and we can chat, if you've got time for a cuppa?'

'Always,' says Elena.

In reality, she doesn't have that much time as she needs to get back to the station for the briefing, but she doesn't want Carol to think she isn't giving her undivided attention. She follows her back down the aisle to a small room at the side of the main door which houses a sink, a small fridge, and a couple of kitchen units. A kettle, a row of various-sized mugs, and an open box of teabags sit on the countertop. Carol fills the kettle with water and switches it on.

'I need to take some notes while we chat, if that's okay,' says Elena. She gets a notebook and a chewed biro from her pocket. 'I don't want to forget anything useful.'

'Oh, absolutely,' says Carol. 'This is a murder

investigation, after all. I've seen Murder on the Orient Express. Where would Inspector Poirot be without his notebook?'

Elena laughs. 'Completely lost, and I'm afraid my little grey cells are not as honed as his,' she says. 'I have to write everything down.' She waits until Carol finishes the tea and they are settled in a pew at the back of the church, their steaming mugs of tea balancing on the shelf in front of them, before she begins to question her. 'As you know, Miriam Chadwick was killed on Thursday evening. From what we have gathered, she finished her job cleaning for Claire and her sister, Sophia, around four, and she made her way straight home. Her son, Jack, told us she arrived home just after four o'clock. He then went out to the shop and discovered her body when he returned, around six o'clock, in their kitchen.'

'Dreadful, dreadful business.' Carol shakes her head.

Elena wonders how dreadful it really is, or whether this is exactly what people like Carol were waiting for; something exciting and dramatic to pull them from their overwhelming boredom, stuck in this sleepy Lancashire village miles from anywhere. 'Did you know Miriam well?' she asks.

'Everyone knew Miriam. She wasn't a friend of mine,' says Carol. 'I couldn't stand the woman.' She makes the sign of the cross on her chest. 'May God forgive me, but she was horrible, anyone will tell you that.'

'In what way?'

'In every way, but mainly in the way she treated that poor boy of hers. Well, he's not a boy, is he? Jack's a full-grown man, but he's like a child sometimes. He needs looking after. Goodness knows how he'll cope now, all alone.'

'Can you be more specific? About Miriam, I mean, not Jack. What horrible things did she do?'

'She used to shout at him all the time, and she never bothered who heard her. She'd tell him off for looking scruffy, that kind of thing. Stand up straight. Brush your hair. Fasten your coat properly. Always picking at him. He never said anything back to her, just yes Mum, no Mum. She made his life a misery, from what I could gather.'

'And what about other people? How did she treat them?' Elena flicks through her notebook to the notes she wrote yesterday. 'You made a comment yesterday that she could argue with her own shadow.'

Carol nods vigorously. 'She fell out with them in the shop a few months back. Something about not stocking the right brand of ciggies. Very particular, she was, and if she didn't get her own way, you knew about it.' Carol takes a sip of tea. Elena waits for her to continue. 'Her and Adam had a falling out. I mean, who would fall out with a vicar, a man of God? I don't think she was even a Christian. She just liked to appear as though she was. She came to church to catch up on the village gossip, in my view. She never sang the hymns with particular enthusiasm.'

'What did she and Adam argue about?'

'Oh, it wasn't him.' Carol looks shocked. 'He wasn't to blame.' She points to Elena's notebook, seemingly concerned that Elena might write something disparaging about the beloved vicar. 'I don't want you to think it was him, because it wasn't. Miriam took against him one day because she said the church smelled of bleach. She said you should never use bleach on a floor like this, it would ruin it.'

'Bleach ruins stone tiles?'

'Not the tiles, but the marble at the altar. I don't know, but with Miriam being a cleaner, I assumed she knew what she was talking about. But there are ways of going about it, aren't there? She came in, nose in the air like she was some sniffer hound, and then she marched up to Adam, right in front of a group of people, and started going on about the bleach, raising her voice and pointing her finger.' Carol shakes her head. 'Horrible, horrible woman. I don't care about speaking ill of the dead, sometimes you have to tell the truth, don't you?'

'Yes, you do,' says Elena. She scribbles in her notebook quickly. 'Thank you for painting a picture of Miriam. It's important to get to know her, and to get to know those around her. So, given the way she was with people, would you be aware of anyone she had fallen out with recently?'

Carol laughs. 'Apart from everyone in the village, you mean?' Elena nods. 'Well, not in that way. No, no, I mean not that anyone would want to murder her. Eldenbridge is a quiet little village. Nobody would do that, not that I know of.'

'We can't rule out that it was someone from outside the village,' says Elena.

'It must be,' says Carol. 'Not that I saw anyone strange hanging around, if that's your next question.'

'It was going to be,' says Elena. 'Were you out and about in the village on Thursday?'

'I came to church in the morning, like I usually do, but I had a hair appointment in Wellington in the afternoon, so I didn't stay here long. I got the eleven o'clock bus, had lunch in that nice cafe on the high street, and then I went to get my hair done.' She pats her perfectly coiffured hair. 'I live a few steps from the bus stop, so I went straight home afterwards. I didn't go out again until the following morning. I saw the police cars whizzing past the house though, but it wasn't until the next day that I found out what all the fuss was about.'

'What time did you get home on Thursday?'

'I don't know exactly, around three I think.'

'Am I right in thinking you saw Miriam on Thursday morning?'

'Yes, but I didn't speak to her. She was leaving as I was walking up the church path. I said good morning to her and she mumbled a reply and walked off. She was like that sometimes. You never knew if she was in the mood to speak.'

'So you don't know why she was here? Because she doesn't normally clean here on a Thursday, does she?'

'No, like I said yesterday, I presumed she was here to see Adam about something. Something to do with cleaning the vicarage and the church, I don't know, you'll have to ask him that.'

'Did Adam mention her to you at all? Didn't he say why she had been here?'

'No, but I wouldn't expect him to really. I saw him disappearing into the vestry and he closed the door, so I got on with my jobs and left him to it.'

Elena picks up her mug and drains the last of the tea. 'Thank you very much, Mrs Turner, you've been extremely helpful. If there's anything else you think of that might be useful, please ring me at the station. Just ask for the Incident Room.' She hands Carol a square business card and leaves the church. On the way out, she has another glance around and wonders whether the silver vase or the bronze bust could be possible murder weapons. She makes a mental note to ask the pathologist when she speaks to him later.

Sunday 9th October 1976

Elena

Elena paces up and down the Incident Room in front of the blackboard, twisting a piece of chalk between her fingers. 'Right team, settle down. Let's go over what we know again. On Thursday 6th October, Miriam Chadwick was found dead in her kitchen at approximately six o'clock by her son, Jack, who says he discovered her after returning from the shop. She was killed at some point between four and six - four being the time she left Claire Simons' house and six being when the triple nine call was made by Jack Chadwick. The time the deceased left Claire's has been verified by her sister, Sophia, and I've no reason to disbelieve her.'

Geoff nods. 'Claire and Sophia are both salt of the earth.'

'So let's go through the people close to Miriam, and what we know about them. The most significant people in her life are her son and the people she worked for.' Elena writes *Adam Hargreaves, Angela Bennett,* and *Jack Chadwick* on the blackboard and draws a line between them, making three columns.

'What about Claire and Sophia Simons, ma'am?' asks Imogen.

'Absolutely not,' says Geoff.

'No, no, it's a fair question,' says Elena. 'Imogen doesn't

know the family like we do, Geoff.'

'I know, but Claire Simons, being an ex-detective and a close personal friend of Detective Inspector Holt is above reproach,' says Geoff. 'Her sister is a writer. I've only met her once, but she's a soft-spoken, gentle woman. Like I say, salt of the earth, the pair of them.'

'Sorry, ma'am,' says Imogen. 'I didn't know you are friends, but I just thought with them being one of Mrs Chadwick's employers that at least one of them would be a person of interest.'

Geoff shakes his head. He takes a large bite of his bacon sandwich, leans back in his chair, and waits for Elena's explanation. He wonders how much detail, if any, she will give about Claire and the reason she left the police force.

'Ordinarily, yes,' says Elena. She pauses, tapping the stick of chalk on her bottom lip. 'But you're right. People do act out of character sometimes and just because some people in the team know Claire and her sister well, doesn't mean we should discount them. They should be considered until evidence proves otherwise. Geoff, I can hear you tutting. You just concentrate on keeping that ketchup from dripping on your trousers.' Geoff looks down at his trousers and flicks breadcrumbs onto the floor. 'Why don't you go and speak to them, Imogen, and take a statement from them? Ask them about their relationship with the deceased, and what their movements were on Thursday. It will be good practice for you.'

'Yes, ma'am, thank you, ma'am,' says Imogen. 'And shall I speak to her lodger and the nanny too?' She looks at her notepad. 'I believe they have a man called Trevor as their lodger and a lady called Helen Billington looks after the little girl in the house and does some cooking for them.'

'Bloody hell, Miss Marple, how do you know about them?' asks Geoff.

Imogen smiles. 'Harry and I spoke to Mrs Billington's sister yesterday, a lady called Eve Hardy. She's Miriam Chadwick's next-door neighbour.'

'Excellent police work, Imogen. We'll make a detective out of you yet,' says Elena. 'Okay, so while you have the floor, tell us what the next-door neighbour said. She is the same one who told the house-to-house team that she heard shouting through the wall on regular occasions, isn't she?'

'Yes, she is,' says Imogen. 'She lives alone after her husband died a couple of years ago, and she has known Miriam and Jack for around ten years. She said that Jack has always been a quiet man and she doesn't usually hear his voice through the walls - just Miriam's. She said that Miriam was a nasty piece of work and treated her son like her servant.' Imogen waits for the murmurs throughout the office to die down before she continues. 'She said last week, on Wednesday, she was putting something in the bin in the back garden when she heard a particularly ferocious argument coming from number eight. Miriam called Jack a useless piece of shit and said she wished he had never been born. Mrs Hardy said she could hear Jack crying, but then Miriam's kitchen door slammed closed and she didn't hear anything else.'

'I must say that Carol Turner, the churchwarden at St. Mary's, said similar things,' says Elena. 'By all accounts, Miriam wasn't a nice person and rubbed quite a few people up the wrong way.'

'So if she was a battle-axe, which we can safely say she was, do you think her son flipped his lid and killed her?'

asks Harry.

Elena nods. 'I am not ruling anything out at this stage, We need to question him further, there's no doubt about that.' She scribbles *Difficult relationship with mother* on the blackboard underneath Jack's name.

Imogen holds up her notebook. 'Can I add, I noted down several other incidents of shouting that the neighbour overheard, but also she told me yesterday that Jack Chadwick lost his temper with her and shouted at her over the garden wall. She said he was 'aggressively angry' - those were her words – because he found out she was the one who said she heard arguments through the wall.'

'Yes, I did tell him that when I first spoke to him,' says Elena. 'Although I didn't expect him to have a shouting-match with her.'

'Shall I make my notes into a witness statement for Mrs Hardy and ask her to sign it?' asks Imogen.

'Yes, that would be advisable. Thank you, Imogen. Well done.'

'Funny that Jack never mentioned any arguments between him and his mother when we interviewed him, boss,' says Harry.

Elena writes *Failed to mention arguments* underneath Jack's name. 'Okay, so moving on to the vicar of St. Mary's Church, Adam Hargreaves.' Elena points to his name with the end of her chalk. 'I spoke to him yesterday and he claims he last saw Miriam on Tuesday morning at the vicarage at around eight-thirty in the morning, but—' she pauses, raising an eyebrow, '—I know that's not true because the churchwarden saw Miriam at the church on Thursday, at the same time Reverend Hargreaves was there.'

Geoff takes another bite of his sandwich and licks ketchup from his fingers. 'He's hiding something, no doubt about it. Why lie about something as simple as the last time he saw her?'

'There could be an innocent explanation. Maybe he forgot. People panic, especially around us,' says Harry.

Geoff snorts. 'Panic? Come on, Harry. The man runs a church. He's supposed to be honest, and lying about something this basic reeks of guilt. What if he had an argument with Miriam? From what we know, she wasn't well-liked. What was it the churchwarden said to you, boss, she could argue with her own shadow? Well, what if they argued and it all went wrong? These things happen. There are plenty of murder weapons in a church. Don't they have gold statues everywhere? He could have picked one up and…'

'She wasn't killed in church, boss,' says Harry. 'Are we to think that the vicar took a weapon with him? That suggests he planned the murder.'

'Well, why not?' says Geoff.

'I was thinking it was a moment of madness in the house,' says Harry.

'That's because you're fixated on it being the son.'

'Let's not jump to any conclusions,' says Elena. 'The murder weapon hasn't been found, so we need an open mind. But I agree, the vicar's hiding something, yes. In addition, he told another lie,' she pauses, 'or was mistaken about what he was doing on Thursday evening. He told me he was at home with his children, but then his wife said he was out all evening with a young couple who want to be married in the church.'

'I suppose it's possible he was mistaken,' says Harry. 'I mean, who remembers what they did on a particular night after work?'

'Let's be honest here,' says Rahul. 'I agree with DS Miller, Harry, you are a bit fixated on Jack Chadwick, and that's why you don't want to believe it could be someone else.'

'No, that's not it,' says Geoff, laughing. 'He's one of those God-botherers, aren't you? He can't accept that a vicar might do something untoward.' He rolls up his paper napkin, smeared with bacon grease and ketchup, and throws it across the room at Harry. It floats in the air and lands two feet from Harry's feet, missing its mark. 'Maybe the vicar's playing away,' he says.

Elena has to admit that it seems like a likely scenario, but then again, it could just be that Geoff is tarring all men with his own brush. 'Right, come on, let's focus on the job in hand. I know it's Sunday morning, but..'

'Sorry boss,' says Geoff. He clicks his feet together, sticks his tongue out of the side of his mouth, and gives Elena a Benny Hill-type salute. She laughs it off but makes a mental note to speak to him about his insubordination later.

'Let's stick to what we can prove.' Elena writes *Lied about when he last saw the victim* in the column underneath Adam's name, and *Lied about his whereabouts on Thursday evening.* 'What about the flower shop owner, Angela Bennett? You seem keen on her as a suspect, Geoff.'

Geoff leans forward, resting his elbows on his knees. 'For the benefit of Imogen and Rahul who might not be aware, Angela Bennett has been on our watch list for some time, isn't that right, boss?' Elena nods. 'She portrays herself as an above-board businesswoman. She totters about in tight skirts and high heels, flicking her long blonde hair and batting her false eyelashes, trying to give the impression that butter wouldn't melt. But her lifestyle doesn't match her legitimate income. The flower shop in Eldenbridge isn't particularly busy and I can't see it giving her enough of an income to keep that big fancy house going, and the Porsche 911 she likes to razz about in. In fact, yesterday when I turned up at lunchtime, she was only just opening up.'

'Where do you think she gets her money from, Sergeant?' asks Rahul.

'Drugs, no doubt about it. We haven't been able to pin anything on her yet, but trust me, never take her at face value.'

'Unfortunately, as Geoff says, we have never been able to prove anything,' says Elena. 'We managed to get it out of one scrote where he bought his stuff from, and he implicated her, but a search of Angela's house and car gave us nothing.'

'She's a horrible piece of work and she's got a temper,' continues Geoff. 'And she turned up outside the victim's house less than half an hour after the nine nine nine call. I think that is more than a coincidence. Knowing her, she was getting a kick out of watching the police.'

'But what exactly is her motive for murder, Sergeant?' asks Harry.

'That, I don't know right now. But with Bennett's dodgy dealings and Jack Chadwick's temper, it's a start. Maybe they killed her together. Bennett's alibi is weak, non-existent in fact. She says she was in the shop alone, but no one can back that up. The sign on the door says that closing time is four-thirty, but she claims she was there until six and then drove to Mrs Chadwick's house to speak to her about something. She could have walked down the lane to the victim's house from the shop in under ten minutes, yet she turned up in her car. It just doesn't add up.'

'She could have been on her way home,' says Imogen.

Elena nods slowly and writes *Possible drugs involvement, Unable to verify alibi,* and *Bad temper* in the column underneath Angela's name. 'Don't forget, Miriam's death wasn't random. There's no sign of forced entry, no robbery. She let her killer in. That means trust. I don't doubt she was killed by someone she knew.'

Harry hesitates. 'It could still be Jack. He's the closest to her, and he found the body. What if he's hiding something?'

Geoff shakes his head. 'I just don't think he's the sort. He relied on his mother too much.'

'It's possible,' says Harry. 'What if it was a crime of passion? Let's assume he didn't mean it. I know he isn't the sort to plot something intricate, but if she was baiting him, getting at him and he hit her, she could have hit her head when she crashed to the floor. He has already exhibited unusual behaviour in the shop because he hasn't wanted to stop and chat like he usually does, which indicates to me that he was upset. I think they had argued, he then went to the shop, when he gets home, the argument continues and he kills her. He didn't go for a walk at all. I think he went straight home. At six o'clock, he pretends that he has just found her, runs outside, and calls the police from the phone box.'

'We are certainly not discounting him,' says Elena. 'There is a lot of time unaccounted for. We don't have any evidence that he went for a walk around the village. He didn't meet anyone or speak to anyone. Do we have anything concrete from the neighbours? Imogen, when you spoke to the next-door neighbour, Mrs Hardy, did she see Jack leave the house?'

'No, I'm afraid not,' says Imogen.

Elena writes *Time unaccounted for* underneath Jack's name.

'I've just remembered something, boss,' says Geoff. 'I asked Angela Bennett whether she knew Jack and she said she did, but didn't you say that Jack said they had never met? One of them is lying.'

'Good point,' says Elena. 'Why would Jack say he doesn't know Angela if he does? Clearly, because he doesn't want to be associated with her, whether that's because of her drug dealing or some other reason.' She writes *Denied knowing Bennett* in Jack's column. 'Now, let's focus on the time line. Miriam was alive at 4pm. Sophia Simons has confirmed she saw her at that time. Jack claims he finds her at 6pm. That gives us a two-hour window. Angela, Jack, or the vicar could have been with her during that time, apart from the few minutes when Jack was seen in the shop. However, we've got no hard evidence against any of them. Let's not speculate without further facts. Harry, you can go with Imogen to speak to Claire and Sophie. Also, speak to Trevor whatever-his-name-is and Helen Billington. Rahul, can you please stay here and man the phones? There's an appeal for information in this morning's paper, so you never know what might come through.'

'What about us, boss? Where will we be?' asks Geoff.

'Having another chat with our good vicar. We need to make the interview a little more formal, which might mean bringing him to the station. Something tells me he will remember a lot more under formal interview conditions. If Adam Hargreaves is protecting someone, or seeing someone, I want to know who.'

Adam

Adam wants to pray today. He wants to ask God to forgive him. He has broken at least one of the Ten Commandments, possibly two. He is disgusted with himself. But during the morning service, as he watches his loyal congregation silently following his prayers of intercession, he can't bring himself to focus on what he has done. He buries it deep within his subconscious. He will deal with it another time. Today, he needs to forget the outside world as much as he can and focus on his wife and family, otherwise, he will send himself mad.

As the prayers finish and the final hymn begins, the congregation stands to belt out *Dear Lord and Father of Mankind*. Adam wishes he could get back onto his knees and beg the Lord to *forgive his foolish ways,* but he can't. Anger and frustration are blocking any conversation he might want with his maker.

Last night's conversation with Claire didn't help him. He was taking a great risk by phoning her from his study. Cheryl could have walked in at any time and the guilt on his face would have told her that he was talking to someone he shouldn't have been. But Adam needed to hear Claire's voice. He wanted her comfort and her understanding. He didn't get either of those. Instead, they had their first argument.

Claire didn't understand why he had lied about where he was on Thursday night. Why had he been so stupid? The police always find out about lies, and this was a murder investigation, for Christ's sake. Being already at the end of his tether, Adam didn't have any patience left and had snapped at her. He told her to stop taking the Lord's name in vain and to stop investigating him. She wasn't a policewoman anymore. That was a low blow, which he knew would hurt. He knew it had been a difficult decision for Claire to make when she left the job she once loved. What she really needed after Stephen's death was some time away, some compassionate leave for a couple of weeks, after which she may have been well enough to go back to the force. But instead, she shouted at her boss and her best friend, and stormed out. When she had calmed down, her injured pride prevented her from asking for her job back. She told Adam that, initially, she ignored Elena's calls because she was upset; she needed to be on her own, to cry herself to oblivion within the privacy of her bedroom in the house she shared with Sophia. But as the days passed, she ignored Elena's calls for different reasons. Embarrassment and shame had begun to creep in, like an overflowing river that seeps under the back door during the night while the family is sleeping. At first, it wasn't noticeable, until she eventually realised that everything she held dear was ruined.

After a few weeks, Elena stopped calling and Claire began to think of how else she could earn a living now that her career in the police force was over. When the office above the florist shop became vacant, she snapped it up and began to take work as a private investigator. Work was slow at first, which left Claire with plenty of time on her hands. Winter was beginning to blanket the village; its icy tendrils touched those brave enough to venture out, which meant the church was generally quiet during the day. Claire began to call in when she wanted to take a break from the cramped office. Initially, she only stayed for a few moments. She lit a candle for Stephen, shed a few tears, and left. After a time, she would sit in one of the pews and say a prayer. Adam acknowledged her and asked if she was okay, but more often or not, she dismissed him, telling him she was fine. He knew when someone wanted to be left alone and when someone needed to talk.

On a particularly cold day in January, Carol made Claire a cup of tea and the two women sat together talking, putting the world to right. When Carol left to collect her grandchildren from school, Claire was about to leave too, but Adam asked if she would like another drink. It was so cold, he needed something to warm his hands, he told her. Of course, if she needed to get back to work, then he didn't want to keep her. Claire said that if she was giving the impression she was busy, that was exactly what she intended to do. Her sister, Sophia, was worried about her, so she didn't like to go home until after four-thirty, otherwise, Sophia would bombard her with questions. Was she doing the right thing? Where was her next pay cheque coming from? Would anyone see her advert in the Yellow Pages? Is being a private investigator a secure enough career? Is it even a career?

Adam laughed and said that, in all honesty, he didn't want to go home until much later either. The boys drove him mad when they first came out of school and he needed to give them an hour or so to run off the energy they had been forced to keep under control in the classroom all day. He liked to go home after five-thirty when they were usually playing a little quieter, a little calmer, when their stomachs were full and they were beginning to wind down before their bath.

A look passed between them as Adam passed Claire a cup of hot tea. He held her gaze a second or two longer than he should have. She had the most beautiful eyes he had ever seen, flecked with green and gold. She had long dark eyelashes and carefully applied khaki green eyeshadow. Her hair fell loose around her shoulders. They sat side by side in one of the wooden pews and she touched his arm as they laughed together. When she was leaving, their hug was that little bit too tight, and went on that little bit too long. Someone who was watching, someone who didn't know them, might have said it was an intimate hug, one reserved for a husband and wife, or a boyfriend and girlfriend.

The following week, Claire called into church after three o'clock, when she knew Carol wouldn't be there. Adam made them tea. He had bought a packet of her favourite biscuits, chocolate Club biscuits, which he had kept hidden in his desk drawer, waiting for her. He told her he had bought them for himself, a little snack to see him through to dinner, but then he laughed and said he shouldn't lie. He put his hands together in prayer, looked up towards Heaven, and said, 'Father, you know I haven't bought these biscuits for myself. I'm sorry for lying. Truth must prevail.' He looked to Claire, who was sitting so close to him that their legs were almost touching, and confessed he had bought them for her. She laughed. He blushed like a schoolboy and she said that was the sweetest thing ever. He hadn't meant to kiss her then. He shouldn't have kissed her.

But she was inches away from him and her mouth was so inviting, like the forbidden fruit Adam and Eve shared. Not quite the original sin, but almost.

When he pulled away from her, he thought they would apologise and say it should never happen again. Isn't that what normally happened? Passion overtakes good sense, but then sense is restored again and each person goes their separate ways, never to speak of the transgression again. But it didn't happen like that. Neither of them were sorry. Adam kissed her again and Claire kissed him back. Any thought of repentance was thrown out of the window.

Now, Adam looks up from his hymn book and spots Detective Inspector Elena Holt sneaking into the church. A man follows her. For a moment, he wonders whether he is her husband, but their demeanour is one of colleagues. They are dressed in the formal wear of detectives, dark suits, white shirts, and black shoes. They refuse the offer of a hymn book from the volunteer at the back of the church. Elena closes the door quietly behind them and they wait in the foyer. They are clearly here to speak to him. Probably hoping to speak to him on his own, to get to the bottom of why he has lied to them. He can see Cheryl and his sons in the front pe, oblivious to what is about to happen. Oblivious to what he has done.

Adam loses his place in the hymn. The words begin to swim on the page. He keeps his head down and tries to concentrate, but the detectives' glares burn through him. Adam can feel a line of sweat developing on his top lip. He hopes nobody can see it, and resists wiping it away until it becomes too much. Then he wipes the sweat with his forefinger, pretending he has an itch on his nose.

As the hymn ends and the last of the organ notes

reverberate around the church, he wishes the congregation a loving and peaceful Sunday. 'Go in peace to love and serve the Lord,' he says. He smiles as widely as he can and hopes it appears natural and warm. May the love of God and the fellowship of the Holy Spirit remain with you always. Now and forever.'

'Amen,' the congregation responds.

As the people begin to collect their bags, chattering about their plans for the day and what they are having for lunch, filing to the back of the church where tea and biscuits are waiting, Adam makes his way to the vestry. He can see Elena and the other detective pushing their way through the tide of villagers, as they walk up the aisle. He knows there will be a knock on his door within a minute or so, so Adam keeps the vestry door open. He has nothing to hide, he tells himself. He will welcome the police. He will answer their questions as best he can, like a good citizen. Like Cheryl. He will tell them he made a mistake about Thursday, that's all. People do make mistakes, after all. He is a busy man and most days he would lose his head if it wasn't fastened on.

The loud knock on the open door makes him jump, even though he is expecting it.

'Reverend Hargreaves, can we have a word?' The man strides into the vestry, closely followed by Elena. 'My name is Detective Sergeant Miller. I believe you already know Detective Inspector Holt.' He flashes his police warrant card, before putting it back in the top pocket of his jacket.

'Yes, come in, please take a seat,' says Adam.

Carol appears at the door, loitering on the threshold. She is holding the silver jug and tray used to hold the communion bread and wine. 'I just need to put these in the safe,' she says.

Adam squashes his irritation with a forced smile. 'Thank you, Carol. Would you mind just leaving them on my desk? I'll put them away.' He watches as she slowly puts them down, pushing his notepad and a Bible to one side, making the job seem ten times more difficult than it should be. He wants to tell her to hurry up, get gone, and stop being so bloody nosy. But he holds the plastered smile and his nerve until she leaves.

He watches Elena examine the jug. She catches DS Miller's eye and a look that he can't quite decipher passes between them. She picks it up by the handle, using the edges of her forefinger and thumb. She bounces it up and down, as though trying to figure out how much it weighs.

'It's heavier than it looks,' she says, as she places it back down on the table.

'Solid silver,' says Adam.

'Is that tray silver too?' she asks.

'Yes. Silver is a symbol of purity and it also has anti-bacterial properties, so it doesn't spread germs between the congregation when they take the wine.'

'Interesting,' says Elena.

Adam isn't in the mood for small talk. He shrugs off his cassock and hangs it on the coat hanger on the back of the door. He pushes the door closed. 'How can I help you?' he says.

'Yesterday, my colleague Detective Inspector Holt asked you to confirm your whereabouts on Thursday evening…' The sergeant, a tall and heavy-set man, is standing too close, his feet spread wide apart, looking down his supercilious nose.

'Yes, I made a mistake,' says Adam. 'My wife told you

that, didn't she, Inspector?'

'Mistakes are often called lies,' says DS Miller. 'Did you make a genuine mistake, or were you caught telling a lie?'

'Well, I…'

'Because from where I'm standing, it seems you were quite adamant about where you were until your wife came home and dropped you in it.'

'With respect, Detective Sergeant Miller, you weren't there, so you didn't get the nuance of the conversation.' Adam pushes past the sergeant and sits at his desk. As soon as he lowers himself into the chair, he regrets his decision. Any confidence he may have been clinging to has now vanished, now that the sergeant and the inspector are both standing over him.

'Don't try and bamboozle me with big words, Reverend. I know a lie is a lie is a lie.'

Elena puts a placating hand on her colleague's arm. 'Adam, I wasn't entirely confident that you were telling the truth yesterday,' says Elena. 'If there is something you can tell us, without your wife being in the room, then please do so. We just need to get to the truth.'

'I don't know what you mean,' says Adam.

'She means, if you've got a bit on the side and you didn't want to let your wife in on the secret, you need to tell us now,' says DS Miller. 'Otherwise, give us the name and address of that young couple you supposedly spoke to and we can check out your alibi for you.'

'My alibi?'

DS Miller leans forward, resting his giant hands on the desk. 'This is a murder investigation, Reverend. Everyone needs an alibi, otherwise, they're a suspect. Now give us the name and address of that couple.'

Adam wishes it were that simple. He wishes he could tell the police that the young couple doesn't exist. He wishes he could tell them he was with Claire all evening and trust them to keep the secret from Cheryl. Then maybe his worries would be over. He would be in the clear. But he wasn't with Claire, and Claire has already told them she was at home, and her presence there has been verified by Sophia and that lodger of hers.

Nobody can help him now.

DS Miller stands up straight and puts his hands in his pocket. His cold eyes bore through Adam, no doubt waiting for a satisfactory response. Adam doesn't know what to say.

'What this?' Elena looks to the door. Underneath where his cassock hangs, a scrunched-up piece of paper lies on the floor.

'It's nothing,' says Adam. He jumps up. 'It's private. Don't touch it.' But his passage is blocked by DS Miller.

Elena unfolds the paper and smooths it out. Adam watches, feeling his life unravelling, as Elena reads the note that has fallen from his pocket, the note he was meant to destroy on the fire.

'Miriam, You can't tell anyone what you saw this morning,' she reads. 'You might want to gossip, but it is none of your business. As your employer, I am warning you to keep silent. If you refuse and news of this gets out, there will be consequences. Adam.'

'It isn't what you think,' says Adam. 'I was just warning her. I thought…'

'Adam Hargreaves, you are under arrest for the murder of Miriam Chadwick. You are not obliged to say anything unless you wish to do, but anything you say may be given in evidence.' DS Miller grabs Adam by the upper arm and marches him out of the vestry.

Angela

Angela is waiting outside the church.

A few minutes ago, she saw the police car at the give-way sign as she came out of the shop. It indicated right at the village green, to turn into the tiny church car park. She waited for the car to pass. She wouldn't dream of attempting to cross the road in front of a police car. She doesn't trust those bastards, not one little bit.

She spotted DS Miller at the wheel and knew she had made the right decision to stay where she was. She could imagine him pressing his foot to the accelerator, the bonnet crashing into her shins as it knocked her down. As she lay bleeding in the road, the eggs and the loaf of bread she had just bought from Robertsons splattered all over the tarmac, he would explain to the ambulance drivers how she had stepped into the road without any notice. He had no chance of stopping in time.

So she stepped back and waited for the car to move on.

The woman in the passenger seat, wearing a serious expression and a black suit that contrasted starkly with her short red hair, stared straight ahead. She hadn't seen her before. A detective who works with DS Miller, no doubt.

Now, despite the cold, she is waiting for them to come out of the church. Knowledge is power and Angela likes to be one step ahead of the police, where possible.

Jack

Jack waits in the queue for a drink in the church foyer. He gives a donation of ten pence for his cup of tea and is handed a tiny white cup on a delicate saucer. His mum used to love these. He can feel a tightening in his chest, as emotion rushes through him. Carol wants to know if he's okay. She is hovering next to him with a tiny plate in her hand, piled high with custard creams. He assures her he is well, thank you, as he busies himself pouring milk into the cup. He can hear his mother's voice telling him that the correct way of doing things would be to put the milk in first. Everyone knows that. That's how the queen takes her tea. Milk first, then tea. Jack smiles at Carol and takes a biscuit from the plate. He asks her whether she thinks the queen has a cup of tea after her church service, or whether she goes straight back to the palace for lunch. Carol laughs, but he can sense she isn't laughing *at* him, she is laughing *with* him. I'm absolutely certain she will have a cup of tea in church, says Carol. Maybe some triangles of cucumber sandwiches on the side. You know, those little ones with no crusts. Carol squeezes his arm and walks away, holding the plate of biscuits in front of her.

She is a nice woman. His mother didn't like her. She said the power of being a churchwarden had gone to her head. But then again, his mother never liked anyone. She was always quick with her criticisms.

How are you, Jack? It's Mrs Hargreaves, the vicar's wife.

She is standing so close to him that he can smell her perfume. It smells expensive and sophisticated. She is looking deep into his eyes. Are you okay? It's your first time in church without your mother, isn't it? She wants to know how he is, but then she doesn't give him time to reply. Why do people do that with him? She carries on talking about how lovely it is that he is here. He has a cup of tea, she can see. She's glad Carol is looking after him.

One of her little boys is tugging at her sleeve. She shakes him off and tells him to go and play outside. Find your brother, but don't go anywhere near the road. The boy lets go and runs outside.

Mrs Hargreaves shakes her head. They're never still, she tells him. It's a wonder they manage to sit still throughout the service. Goodness knows how their teacher copes with twelve of the little buggers in her class. It's only the threat of God watching them - she stops talking and laughs. Well, it works throughout December, she says, when they think Father Christmas is watching. They are on their best behaviour then. Nobody wants to go on the Naughty List, do they?

Jack shakes his head. He remembers his mother telling him the same thing when he was a small boy. Father Christmas must have been so busy watching his every move, that he wondered how he would have had time to watch over all the other children in the world. Despite Jack's best efforts, it always seemed that he wasn't quite good enough to warrant any decent presents to be left under the tree. His mother blamed the post. His letter to Father Christmas obviously didn't get to the North Pole. It's no wonder, really. It's a long way, and the weather has been particularly bad this year. It didn't make sense to nine-year-old Jack. How was that the case, that the weather was always *particularly bad?* Father Christmas and his reindeers loved the snow. They were used to bad weather. Jack asked her one Christmas Day how the letters from the other children always seemed to make it in time. He knew they did, because everyone talked about what presents they had when they went back to school in January. He got a punch to the side of the head for his impudent question. Ungrateful little sod, his mother called him. She spent the rest of the morning on the sofa, smoking one cigarette after another, and making her way through a bottle of *medicinal* brandy. When Queen Elizabeth gave her speech to the nation at three o'clock, which most families followed by a roast turkey dinner, Jack made himself and his mother a jam sandwich and then took himself to bed.

Mrs Hargreaves is still talking to him. He tries to concentrate and ignore the thoughts of his mother. Mrs Hargreaves begins to talk about suitable hymns for the funeral. Jack hasn't thought about it. He doesn't want to go to his mother's funeral, he tells her. Mrs Hargreaves gives him an unexpected hug and tells him that funerals are awful, she knows that, but he will have lots of support. Lots and lots of it. He will be fine. Most people find funerals to be quite comforting actually.

Someone calls out 'Cheryl!' The urgent voice sounds frightened and Mrs Hargreaves reacts by dropping her tea onto the floor. The cup smashes onto the stone tiles and tea splashes onto the toes of Jack's shoes.

Her face is pale and Jack wants to tell her that it's okay. He will find the mop, it will be around somewhere, and clean it up for her.

The clatter of teacups against saucers becomes quieter

and the chatter of voices around him diminishes to faint whispers. Someone gasps. Then whispered voices. What's going on? What are they doing?

Adam! Mrs Hargreaves cries. What are you doing with my husband?

Jack turns to see the vicar, pale and trembling, being escorted down the aisle. Detective Inspector Elena Holt is on his right side and another detective is on his left. Jack remembers he was one of those who came to his house on the night his mother died. He was bossy and rude, and Jack took an instant dislike to him. They are both clinging to the vicar's arms. They begin to walk quicker now, asking people to give them space. Move out of the way, please. Let us pass. Thank you. Like Jesus making his way into Jerusalem on Palm Sunday.

Mrs Hargreaves runs to her husband. Darling, what on earth is going on? She is crying now. Jack backs away as the detectives approach the door, and stumbles into the table behind him. Empty cups and saucers rattle on the table. He holds onto it, feeling as though the floor may give way beneath his feet if he doesn't have something to keep him upright.

The vicar tells his wife there is a misunderstanding. Everything will be fine. He will be home soon.

Jack watches as the sobbing Mrs Hargreaves is led away into the vestry by Carol, and the sobbing Reverend Hargreaves is led away to the police car by the detectives.

Claire

It is Sophia who picks up the phone when Adam calls from the police station later that afternoon. Despite the arrangement between him and Claire that he will only call the house after six o'clock in the evening and only on the days when he knows she will be at home to answer, it seems he took a chance and called anyway. The fact that she answered the phone yesterday must have given him courage. Claire isn't sure whether she should be flattered by his couldn't-care-less attitude, or whether she should be angry with him. Earlier, in the church, she struggled to keep a neutral expression as she watched him being marched to the police car, as those around her declared it a 'disgrace' and 'unbelievable' and 'shocking' that their wonderful, virtuous vicar should be arrested for such a heinous crime - any crime at all really, but certainly not murder. She bit back the tears and sipped her tea as she watched the melee play out in front of her, the congregation uniting in their public outcry.

When they arrived home, with Wendy put down for her nap, and she, Sophia, and Trevor were settled around the kitchen table, Sophia hadn't asked Claire if she was all right, despite the fact she was quiet and sombre. The anniversary of Stephen's death gave her an excuse. Claire couldn't tell her sister that it wasn't Stephen she was thinking about, but instead, she was worried to death about Adam, the married man she has been sleeping with for the past nine months. Everyone at church seemed to think he had been wrongfully arrested, and no doubt he will be having a traumatic experience, but she was more than a little worried about *why* he had been arrested. Why him? Elena and Geoff knew what they were doing and they had to have some kind of solid evidence before they arrested someone. She hated herself for thinking such a thing, but she knew how diligent Elena and Geoff were, and she knew they would have their reasons for arresting Adam. She needed to find out what those reasons were.

Now Sophia is waiting in the hall while Claire speaks to him. Claire considers asking her to give her some privacy, but what's the point? The secret will be out soon enough, and she needs someone to confide in. It is about time she came clean.

She imagines Elena standing behind Adam in the custody area of the police station as he presses the receiver close to his ear. They would both have been watching the numbers as they spun around the dial unbearably slow. Five, seven, eight, five, three, six. Elena must surely have cottoned on to who he was calling by watching the familiar numbers that she herself has dialled so many times in the past. Even if she didn't recognise the number, or didn't see him dial it, now she would know for sure who he wanted to speak to, as she would have heard Adam ask for Claire to be brought to the phone.

'Claire, is that you?' His voice is heavy with emotion; unshed tears and fears. He hardly sounds like himself.

'Yes, it's me,' she says. 'I'm sorry I didn't answer the phone, but I wasn't expecting you to call me.'

'It's okay. I don't care about that.'

The few seconds of silence that follow seem to drag on for a lifetime. Claire doesn't know what to say. Her instinct is to put the phone down. She wants to tell her anxious sister it was a prank call, nobody important, just someone heavy breathing. They will laugh and go back to their lunch of roast chicken and mashed potatoes, and they will chat over their meal about insignificant things, about who was in church this morning, and how pretty Mrs Hargreaves looked in her new coat, and how those boys are growing each time you see them. But she can't do that to him.

'I need your help, Claire,' says Adam.

Claire looks at Sophia who is now seated at the telephone table, only inches away. Claire isn't sure whether Sophia can hear the voice at the other end of the phone, but she can tell that Sophia instinctively knows her sister needs her. Sophia holds out her hand and Claire grabs it, thankful for the emotional and physical support.

'What do you want me to do?' Claire asks. 'I don't know what I can do?'

'They arrested me for Miriam's murder. Can you believe it? But I didn't do it,' he says. 'You know that, don't you? You need to get me out of here.'

'I can't do that,' she says. She wants to laugh. It isn't funny, not at all. But if she laughs, it might mean this isn't real. It might mean someone is playing a joke. The man she is sleeping with cannot seriously be in a police cell accused of murdering someone. It cannot be happening. Not to a vicar. Not on a Sunday.

Suddenly, she wants to end things; whatever this *thing* is with Adam. She doesn't want to have a secret lover anymore. The joy has been sapped by his arrest, whether wrongful or not. She didn't sign up for this kind of commitment. She doesn't want a man who *needs* her, not in this way. She isn't his wife, or his mother, or even his friend, not really. She is his part-time lover. They have been there for each other over the past nine months, but they both knew it couldn't last. He has been keeping her sane while she gets over the death of the man she was meant to marry; helping her to see she has a future that doesn't contain Stephen. He is serving a purpose, temporarily. In return, she has been keeping him sane while his children are young and demanding; helping him to see he has a future that doesn't contain toy cars and temper tantrums. She wants to tell him it's over. Whatever this is between them, it has to stop. He shouldn't be calling her from the police station. He should be calling his wife.

'You should have called Cheryl,' she says. Her voice is laced with icy reproach, each word a subtle, unspoken indictment.

'Claire, please.' He doesn't want him to beg. That one word, *please,* which comes out as a strangled sob, is enough to make her change her mind. She knows she can't abandon him now. Not until she speaks to Elena and finds out the reason for his arrest.

'What can I do?' she asks with a sigh as heavy as a thundercloud about to drop its deluge of rain.

'Get me out of here.'

'I'm not a solicitor, Adam. I know the law, but you need a solicitor. I'm not enough. I don't know what evidence they have…'

'They don't have any bloody evidence.' His voice is loud and sharp. 'I can't believe you would think they do. Don't you know me at all?' He has never before spoken to her with anything other than compassion and love. She doesn't know this side of him. She doesn't want to know this side of him.

She holds the earpiece away from her ear. Sophia jumps up and Claire can see her hand hovering over the telephone cradle. One movement of her index finger, one push on the button, will cut off the call. Sophia won't stand for anyone shouting at her sister, Claire knows that. Not now. Not days away from Stephen's anniversary. Not when Claire is on an emotional precipice.

'Claire, it's Elena.' Adam has gone.

'Oh, hello Elena,' she says. Sophia withdraws her finger.

'I'm afraid Reverend Hargreaves has had his allotted time on the telephone. He wanted you to know he's here.' Elena's voice is cold and professional.

'Thank you.' She doesn't know what else to say. Then she says, 'Shall I organise a solicitor to come and see him?'

'You don't need to. If he asks for one, we can telephone the Duty Solicitor and arrange it for him. Unless you know someone you want to use?'

'No, not really. The only ones I know do conveyancing and divorces.'

'Okay, leave it with me. I need to go now.'

'Can you tell me…'

But she's gone. The dialling tone buzzes down the line. Sophia takes the receiver from Claire and puts it back on the cradle.

'Why did he call you?' asks Sophia, although it is clear she has guessed the answer. 'Rather than his wife, I mean? Don't tell me you and him are together? You're not, surely.'

Claire nods as tears fall down her cheeks.

'Is everything all right, ladies?' Trevor is standing in the kitchen doorway. The remains of their lunches on the table behind him are now cold. Half-eaten mash and congealed gravy will be scraped into the bin. Trevor's efforts at a Sunday lunch will be wasted.

'It was Adam on the phone,' says Sophia. 'Reverend

Hargreaves. He was ringing to see if Claire could help him with legal advice.'

'Ahh, yes,' says Trevor. 'With her being an ex-detective and all?'

'Yes, that's right,' says Sophia.

Claire wipes her eyes and follows her sister back into the kitchen. They sit down and Claire pushes her plate of food towards the middle of the table, so she has space for her elbows. She rests her head on her hands. Sophia looks at her, her expression full of disappointment.

'It is time for the truth,' says Claire. 'Adam didn't phone me because I'm an ex-detective. I can't lie to your face, Trevor. Lying by missing out information and keeping you in the dark, is one thing, but I can't lie while you look me in the eyes.' Sophia shoots her a look that tells her she doesn't need to spill her secret. It's okay to keep it quiet for a little while longer, maybe forever. That way, people won't get hurt. But Claire shrugs, letting her know it is time to unburden herself. The secret is ready to be revealed, whether Adam likes it or not. 'Adam rang me to get legal advice, yes, but he rang me, rather than his wife, because we're having an affair. There. I've said it. I'm sorry to disappoint you, both of you, by carrying on with a married man but you have to believe me when I say I didn't want it to happen. Adam was in the wrong place at the wrong time, I suppose. I was grieving and he was there, offering comfort, and one thing led to another.' She is crying freely now, unable to stop the torrent of tears.

'No need to apologise, dear,' says Trevor. He hands her the box of tissues from the kitchen counter. 'Not at all. Love is a complicated thing. Sometimes it comes and grabs you when you least expect it, and who are you to stand in the way of Cupid's arrow?'

'That's very magnanimous of you, thank you,' says Claire, as she takes a tissue from the box. 'But I know it's wrong. I should have just walked away.'

'Yes, you should. He has children, for God's sake,' says Sophia. Any support Claire thought was hers is snatched away with Sophia's sharp words. Claire knows she cannot begin to defend herself to her sister, a woman whose accidental pregnancy resulted in Wendy's father admitting he was married and declaring he would never leave his wife. Sophia, as the wronged and innocent party, has never understood anyone who could get involved with a married man. If only Claire had taken a leaf from Sophia's moral book, she wouldn't be in this position. 'How could you do it?'

'I don't know.' Claire pushes her chair back and begins to pace up and down the long kitchen. She stops to take time at the window, resting her hands on the sink, and stares out into the garden.

Trevor collects the plates, scrapes the forgotten food into the bin, and piles the plates onto the countertop. Claire begins to fill the washing-up bowl with hot water.

'Don't tell me he forced himself onto you, because I won't listen to that argument,' says Sophia.

'He didn't, but neither did I force myself onto him. I'm not a slut.'

'I never said you were, but you can say no to temptation, you know. Isn't that what churches are all about? It doesn't matter how charismatic or good-looking a man might be. No is a very easy word to say. It's one small syllable.'

'I was going through a bad time.' Claire's voice is loud and full of pent-up tears. 'You know how hard it has been for me, and he was there. Like I said, one thing led to another. It wasn't as though it was planned.'

'Oh, rubbish. That's a terrible excuse.'

'Ladies, please,' says Trevor. He waves his hand up and down in an effort to lessen the rising volume of their conversation. He watches both women with concern, his head moving from one to the other as though watching a particularly tense Wimbledon final. 'Shouting at each other won't solve anything, will it?' Sophia shakes her head and Claire turns her back to them and continues watching the garden. She reaches over for the plates, places them in the washing-up bowl and leaves them to soak.

Trevor comes up behind her and rests a gentle hand on Claire's back. 'So what's your plan of action now?' he asks.

'Nothing,' says Claire. 'Elena said she will arrange a solicitor for Adam if he asks for one. Honestly, there's nothing I can do for him. I wish he hadn't rang me.'

'He should have rang his wife,' says Sophia. 'She will be going out of her mind wondering what's happening to him, and all the while he's on the phone to his mistress. Men like that make me sick.'

Claire knows Sophia is more angry with Adam than she is with her, and she is more angry with Wendy's father than she is with Adam. But even so, her words sting because she knows she is right.

She turns to face her sister. 'I wish I had never got involved with him,' she says. 'Please believe me. I wish I hadn't been so sad and desolate that I needed the comfort of the church, then I wouldn't have felt the need to go in. I wish I had been busier at work and that I hadn't had time to think.' The tears are coming quickly now, falling down her flushed cheeks. 'I wish Adam hadn't been so kind and given me a shoulder to cry on.' Trevor hands her the tea towel to mop her tears. 'But most of all, I wish Stephen hadn't died and I would now be his wife and I wouldn't have to steal another wife's husband. I would have my own.'

She throws the tea towel onto the floor and runs from the room, taking the stairs two at a time.

Sophia and Trevor listen to the echo of her bedroom door as it slams shut.

Elena

The interview room at Wellington Police Station is cold and bleak, despite the huge radiator humming in the corner. The grey-painted walls do nothing to add any warmth to the room. Even the red plastic chairs, a welcome burst of colour in any other setting, seem drab. The air is heavy with other people's despair.

Geoff holds Adam tightly by his elbow and leads him to one of the chairs at the square Formica table. He sits down wearily. Elena and Geoff sit on the opposite side.

'You know why you're here, Reverend Hargreaves,' says Elena, nodding in confirmation. 'We need to chat to you about the murder of Miriam Chadwick.'

'Yes, I do know why I'm here,' he says. 'but I'm not guilty of anything. I've got to say that now, before we start.'

'Well, we'll talk in detail in a moment and you will have a chance to tell us your story. We're just waiting for a colleague to join us.'

'You haven't really explained why I've been arrested,' he

says. 'I mean, I know it's in relation to Miriam's murder, but why me? You know the real murderer is still out there, don't you? You're wasting your time with me when you should be out there catching him before he kills someone else.'

Adam's deep brown eyes have lost their flirtatious twinkle. They are pleading with Elena, like a small boy begging his mother for more biscuits, but she can see him now for the man he really is. An adulterer and a liar. Whether he is lying about Miriam's murder, she isn't sure, but there is no doubt in her mind that something is going on between Claire and Adam. Why else would he ring her? She doesn't believe for one moment that he rang her for legal advice, just because Claire is the only ex-police officer who lives in the village. She isn't surprised that his charms worked on Claire. Disappointed, yes. Dismayed, yes. Surprised, no.

Claire told her when she first began dating Stephen that it was his eyes she fell in love with first. The window to the soul, apparently. Elena can't tell whether Adam's eyes are portraying innocence, or whether he is a cold, calculating, and very clever killer who has so far managed to fool everyone around him. She has never before been so confused about a suspect. Maybe the fact that he is a vicar is clouding her judgement. If he was one of the lads from the Hilltop Estate in Wellington, or that family from Moorside Close whose every member has a criminal record, except for the tiny baby of their youngest sixteen-year-old daughter, she would know where she stood. She knows what to expect from people like that, and she knows how to deal with them. But Adam is a conundrum.

There is a knock on the interview room door. Imogen

enters carrying a tray of drinks. A large notepad is tucked under her arm. 'Sorry if I kept you waiting, ma'am,' she says. She places the tray on the edge of the table and hands out the mugs of steaming tea, first to Elena, then to Geoff, and finally to Adam. He takes it, mumbling his thanks, and wraps his hands around the hot mug. Imogen pulls the empty chair beside Adam away from the table and sits in the corner of the room behind Elena and Geoff. She places the notepad on her knee and takes a ballpoint pen from her jacket pocket. She opens the notebook and scribbles *Interview with Reverend Hargreaves* on the top line of a blank page.

'This is WPC Imogen Winters,' says Geoff. 'She will take some notes of what is said in this interview room. At the end of the interview, those notes will be made into a witness statement, which you will be asked to sign. Understood?'

Adam nods. 'Do I have the right to a solicitor?'

'You're kidding, right?' Geoff slams his mug of tea onto the table. Adam watches the tea sloshing about. A tiny storm in a porcelain teacup. 'We've just sat down. Why didn't you say something before?'

'Yes, you do have the right to a solicitor,' says Elena, resting a placating hand on Geoff's arm. 'Do you want one?'

'It's too late now. You should have asked for one before now.' Geoff leans across the table until his personal space and Adam's are one and the same. He pushes his chair back and stands, legs wide, feet firmly planted on the floor as though bracing himself for a hurricane. 'Wasting police time and resources…'

'It's okay, it's okay,' says Adam. 'I'm happy to continue

with the interview. Please sit down.'

'Are you for real? Telling me what to do?'

Spittle is forming at the edge of Geoff's mouth and Elena can see his ears burning with the desire to punch Adam from here to next week. It is well known throughout the police station that Geoff's suspects are more susceptible to unexplained cuts and bruises than any other. They tend to 'fall' over their feet on their way from the cell to the interview room. Their clumsiness when entering a room results in black eyes on a regular basis. The custody sergeant is so used to it that their injuries hardly get a mention in the paperwork anymore. There are never any witnesses, except Geoff, and the suspects never ask to press charges and they never ask to see a nurse. Except for one suspect who was rushed to hospital in the back of the police car when Geoff heard his arm crack when being held in a precariously unnatural position too far up his back. The twist resulted in a nasty fracture to the ulna. Geoff's informal caution by the custody sergeant was dealt with over a couple of pints of ale at the end of the shift. Geoff promised not to be so rough in the future and the custody sergeant promised only to give him those suspects who had enough meat on their bones to prevent injury. Geoff blamed the suspect's injury on the fact that he was *a skinny bastard.* Both men laughed.

'Reverend Hargreaves, let me remind you that we are the ones conducting this interview and as such, we will be the ones who give out the orders. Don't order one of my detectives to sit down. Is that clear?' says Elena.

Adam frowns and the slight pause tells her he isn't used to being spoken to in that way. He seems about to answer back, but then he nods slowly. Defeated.

Geoff takes a packet of cigarettes from his pocket, puts one in his mouth, and lights it with a match from a book inscribed with *Hare and Hounds*, his favourite watering hole, across the road from the police station. He leans back in his chair and blows smoke across the table towards Adam's face.

'Can I smoke?' asks Adam. 'I could really do with one. It's been a hell of a day.'

'You're priceless, you know that?' says Geoff. He holds the packet of cigarettes across the table. Adam takes one and lights it with the urgency of someone desperate for a momentary escape from the weight of his thoughts.

'Thank you,' he says.

Geoff holds the open packet to Elena, but she shakes her head, pleased with herself for going five days without a cigarette.

'Reverend Hargreaves, you've been arrested in connection with the murder of Miriam Chadwick. I will remind you of the caution. You are not obliged to say anything unless you wish to do so, but anything you say may be given in evidence. Do you understand?' she says.

'Yes,' says Adam.

'You are here because of a number of things, which I will explain to you in detail. This is your chance to give us your side of the story and to explain any discrepancies.' Elena looks across at Imogen, who is already scribbling in the notepad. 'When I spoke to you on Friday 8th October, the day after the discovery of Miriam's body, you told us that you last saw the deceased on Tuesday. You told me she cleans the vicarage every Tuesday, is that correct?'

'She does clean every Tuesday, yes. But…'

Geoff holds up his hand. 'Just answer the questions Detective Inspector Holt asks you, Reverend Hargreaves. If at the end of the interview, you have anything else to say, you will have an opportunity, is that clear?'

'Yes,' says Adam. He takes two puffs of the cigarette and inhales deeply.

'You were quite specific about the circumstances in which you last saw Miriam,' says Elena. 'I got the impression you weren't mistaken. You were pretty clear and could remember relevant details. You told me she arrived at your house around eight-thirty in the morning. The children had gone to school and you were about to leave for the church. Can you remember me asking that question and can you confirm that was your response?'

'It was, yes,' says Adam.

'It was, yes,' repeats Elena. 'There was no ambiguity.' She pauses a moment to make sure Imogen can keep up with her note-taking. 'Yesterday, that is Saturday 9th October, I wanted to clarify what you had said, so I went to see you again. Do you remember me attending the vicarage yesterday morning?'

'Look, I was…'

'Just answer each question,' barks Geoff. 'Do you remember the inspector visiting you at the vicarage yesterday? Yes or no.'

'I do, yes,' says Adam. A line of ash balances on the edge of his cigarette.

'I told you I was trying to piece together Miriam's movements on Thursday and, again, you confirmed you last saw her on Tuesday.' Elena opens her notebook and flicks to her notes from yesterday morning. 'It says it here, look.' She points to her handwriting on the page. 'I then asked you what you had done on Thursday. I wrote down what you said.' She reads from her notes. 'Reverend Adams says he was in church for most of the day. He was preparing for a church council meeting. He wrote some letters. He went home at lunchtime, had a sandwich with his wife, and returned to church for a couple of hours. He was there until around three o'clock.' She looks up. Adam is watching her intently. 'You told me that, didn't you?'

'Yes.'

'Then you stayed at home for the rest of the evening. You told me that, didn't you?'

'Yes, I did, but I explained to you, that was a mistake.'

'If you had only said it once, I might be able to concede that it was a mistake. A busy man like you could be prone to a mistake or two, but you told me the same thing twice, which I would say was deliberate. What I want to know is why.'

'Well, I made the same mistake twice,' says Adam. 'Why is that so hard to believe? You're not serious about this, surely? You can't honestly think that I'm the murderer? I'm a man of God.'

Geoff laughs with genuine mirth. 'I've heard it all, now.'

'I think I need a solicitor,' says Adam. He puffs at his cigarette frantically until only the stub remains between his shaking fingers.

'All in good time,' says Geoff. 'If you answer a few more questions, I'm sure we can all go on our merry way a lot quicker. Or would you prefer to wait in your cell for a few more hours until your brief arrives?'

Adam looks at Elena. 'Okay,' he says. 'What else do you

want to know?'

'Thursday evening. Where were you and what were you doing?'

'I told you yesterday, I was out interviewing a young couple who wish to be married in the church.'

'Where did you interview them? At their home, I presume?'

'Actually, no. I met them in a pub on Wellington Road, about a mile north of the town centre. I can't remember the name of it. It's a big one, whitewashed walls and a beer garden.'

'There are half a dozen pubs on Wellington Road that look like that. You'll need to be more specific,' says Elena.

'I think it was called the Hare and Hounds.'

'Really?' Elena fiddles with the book of matches and turns it to face Adam so he can read the name clearly. 'This Hare and Hounds? Because, this is the pub across the road from the police station? It wasn't this one, was it?'

'I don't know. I can't remember.'

'Why didn't you go to their house for the interview? Wouldn't it be more private there?'

'He suggested the pub and I thought, yes, why not? We weren't discussing anything particularly private or contentious.'

'Can you give me the names of this couple?'

Adam pauses. 'Peter and Jane something or other. I can't remember off the top of my head.'

'Peter and Jane? Good one. Like the Peter and Jane in those Ladybird books your children have?' Geoff laughs. 'Pull the other one.'

Adam throws him a dirty look. He drops the stub of the cigarette into the ashtray on the table and fiddles with the handle of the mug of tea.

'But you will have their details somewhere in your office, will you?' asks Elena.

'Yes, probably. Maybe.' Adam shrugs. He inspects the edge of the desk and runs his finger along a crack in the surface. A splinter of wood pierces his thumb.

'You can't remember the name of the pub, you can't remember the surname of either of them. I don't suppose you can remember where they live or work?' asks Geoff. Adam doesn't reply. 'Let me go and get you a shovel,' says Geoff. 'It looks like you're digging yourself a great big hole.'

Adam

Adam knows that DS Miller is right. He is digging himself a huge hole, and right now, he isn't sure how to get out of it. The police will want to know the names and addresses of the couple he claims he spoke to. Of course, they will. Like they keep telling him, this is a murder investigation and things need to be done, and will be done, diligently. If he has offered an alibi, the police will check it out.

What can he do? He is in a mess, and can't see the way out.

He knows they won't find anything in his diary for Thursday night. No address or telephone number will be listed there. There won't be any appointment time written down for the meeting with the young couple. They will find a blank page instead.

Why on earth did he say the pub was called the Hare and Hounds? He has no idea. He saw it on the book of matches and spurted it out without thinking. Even if they visit every pub between Eldenbridge and Wellington, they won't be able to find anyone who will remember a vicar sitting with a young couple for hours and hours, because it didn't happen.

If he were conducting this interview, he would ask the suspect what they managed to talk about all that time. He expected Cheryl to ask him when he got home that night, and she didn't disappoint him. As he drove home to the vicarage, he tried to think of suitable subjects one would discuss with young people you had never previously met. He thought they might be interested in world politics. Students are always marching in protest of one thing or another. It was feasible they might be interested in the presidential election campaign and the pros and cons of voting for Gerald Ford or Jimmy Carter. Then he decided they would want to talk about music and the pros and cons of disco versus punk rock. Adam hates contemporary music, and he was hoping Cheryl wouldn't ask him what bands they had talked about. He has only heard of Abba and the Bee Gees, and only because she insists on singing their songs around the house on a daily basis. Sport is a nice general subject, too. He decided they would have talked about the Olympics. Everyone takes an interest in that, don't they? Especially as this year's boycott links closely to the subject of world political issues. He was hoping Cheryl wouldn't want lots of detail, as he couldn't name any of the athletes.

But they don't ask him what they talked about. Probably for the best really. The more detail he goes into, the more he will trip himself up.

Detective Inspector Holt is watching him, chewing on

the end of her pencil. She smells familiar. He recognises her perfume as the same one he bought Cheryl for her birthday – Shalimar by Guerlain. It's funny how smells evoke powerful emotions. It makes him want to cry as he pictures Cheryl's face lighting up with joy as she ripped the paper off her gift and kissed him passionately.

He sends up a silent prayer for God to help him and to forgive him his sins.

Elena

It is approaching three o'clock and nobody has eaten lunch. Elena can hear her stomach complaining noisily and she is beginning to lose focus. This interview is too important for her to cock it up. She can see Adam's face visibly relax when she suggests a break. He looks like he is about to cry. The constant questions and allegations are beginning to take their toll on him, she can tell.

'Can I phone my wife?' he says. 'I need to speak to her. Please.'

She would have allowed it, even though he has already had his one designated phone call, but Geoff jumps in before she can speak.

'No, mate. You had your phone call earlier.'

'But that was in relation to getting legal advice. Aren't I allowed a legal phone call and a private phone call?'

'Nice try,' says Geoff. Sometimes Geoff has no heart. Elena doesn't want to contradict him. They need to appear as a united front.

She closes the door of the interview room behind them

and leans against the wall. 'I need to catch my breath,' she tells Geoff. 'I don't know what to make of him, do you?'

'I don't like him, that's what I do know,' says Geoff. 'But that might just be my Catholic upbringing. I don't trust any priest. All that sinning behind closed doors and then confessing to get yourself a free pass to Heaven. It's all wrong in my book.'

'You know he's not a Catholic priest, don't you?' she says.

'All cut from the same cloth. Come on. I need a brew and something to eat.'

They make their way to the staff canteen on the first floor of the police station, leaving Adam alone with his confessions, if there are any, in the basement interview room, having assured the custody sergeant that he is perfectly safe in there. He can't escape without going past the sergeant's desk and up the stairs to the front office.

Elena is hoping that by giving Adam special treatment, such as plenty of cups of tea and coffee, a cigarette or two, and trusting him to be left in an interview room rather than being locked up in a cell will help with the interview process. He might open up to them. She knows he isn't likely to confess to a murder. Nobody has ever done that in her experience, but if a suspect talks openly and freely, that's when they trip themselves up. They become nonchalant and lazy, and the lies they have told are easily forgotten. Before long, they have tied themselves in knots and given the police the extra bit of rope they need to hang themselves. Before they know it, the charge sheet is typed out and the case is closed.

The canteen is quiet. The officers working the two - ten shift won't take their breaks for another couple of hours and the office workers don't work at the weekends. The detective superintendent is sitting at a small table for two, with a coffee and a newspaper in front of him. He looks up and Elena nods a greeting. He knows the vicar has been arrested, and he is going to want a full update on the interview later.

Elena tells Geoff and Imogen to make themselves comfortable at the large corner table under the window while she orders the food. She collects a wooden tray and bypasses the hot food section, even though she is as hungry as a horse. She can't afford to lose any concentration and a full stomach will make her feel tired and lethargic. She collects four cheese and pickle sandwiches and four large cups of tea, pays for them, and takes them back to the table.

'Feeding the scrote, are you?' says Geoff. 'You're too soft for this job.'

Being too *soft*, too *kind,* and too *female* are insults Elena has heard many times. She brushes them away like cobwebs in a doorway, ignoring them and going on her way. She knows she has worked hard to be a detective inspector; much harder than any man at her level. Her role is coveted by many of her male colleagues, not least Geoff, and she sees their insults as insecure petty jealousies. If she let them get to her, she would be crying in the toilet most of the day. She can't allow that. She absolutely won't allow that.

'Yes, that sandwich is for him, Geoff, so don't even think about snaffling it. He isn't likely to talk if he is hungry. Being hungry brings out the worst in people, in my experience.'

'That's true,' says Geoff. 'My wife daren't speak to me before I've had my breakfast in a morning.'

They eat in companionable silence for a minute or so,

each of them lost in their own thoughts.

'So why do you think Reverend Hargreaves chose to call Claire Simons rather than his wife?' asks Imogen.

'He's screwing her, obviously,' says Geoff. He slurps his tea, washing down a mouthful of barely chewed sandwich.

'You eat like a pig, has anyone ever told you that?' says Elena. 'That's why your wife doesn't want to talk to you in the morning. She doesn't want to watch you eat.'

'You're not wrong. She tells me every day,' says Geoff. He laughs raucously and takes the napkin Elena hands him to wipe a drop of tea from his shirt.

'I was thinking he might have called Claire because she's an ex-detective, isn't she?' asks Imogen. Elena nods. 'She's someone he clearly feels comfortable with and maybe he rang her for some help. I mean, I heard him ask her to get him out of here, but even so, his wife would help him, wouldn't she? So why didn't he ring his wife?'

'Like I said, he's screwing her.'

'Geoff, please.' Elena very rarely gives Geoff a dressing down. She knows he won't take it well. He won't listen to what she is saying and then he will sulk like a child having been told he can't play outside because he has been cheeky to his mother. 'To answer your question, Imogen, I don't know why he rang Claire, but I do think that's something we need to question him about.'

'That's the reason he lied about what he was doing Thursday night, surely? He was with his bit on the side and he doesn't want his wife to know about it, so he made up some story about going out with a young couple.' Geoff takes a large bite of his sandwich and continues to talk through half-masticated food. 'It's the worst story I've ever heard. Why would a couple want to get married in St.

Mary's rather than their own church? It doesn't make sense. Apart from being in a village, what's so special about it?'

'It's pretty,' says Imogen.

'All churches look the same. It's the most made-up story I ever heard since the one about Adam and Eve talking to a snake about some apples. Complete garbage.' Geoff takes the last bite of his sandwich and Elena is pleased that she no longer needs to watch him eat. She makes a mental note to sit by his side next time they share a meal.

'The thing is,' says Elena, 'I might be persuaded to agree with you that there is something going on between Claire and the vicar, but there are two reasons why I am struggling to agree.'

'Why's that then?' asks Geoff.

'Number one, Claire isn't like that. She was my best friend for a long, long time. I've known her for ten years and she just isn't like that. She wouldn't touch a married man with a ten-foot barge pole.'

Geoff nods, 'Maybe the old Claire wouldn't, but you haven't really been on the best of terms lately, have you? She might be a changed person, for all you know.'

Elena hates it when Geoff hits the nail on the head. 'It's a possibility, but I can't believe it. She's still grieving the death of my brother. She isn't ready to start dating again, never mind getting involved with a married man, and a vicar at that. I'm not buying it.'

Geoff looks at her across the table. She can tell he is wondering why she is being so naïve. Affairs happen all the time, between all types of different people. Why should Claire be exempt from the temptation of a handsome man?

'Okay, what's the second reason?' asks Geoff.

'Claire already told me where she was on Thursday

night. Remember, I went to see her at her office on Friday? She told me she was working late and then she went home. She wasn't sure if anyone saw when her office lights were switched off, so there was nobody to corroborate what time she left her office, but on the way home she bumped into Helen. You know, the woman who works for them and looks after her sister's baby? When she got home, Sophia and their lodger were there, and I'm pretty sure all of those three people will attest she got home around seven. That's much earlier than the time the vicar got home.'

'So what you're saying is, even if they are screwing, they weren't doing it on Thursday night?' says Geoff.

'Correct,' says Elena. 'If they are an item, then they weren't together at the time of the murder, that's for sure.'

'Unless Claire is lying, too,' says Imogen.

Elena hadn't considered that to be a possibility.

'She could be,' says Geoff. 'But if she is, then her sister and the lodger and the nanny are all lying too.'

'This is so complicated,' says Imogen. 'I don't know if I could ever be a detective. My head is scrambled now. I don't know who's telling the truth and who isn't.'

'It's not an easy job,' says Geoff. He sits back in his chair, chest puffed with self-importance. 'There's a really important job detectives must master before they start to consider interviewing suspects,' says Geoff.

'What's that?' Imogen's face lights up, watching for the nugget of advice from an old professional like Geoff.

'Getting the tea in.' He pushes a pound note across the table and nods towards the counter. 'Off you go then.'

Angela

Angela doesn't know what to do with the information that Jack has just landed on her. It's too much. Being nosy and watching the police going into the church was meant to be to her advantage. She likes to keep her finger on the pulse of the village. She likes to be aware of what's going on. In truth, she was a little surprised when she saw the detectives walking out with the vicar held tightly between them. But anything is possible in the world she lives in. All kinds of respectable people - bankers, school teachers, doctors, even Crown Court judges - buy the cocaine and the weed she very gladly supplies, which means that all kinds of respectable people take a chance they could be arrested. She wondered whether the vicar had bought a little stash from Kamal and it had somehow been discovered during the police's recent enquiries. She planned to ask Kamal when she got home, although now she doesn't need to. She now knows why he has been arrested.

It never occurred to her that the vicar had been arrested for murder.

She watched from across the road as he was bundled into the car. She was about to walk away when she spotted Jack coming out of church. He looked upset, which was understandable, having come face-to-face with his mother's killer. She went to him and asked him how he was. Carol came out of the church behind him, crying hysterically. She told Angela the police were accusing Adam of the murder of Mrs Chadwick and what a terrible travesty of justice this was. 'They have got the wrong man,' she said, twisting a sodden handkerchief in her hands. 'Adam would never do something like that. What can we do? I don't know what to do?'

Angela wanted to slap her across the face like they do in those Hollywood films when women become too hysterical.

'There's nothing we can do,' she said. 'I'm sure things will work out. If it's a mistake then…'

'Of course, it's a mistake,' Carol said, interrupting her with the passion and vehemence of someone who had a huge social injustice to fight and was up for the challenge.

'Then he will be questioned and will be released. He'll be home by tea-time, mark my words.'

Carol brightened at Angela's words, as though she was the Oracle, the fountain of all legal knowledge. Angela told her to get back inside the church and make some more tea. People like tea in an emergency situation, it will make them feel better. Carol nodded and did as she was told, which gave Angela the opportunity to grab Jack's hand and walk him away from the hysteria the members of the church congregation were working themselves into. He didn't need to be part of it. In his fragile emotional state, it wouldn't do him any good.

They walked round the village green towards Jack and Miriam's house. As they rounded the corner into Southgate Drive, Angela told Jack she would stay with him for a while. 'I'll make you some lunch,' she said, opening the fridge to examine the contents. There was half a pint of milk, a slice of ham wrapped in some greaseproof paper, and six eggs. No potatoes. No vegetables. No fresh meat. 'How long have these eggs been in here?' she asked.

'I don't know,' he said. 'My mum brought them home

with her one afternoon last week.'

Angela picked them up one by one and dropped them in the bin. 'There's nothing to eat, Jack,' she said. 'What were you going to have?'

'There might be some tins of soup in the larder,' he said. 'Or some spaghetti hoops.' He opened the door to the larder under the stairs. 'Well, there was, but I think I must have eaten them.'

Angela told him she would take him to her house for a proper meal. She said Kamal was cooking a joint of beef and roast potatoes and there was always too much for the two of them. He would be very welcome.

'Thank you, but I want to stay at home,' he said.

Angela told him that in that case, she would leave him the eggs and the loaf of bread she had just bought from Robertsons, so he could make fried eggs on toast when he felt like it later. She made him promise to go and get something more substantial in the morning. He said he would. She made them both a cup of coffee and they went into the living room and sat side by side on the sofa.

It was then that he dropped his bombshell. The grenade that Angela is terrified of dealing with.

She asked him how he felt about seeing the vicar being arrested. Jack shrugged. Angela, having known him for a number of years, knew that Jack sometimes struggled to process his emotions. 'It's okay, it's over now,' she said. 'You're safe now, Jack.'

He asked if he could talk to her about a secret. Angela told him of course he could. He could tell her anything.

Jack told her how the police confused him at the police station on Thursday. Firing questions at him from right, left, and centre. He couldn't think. It was so hot in that tiny room and he was tired and upset. The police lady told him he had been through a trauma, seeing his mother's dead body like that. Angela agreed with him. 'It's no wonder you weren't thinking straight,' she said. She put down her coffee cup then and said she was sorry for everything he had been through. The policewoman was right, it must have been dreadful. She put her arm around his shoulder and allowed him to rest his head on her shoulder.

Jack had closed his eyes and, without pausing for breath, told Angela 'all the gory details' she had asked for yesterday about the night of his mother's death. How his temper had flared unexpectedly. After all the years of unwarranted criticism from his controlling mother, she had finally pushed him to the edge of insanity, to the point where he hadn't felt in control of what he had done.

'It was silly to argue over something as insignificant as food, but these things happen, don't they?' he said. 'It was bound to happen. We argued almost every day, even though I did everything I could to make her happy. She was never happy. Nothing I did was ever good enough for her.

Angela had pushed his head away from her shoulder and turned to face him. She was beginning to feel dizzy. She could sense what he was about to tell her. She wanted to tell him to keep his mouth closed and to keep the secret to himself, but she also needed to hear it. She could feel her heart hammering in her chest and she was beginning to sweat.

'You look a little pale,' Jack said.

'I'm fine,' she said. 'I might be coming down with something, that's all. Go on.' She needed him to continue with his story without getting distracted. 'Tell me what happened.'

So Jack told her.

'It wasn't him,' he said. 'It wasn't the vicar who killed Mum. It was me. I did it.'

He told Angela how his mother had shouted that he needed to watch his mouth and she was sick to the back teeth of his back chat. When she complained of too much salt in the potato hash, he had picked up the heavy pan of simmering stew and swung it at his mother's head. There was enough force to knock her over. She wasn't a big woman and she went down like a rock in a lake. Hot potatoes and chunks of corned beef had poured down her neck, as she lay on the floor. She stared up at him, fury giving her strength, despite the open wound to the side of her head. Jack said he knew that he had to finish her off, before she had the opportunity to do the same to him. So he hit her again.

'She would have killed me,' he said. 'I could tell. I have never seen her so angry. She would have finished me off. I'm afraid it was me or her.'

Angela was quiet for a long time. She sipped her coffee and mumbled, 'Fuck, fuck. Wow, I would never have thought it was you.'

'Are we still friends?' asked Jack. Angela nodded. She drained her coffee and buried her face in the still-steaming cup. She didn't know what to say. She didn't know whether she should be scared. She wouldn't have said Jack was a violent man, but he clearly had the propensity when pushed to his limits, and here she was, sitting alone with him in this house. 'I knew you'd still be my friend.' Jack smiled at her. 'I know you sell drugs and I know Kamal distributes them for you, my mum told me she saw them in your house, in little bags of foil, so I knew you'd be on my side. You break the law, too.'

'Look,' said Angela, 'I might not be on the right side of the law, not one little bit, but selling drugs and killing someone are two different things.'

'I know that, but I won't kill anyone else.'

Angela realised then what a vulnerable position she was in. She could no longer trust Jack. If she said anything to spark his temper, who knows what he would be capable of. But she couldn't let him know how she felt. She just had to get herself out of there. She forced herself to laugh. 'Well, the useless bastards in the police will never solve this one, will they? Let's see how it all works out,' she said. She looked at her wristwatch. 'Goodness, is that the time? I've got to go. Kamal will hate it if the beef is overcooked.'

Jack asked her to come back and see him tomorrow and she promised she would, but she couldn't look him in the eye. She fastened her coat with stumbling fingers and shouted *see you* as she hurried down the path and into her car.

Now, as she sits at her dining room table watching Kamal slice the beef that he has cooked to perfection, she wonders what she should do with the knowledge she now has. She knows who killed Miriam Chadwick. She knows she should tell the police. But Jack would never survive in prison. He would be eaten alive by the other inmates.

Let's hope the evidence against the vicar is flimsy enough to fall apart, then he can be released, she thinks. Then Jack's secret can be kept safe.

Jack

It was his mother's fault. She had it coming. Jack's fuse had been lit and was ready to blow a long time ago. He is amazed he had managed to control the flickering spark of fiery anger for so long.

In his mind's eye, he can see himself grasping the handle of the heavy porcelain pan, lifting it high in the air, and bringing it crashing down onto his mother's head.

There! That will stop you from going on at me, won't it?

That has shut you up.

He lies in the bath, surrounded by the bubbles from his mother's precious Lily of the Valley bubble bath by Avon, the bottle he was never previously permitted to touch. He smiles and tells himself that his life will be wonderful from now on. He doesn't have anyone bossing him about, telling him what to wear, and treating him like a child. He can eat whatever he wants for his tea. He can have eggs on toast every day if he wants to. He can have cake and custard, or a tin of rice pudding. He will go shopping tomorrow and will stock the larder with his favourite things. Angela told him he should do that. He will never make potato hash again, he knows that for a fact. He will never buy corned beef again.

But after a few moments, as he breathes in his mother's familiar scent, tears spring to his eyes. He clenches his fist and knocks his knuckles against the side of his head to dispel her memory. He doesn't want to have nasty thoughts. He wants to be happy. He opens his eyes. He must stop hitting himself. He will have a bruise if he's not careful.

Stupid boy, he can hear his mother say. You should never have told Angela. You were stupid to trust her.

He lets himself cry then. He holds a wet flannel onto his face and sobs and sobs.

Jack can't decide whether his mother deserved to die, or not.

But still, he misses her.

Elena

Adam seems grateful for the sandwich and the hot drink. Elena notices that he looks to have paled since she left the room. During the past half hour, maybe the frightful position he is in has hit him. He looks like a lost soul, frightened and bereft. She asks him again whether he would like a solicitor present. After a moment, he confirms that he is agreeable to carrying on with the interview. She feels sorry for him then. He thinks he's going home. He thinks the sooner the interview is over, the sooner he will be released, so he doesn't want to waste time waiting for a legal representative to arrive. She hopes that the sooner the interview is over, the closer they will be to finding their man. Right now, she isn't sure whether the killer is sitting on the other side of the table, or whether they have arrested an innocent man. What she does know is that Adam still has many questions he needs to answer.

'I need to remind you that you are still under caution.

Do you understand?' asks Elena.

'Yes,' says Adam.

'Just to recap, before we took a break, you were telling us about the young couple who you went to see on Thursday night. The couple who want to be married in your church. That's right, isn't it?'

'Yes,' says Adam. He sighs deeply.

'Peter and Jane,' says Geoff. He smirks at Adam and digs Elena in the ribs to get her attention, but she has no intention of joining in the joke.

Elena wishes now more than ever that she had asked Harry to assist her with the interview. He is ten years younger than Geoff but is a thousand times more mature.

'You said you couldn't remember their address, but my question is, would you have any documentation in the vicarage or at the church that proves their address?' she asks.

Adam picks at a hangnail on his thumb. 'I can't remember where I wrote it down, but I must have done. It will be there somewhere.'

'So if we search your offices, at the vicarage or at the church, we may find it?'

Adam takes a deep breath. He looks terrified, as though he is standing on the edge of a cliff and about to jump onto the rocks below, certain that he will not be saved. 'Okay, look, I didn't tell you the truth about that night.' Adam leans forward onto the table. 'But I had a good reason. Please believe me when I tell you I didn't kill Miriam. I'll tell you the truth now. I'll tell you where I was and who I was with.'

'I wish you would,' says Elena. 'It would save us a lot of

time.'

Adam takes a deep breath and clasps his hands firmly together, as though in prayer. 'I'm having an affair with a lady called Claire Simons, the person I telephoned this morning. I believe you know who she is. She used to work at this police station. As you can imagine, when you asked me where I was on Thursday, I didn't want my wife to know, so I made up a story about being out with a young couple, but the truth is, I was with Claire that night. I'm sure she will confirm that, if you ask her.'

Elena shakes her head. 'The problem is, Reverend Hargreaves, I already did ask Claire what she was doing on Thursday, as we asked everyone we have spoken to. Unfortunately, Claire does not corroborate your story. She told me that she was working that night. She finished late and then she went home to her sister and her lodger.'

'But ask her again.' Adam's knuckles are white. 'She probably didn't want to tell you about me and her. For obvious reasons, we have been keeping it a secret. But tell her I've told you now. I'm sure she will tell you I was with her.'

'That remains to be seen. For now, let's move on,' says Elena.

'Yes, let's move on,' says Adam. 'Because I'm getting a little bit sick and tired of these four walls. I want to know exactly what evidence you have against me because from what I know, telling lies to the police is not illegal.'

'It's not illegal no,' says Geoff. 'But it's dodgy. People who have nothing to hide don't tell lies to the police.'

'But I told you why I lied,' says Adam, his voice suddenly rising. 'I didn't want to admit that I was having an affair. Surely even *you* can understand that.' He stares at

Geoff defiantly.

'Even me? What the bloody hell does that mean?' Geoff leans over the table.

Both men are getting angry now. Elena can feel the palpable tension in the room rising. Both of them are raising their voices. But before she can calm them down, before she can take control of the interview, in a sudden explosive moment, Geoff swings a punch at Adam and hits him square in the nose. The crack of the impact echoes through the room as blood splurts from his nose onto the desk. The dregs of tea in Adam's cup, which is now on its side, drip onto the floor. Imogen screams and drops her notepad and pen onto the floor.

'Geoff, leave the room now,' orders Elena. 'Imogen, calm yourself down and go and get a paper towel from the toilets. Soak it with cold water first.'

Both officers leave the room.

'If he's broken my nose, I'll sue him,' says Adam. 'I'll have him for assault.'

'Tip your head back and squeeze tightly onto the bridge of your nose,' says Elena. 'I don't think anything will be broken. He didn't hit you that hard.' She curses Geoff and his uncontrollable fists.

Within a minute, Imogen returns with a handful of soaked paper towels, which she places on the table in front of Adam. Elena tells her to sit down in Geoff's place. They wait until Adam has gently wiped his face with various towels and the blood flow has dried up.

'Do you want to see a solicitor?' Elena asks him.

'My patience is being sorely tested,' says Adam, 'but I would rather get on with it and get home. I'll answer any questions you have, but mark my words, I will be seeking legal advice as soon as I get out of here.'

If you get out of here, thinks Elena.

'Before you tell me what evidence you have,' says Adam. 'can you answer me this: have you found the murder weapon, and if so, are my fingerprints on it?'

Adam glares at Elena across the table, barely disguising his disdain for her and the situation he finds himself in. 'Reverend Hargreaves, I can appreciate how frustrating this is for you, but let me make myself clear. I told you before that I'm in charge of this interview and I will be the one asking the questions. Just because Detective Sergeant Miller has left the room, does not mean that you are now in charge, just because you're the last man standing. I am the senior officer, and this is my investigation.'

Adam leans back in his chair, his defeat palpable. 'I'm sorry, I didn't mean to imply anything because you're a woman. I'm not that kind of man. Trust me, my wife is the one in charge at home. I just do as I am told.

Elena can see that he probably isn't that kind of man, but even so, she needs to put her stamp on the interview. 'To answer your question, the murder weapon is still outstanding. That is to say, we haven't found anything in the fields and the streets surrounding Miriam Chadwick's house. However, that doesn't mean to say that the murder weapon isn't hiding in plain sight.'

'What do you mean by that?' asks Adam.

'The silver jug, for example, the one you give the communion wine in. It's heavy, isn't it? Perhaps that could be used with sufficient force to knock someone over. Or the paperweight on the side of your desk in the vestry. Or perhaps something that was picked up in Miriam's house.

Many items can be used as murder weapons.'

'Oh, that's ridiculous. But if that's what you think, why don't you take those things from the church, the jug, the paperweight, anything else you want?' asks Adam. 'Have them examined for tiny specks of blood and then tell me if you find anything on them, because you won't. I might as well tell you that now, to save the taxpayer's precious money.'

'Would your fingerprints be found anywhere in Miriam's house?'

'Yes, of course, they would,' says Adam. 'I'm her local vicar and I visit most people in the village on a regular basis. You will find my fingerprints on the door handles, the cups she served tea in, the handle used to flush the toilet. I don't know, all manner of things. You're clutching at straws now, surely. You have no murder weapon with my prints on, you have no witnesses, but most of all, you haven't come up with a motive. Why would I want to kill Miriam? The whole situation is preposterous.'

'I might have agreed with you a few days ago,' says Elena. 'But I'm not in the process of arresting people without evidence.' She doesn't want to admit, to Adam or to herself, that she believes Geoff jumped in and arrested Adam too soon. Her case against him certainly needs more building blocks before it would stand up in front of a jury. This morning, she would have held back and asked him a few more questions but Geoff barged through like a bull in a china shop and before she knew it, Adam was being manhandled down the aisle, watched by dozens of shocked church members. 'However, there is something we haven't talked about yet, and that is this.' Elena takes the crumpled note found on the floor of the vestry and smooths it out onto the table. 'Let me read what it says. "Miriam, You can't tell anyone what you saw this morning. You might want to gossip, but it is none of your business. As your employer, I am warning you to keep silent. If you refuse and news of this gets out, there will be consequences. Adam.". The question is, what did Miriam see that was so damaging for you?'

Adam sighs heavily. 'She saw me and Claire kissing in the vestry on Thursday morning. We didn't know there was anyone in church, and we didn't hear her until it was too late. That's why I denied that I had seen her on Thursday, because of my affair with Claire.'

'Why did you write her this note? What was your intention?'

'I don't know. I wanted to frighten her, I suppose.'

'Frighten her?'

'Not like that, not so she was scared of me, but I wanted to make her frightened she would lose her job. What I was trying to say in a really clumsy way was *I'm your employer and I'm telling you not to say anything.*'

'And if she did say something, if she let your secret out into the community, what would the consequences be for her?'

'Losing her job, of course.'

'Or losing her life?'

'No, no, of course not,' shouts Adam. 'Don't put words into my mouth.' He shakes his head and scrunches his eyes closed for a moment, as though holding in tears. 'I'm sorry, I don't mean to shout, but I'm finding this whole thing extremely stressful.'

'So here's what I think happened, Reverend Hargreaves,' says Elena. 'You wrote that note to Miriam and took it round to her house to give to her on Thursday evening. Whether you expected her to be at home, I don't know. Maybe, if she wasn't in, you would pop it in an envelope and post it through the door, or if she was in, you were going to slip it to her behind Jack's back. You wouldn't want him to know about your affair, too, would you? That's why you had to write your threat down, because there was a possibility you wouldn't have an opportunity to talk to her without Jack being around.'

'That isn't…'

Elena holds up her hand. 'Let me finish. I think that when you got to Miriam's house, you discovered that Jack was out. That was convenient, wasn't it? That's why you didn't give Miriam the note. You didn't need to, because here she was alone, waiting for you to speak to her. Only, the conversation took a sinister turn, didn't it? She wasn't so easy to manipulate as you expected. She probably shouted back at you and told you where to go.'

'No.'

'People have been telling me that Mrs Chadwick wasn't an easy person. She was bad-tempered and not well liked. So I can imagine how she would have reacted to you. Then you lost your temper, too, and killed her in a moment of blind fury, didn't you?'

'No! No! I didn't go round to her house and I didn't kill her.'

'Has anyone examined the saucepan for traces of blood?' asks Imogen.

'The saucepan?' says Elena.

'Yes, the one with the corned beef hash. That could have been the murder weapon. It's heavy enough and it was found right next to the body, wasn't it?'

Elena can't allow Adam to think she hasn't already thought of that. Why hadn't she thought of it? Nobody else on the team has thought of it either. How stupid she has been. The chief superintendent will be furious when he finds out. The pathology report that landed on her desk this morning indicated the cause of death to be two blows to the head. Both impact sites contributed equally. The report confirmed that the deceased was hit over the head with a blunt instrument, which caused a fracture to the skull and an injury to the frontal lobe, resulting in some swelling. There was also an injury of a similar size to the back of the skull, where the deceased very likely fell onto the floor. The skull was fractured and damage caused to the occipital lobe. Both injuries caused the death of Miriam Chadwick.

'I didn't kill her,' says Adam. 'I didn't kill her with a jug, a paperweight, or with a stupid saucepan. I didn't do it.'

'That will be all for now,' says Elena. 'I'm going to ask you to return to your cell while I discuss this case with my superior officer.'

She leads Adam out of the interview and into one of the cells. The door is locked behind him. She opens the tiny flap covering the window and tells him she will ask the custody sergeant to make him a drink as soon as he has time.

'Imogen Winters, I think you may have just cracked this case wide open,' she says, as they walk away.

Monday 10th October 1976

Claire

Claire can see the vicarage from her office window. She started work early this morning, desperate to get out of the house and from under Sophia's disapproval, and she watched as Cheryl Hargreaves ushered the children out of the house and on their way to school. Their little leather satchels were grasped tightly. Their little knees, as thin as sparrows, poked out between the bottom of their grey shorts and the top of their socks. Their little feet skipped in front of their mother. Claire watched their faces for signs of trauma, but all she could see were the usual giggles of gap-toothed seven-year-olds. It seems that they are, so far, unaware of their father's plight. In contrast, Cheryl looked awful. Her pale face, naked of makeup, was etched with sorrow and she looked like she hadn't slept a wink.

The vicar's wife is back home now. She has been back for an hour or more, and Claire has no excuse not to go and see her. She knows she must, but despite the fact that she has thought about nothing else all morning, she still doesn't know what to say to her.

Last night, Sophia asked her whether the affair with Adam was serious. 'Is it a long-term thing?' Claire said no, as far as she was concerned, it wasn't going anywhere. She liked Adam and she enjoyed his company but the thought of taking him away from his boys broke her heart. She knew she wouldn't be able to do it. Sophia gave her a tiny smile then. The kind of smile that said, see, I knew you were a decent person deep down. You have been hurt and used him to help you heal, but you are doing the right thing now by letting him go back to his family.

Claire knows how her sister's mind works. Sophia would be terribly disappointed if their affair morphed into something serious and Claire became responsible for breaking up what was once a solid marriage. But anyone can be forgiven for the odd transgression, especially during a moment of grief, can't they? She would rather die than continue living without her sister's love and approval.

The truth is, before the events of this weekend, Claire had hoped the affair would lead to something. She hadn't allowed herself to think about the future too much, and she wasn't lying when she said the thought of taking Adam away from the boys was heartbreaking, but even so, she would have done it. She would have been *the other woman*. She was prepared to steal someone else's husband in order to make herself happy. She knew that Cheryl would get over it, in the same way she had been forced to get over Stephen. It would be hard for a time. There would be lots of tears and sleepless nights. Then they would all move on.

But yesterday, everything changed after that phone call. When Adam pleaded from the police station for her to help him, all the loving feelings she had for him dissipated like a dream upon waking up in the morning. The magic of their secrecy was gone. The butterflies in her stomach when she heard his voice were replaced by - what? She hates to admit it, but distaste. She bit on her tongue during the call to prevent herself from being cruel and telling him never to speak to her again. She was shocked at how her feelings changed so suddenly. She saw him differently now. He was despicable. What kind of married man kisses someone else in a church? What kind of vicar cheats on his wife and family? What kind of father would jeopardise his marriage? The scales well and truly fell from her eyes. As soon as he comes home, she will tell him it's over.

Right now, she must speak to Cheryl. It's now or never. She grabs her coat and bag, locks the office door, and makes her way down the steps to the street below.

The gentle autumn breezes of the past few weeks have been pushed aside by a restless wind that is stripping the remnants of crisp golden leaves from the trees. Claire fastens her full-length grey leather coat up to her neck. As she struggles with the buttons, she contemplates dashing back up the stairs for her scarf which is thrown over the back of one of the chairs, but she knows she is procrastinating. Her long hair lashes at her face like a whip, stinging her cheeks with tiny jolts of pain that cause her to dip into Angela's florists for a moment of respite.

Angela is behind the counter cutting the bottom from long-stemmed roses and arranging them into bundles. 'The wind blown you in here, has it?' She laughs.

'It did, yes,' says Claire. 'Wow, are we in for a storm or something? It isn't raining, but it's blowing a gale out there.'

'It certainly is. I think it will be a quiet day for me,' says Angela. 'If there's one thing that puts customers off, it's the wind, especially one that can lift old ladies into the air and drop them down like a bag of spuds.'

'I've got to admit, I only came here to find a rubber band in my bag so I can tie my hair back, I hope you don't mind.' Angela laughs while Claire rummages in her bag. 'I'll end up looking like the Wicked Witch of the West if I don't sort my hair out.' She finds a rubber band and pulls her hair into an untidy ponytail. Angela gathers the bunches of roses in her arms and drops them into a bucket of water next to the other flower displays along the back wall of the shop.

'Those roses look beautiful. I'll take a bunch, please.'

'For yourself? Or shall I wrap them in gift paper?' asks Angela.

'Actually, I'm on my way to the vicarage. Thought I'd see how Cheryl is this morning, you know, after yesterday.'

'Yes, I saw the vicar being carted away. What's all that about?'

'Honestly, I've no idea,' says Claire.

'You used to be a copper, didn't you? No smoke without fire, eh? They must have something on him.'

Claire is beginning to regret her decision to pop into the florist. She doesn't want to talk about Adam and she certainly doesn't want to contemplate that there might be any evidence against him, although in truth, the whole village will be talking about him today, so it isn't a subject she will be able to avoid.

'I'm hoping the police have made a mistake,' she says. 'It does happen. Poor Cheryl will be going out of her mind, so I'd better get up there.'

'Yes, of course. I don't suppose you want these red roses? Not really appropriate, given the circumstances, are they?'

'No, absolutely not. Any other colour, but red.'

'If you want roses, I've got some lovely white ones, or these yellow ones? Maybe pink? No, on second thoughts, they can be a bit romantic, too. You don't want to rub it in that her hubby isn't with her, do you?'

'I'll have some white ones, please. I love white flowers,'

says Claire. She wonders whether Cheryl will pick up on their significance, being a symbol of humility and a way of saying sorry. If Angela does, she doesn't say anything.

As Angela wraps them in paper, Claire watches out of the window as the wind increases in speed and strength. The water on the village pond ebbs and flows like a miniature tide. A huddle of ducks is tucked underneath a tall tree at the edge of the pond, their heads tucked safely into their feathers. The postman pulls up outside the shop in his red van and struggles to open the driver's door. As soon as he steps outside his vehicle, his hat is torn from his head. He chases it down the road for a few yards before he manages to catch it and throw it into the van.

'There, all done,' says Angela. 'Please give Cheryl my regards, and tuck these under your coat. The wind will ruin them by the time you get there, otherwise.'

Claire pays for the flowers and battles her way to the vicarage, with the roses clutched tightly against her chest, as the wind tugs at her coat and threatens to snatch them from her grasp. She knocks on the front door and waits in the shelter of the porch for Cheryl to answer. She has almost given up, imagining Cheryl tucked away at the back of the house avoiding all visitors, and is about to turn around and go back to her office when the door opens.

'I wasn't sure whether to come or not, and I know flowers won't necessarily help you to feel any better, but I hope you like them,' says Claire, pushing the flowers towards Cheryl.

Cheryl bursts into tears and ushers Claire into the hallway. 'Thank you so much,' she says. 'These are beautiful. Come in, come in. I'll put them in a vase.' She trudges down the hallway into the kitchen, wiping her eyes with the back of her hand as she walks.

Claire hesitates, her feet seemingly unable to move from the *Welcome Home* mat by the door. She sees a pair of Adam's shoes standing neatly side by side next to the umbrella stand. She has seen him in those shoes often. Leather, the colour of a comforting milky coffee, with darker brown laces. The shoes of a respectable married man; a man with values and principles. Next to them are two tiny pairs of wellington boots, one blue, one yellow. Suddenly she wants to cry. She wants to fall to her knees and confess what she has been doing for the past nine months with the father of the children who own these wellington boots. Instead, she takes a deep breath and follows Cheryl into the kitchen.

'Nobody spoke to me at school, you know?' says Cheryl. She takes a crystal vase from the top shelf of a pine Welsh dresser and fills it with water from the tap. 'Can you believe it?'

'I'd like to say no, but unfortunately, I can believe it,' says Claire. 'People are very odd sometimes. It's times like this when they show their true colours.'

'Yes, you're right. I'll find out who my real friends are, I suppose, over the next few days.'

Claire is glad Cheryl's back is turned as she busies herself arranging the roses. She doesn't see how Claire's cheeks are burning with shame. 'Have you heard from Adam?' she says.

'No, I haven't.' Cheryl's voice is laden with disappointment and sadness.

Claire doesn't know what to say. Should she tell this distraught woman that her husband used his phone call allowance to call his mistress, rather than his wife from the police station? Would she be better kept in the dark, where ignorance is bliss, or be shown the light?

'The roses look beautiful,' she says. She is pleased that, even for a moment, Cheryl has a little something to brighten her day. Cheryl places the vase on the windowsill in front of the sink. She strokes one of the petals, gently and softly, and it is now that Claire is sure her decision to end things with Adam is the correct one. She can't allow her selfish actions to negatively impact this poor woman, especially now when she has so much to deal with. The affair with Adam is over and Cheryl doesn't need to know about it. What she doesn't know won't hurt her. Although she does need to know about Adam's phone call.

'I should have come to see you last night,' says Claire. 'but I assumed Adam would telephone you and speak to you himself, after he spoke to me.'

Cheryl shrugs. 'I expected to hear from him but - I'm sorry, what? He spoke to you? I don't understand why he would ring you.'

'He rang me in the afternoon,' says Claire. 'For legal advice.'

'Oh. Well, that's good that you could give him some legal advice.'

'I'm not sure I helped much. I spoke to the officer in charge, DI Elena Holt, and I offered to get him a solicitor, but honestly, the only good ones I know don't practice criminal law. They do family law and conveyancing.'

Cheryl nods. 'She seemed nice, DI Holt. That is, I thought she was nice before she came to arrest my husband.' Tears well again in her eyes. She pulls out one of the wooden dining chairs and sits at the table.

Claire is beginning to wish she hadn't come. Seeing

Cheryl with the weight of the world on her shoulders is distressing. She seems to have aged overnight. Her pretty face which is usually made more beautiful by blue eye shadow and layers and layers of black mascara looks tired and pale, washed out by emotion.

'I'm not sure if you know, but Elena and I used to be friends. We used to work together when I was a detective at Wellington Police Station.'

'I didn't know that. I'd forgotten you used to be a policewoman.'

'Elena is Stephen's sister.' Claire watches Cheryl's face for any sign of recognition or remembrance, but there is none. Then she realises that Cheryl probably hasn't met Elena before this week. In normal circumstances, she would have expected a sympathetic response, some comment about how awful it was that Stephen was taken so suddenly, and how terrible it was for a sister to lose a brother. But Cheryl's expression is cold and hard, showing not an ounce of warmth towards the woman who has taken away her husband and locked him in a police cell.

'Would you like a coffee?' asks Cheryl. The request is sudden, as though Cheryl has forgotten her manners and just remembered she hasn't yet offered her visitor a drink.

'I'm sorry, I've got to go,' says Claire. 'I've got so much to do, reports to write, and phone calls to make.'

'Yes, of course. I'm glad you're keeping busy and your business is doing well. Thank you for popping in, and thank you for the lovely flowers.'

'Why don't you ring the police station and ask what's going on?' says Claire.

'Will they tell me?'

'They won't give you details, but they should tell you

whether Adam is still being interviewed, or whether they have finished and what time they can release him. You might be able to go and pick him up?'

'Oh, I hope so,' says Cheryl. She gives Claire a tight hug.

Claire fastens her coat again and prepares to brave the wind back to her office. She doesn't tell Cheryl that she will ring Elena to see what evidence they have. Elena shouldn't discuss police business with her, but she hopes she will, as an old friend and an ex-colleague. She waves goodbye to Cheryl and tells her to close the door and not let the cold air into the house.

Claire walks quickly and is almost at her office door when the heavens open and torrential rain soaks her within seconds. A flash of lightning bolts through the grey clouds covering the village. She struggles to find her door key, which has slipped to the bottom of her chaotic handbag. She pushes old tissues, a lipstick, and a felt-tip pen to one side and finally her fingers grasp onto the bunch of keys. Her hands are cold and wet now. She fumbles with the lock and manages to push the door open as thunder blasts overhead.

Adam

People say that they haven't slept a wink, when what they mean is they had a restless night. They probably slept longer than they realise. But Adam is sure he hasn't slept a wink. He lay on his back on the thin mattress on the concrete block that purported to be a bed for hours and hours, staring at the starkly painted ceiling of the police cell, and listening to the strange noises around him. He had no idea that so many people would be arrested at any one time in a small town like Wellington. The six cells were all occupied as far as he could tell, with various vagrants, thieves, and vagabonds. There must have been a pub fight somewhere, as an altercation between two inebriated gentlemen carried on from the custody office, down the corridor, and into the cells. What seemed like dozens of police officers dragged the men into the cells and slammed the doors shut. Two drunken voices continued to shout obscenities and death threats to each other across the darkness, until they eventually fell quiet.

It is morning now and there are different noises on the other side of the cell door. The atmosphere is more subdued as prisoners wake and face the reality of their dire situations.

Through the tiny window in the door, Adam can see the shadows of uniformed officers as they pass, wandering the corridor and checking on the prisoners. A pair of eyes stare at him for a moment. Adam wants to jump up and ask the policeman to let him out. He has been here long enough, surely. He shouldn't be in a place like this, with people like this. But his pleas would be futile, he knows that. He tried during the night when the first pair of eyes checked on him. He was shocked that he wasn't being listened to. He isn't used to being ignored. At church, he is used to people gazing at him with admiration as he speaks, uninterrupted, for twenty minutes every Sunday. At home, he gets cross when his children ignore him when they are too busy playing. He tells them off and gives them a lecture about manners and kindness, and consideration for others.

Last night, he wanted to jump up and bang on the door

and shout for the officer to come back, he was talking to him. How dare he walk away and ignore him? But something told him to stay calm. Anger doesn't get you what you want. In fact, anger can get you in a whole barrel full of trouble.

Adam knows he should use this time to pray. He usually says silent prayers every morning, before he gets out of bed. While Cheryl is making coffee and pouring cereal for the boys downstairs, he stays in bed, closes his eyes, and connects with his maker. A few moments of quiet before the madness of the day begins. He should pray now for God's grace, for help, for comfort, and for forgiveness. There is so much he should ask for, but he doesn't feel worthy. He doesn't want to hear God's displeasure. If he doesn't ask for anything, then he can't be upset when his prayers are not answered. He considers praying to God to look after Cheryl in her time of despair. She must be out of her mind with worry. But right now, he can't focus on anyone else, other than himself.

He hears a key rattle in the cell door. 'Stand back!' someone shouts. He isn't sure who the man is shouting at. Does he mean him? He can't stand back any further; his back is already to the wall. The door is flung open by a middle-aged sergeant, a different one from the one on duty yesterday when he was brought in. He is carrying a thin wooden tray. 'Breakfast,' he says.

Adam doesn't know whether to accept it or not. He is reminded of visiting his ageing mother in the hospital last year. The patients who were offered meals were the ones who were expected to be kept in another day. The ones who were going home were taken off the list of those who needed food. But before he is given a chance to ask any questions or refuse any food, the sergeant has gone. The tray is left on the floor of the cell, the door is once again locked and Adam is once again alone.

He is longing for a drink, whether or not he will be allowed home soon. He picks up the tray and takes it to his concrete bed. A small cardboard cup is three-quarters full of tea. He tastes it, and even though it has no sugar and is almost cold and stewed, he swallows it in a couple of mouthfuls. Beside it sits a slice of soggy toast, pale on one side and almost burned on the other. It is lathered with white margarine. It looks disgustingly inedible, but his stomach grumbles, so he eats it.

Afterwards, he looks at the bucket in the corner of the room which he was told was for his toilet use. 'Toilet use?' he asked. 'Yes, when you want a piss, you use that as the toilet.' He is desperate to use it now, but surely they will let him out to use a real toilet? How will he wash his hands? He knocks on the cell door, politely at first, and then heavier when it becomes clear nobody has heard him, or nobody is listening.

'Hello, can you let me out to use the bathroom?' he shouts, with his face up to the round window in the door. 'Please,' he adds, as an afterthought, as though politeness will get him what he wants.

'Oooh, listen to him,' shouts the voice from the next-door cell. *'Can you let me out to use the bathroom?'* His voice is mocking. 'Where do you think you are? The bloody Ritz?' The man finds his own joke hilariously funny and another man joins in with the laughter. If they are the two men who were brought in in the early hours, they have clearly made peace with each other now, and they don't appear to be too hungover following their night of revelry.

Adam ignores them and bangs on his cell door. 'Hello,' he shouts.

Any response from the custody sergeant is drowned out by his neighbours hammering on their doors and shouting various commands. Adam's voice is lost. He might as well be talking to himself. In his desperation, he urinates in the bucket and sits on the corner of his mattress, resigned to wait in silence until someone comes along to determine his fate.

Yesterday, DI Holt gave him no indication of what would happen next. He presumes he has to wait for her to come on duty this morning and for her to make a decision. He wonders whether she will be an early starter, or will she be on a later shift, given the fact that she has worked all weekend.

Adam isn't unintelligent. He can often see both sides of an argument and he is able to see why he was arrested. The note to Miriam was the nail in his coffin. If they hadn't found it, if he had pushed it further into his pocket so that it hadn't fallen out, then he would probably not be here. It was stupid of him to put a threat in writing, even though, as he tried to explain in the interview, the threat was that Miriam would lose her job, not that she would lose her life. He asked DI Holt to consider what kind of man he was. It didn't matter that he is a man of God; he could tell she isn't the religious type, but surely she could see he is a good citizen? A nice family man with morals and values. He wouldn't be so stupid that he would threaten to kill someone, and then actually carry it out, would he? She had stared at him, not answering his question. Now, as he relives the interview in his mind, he is scared that is exactly what she was thinking.

He shouldn't have lied, he knows that now. He should have told the police he saw Miriam on Thursday morning. Why on earth didn't he say that? He didn't need to mention that Miriam had seen him and Claire kissing, but he should have admitted he saw her in church. When Carol saw Miriam storming out, it was obvious she would tell the police, but he wasn't thinking. His mind was whirring like a steam engine, just thinking of one thing - him and Claire, him and Claire, him and Claire. That's all he could think about. He had to deny, deny, deny. So he did. Until he could stand it no longer and finally he told them about his affair.

Thankfully, Claire had managed to sneak out of the back door in the vestry before Carol had made her way down the aisle - Carol always barges into the vestry, even if he is busy working. She likes him to know she is there, doing God's work, collecting brownie points – but it isn't important now. All the steps he and Claire took to keep their secret are worthless. The truth is out now and soon everyone will know. He isn't sure whether what he said in the police interview is privileged information. Is it the same as when you tell a doctor or a solicitor something private? Are the police obliged to keep his secret to themselves? He has no idea. As far as he knows, Cheryl still doesn't know about his infidelity, and he would like to keep it that way, if he possibly can.

There's a sharp knock on his door, followed by the turning of the key. The door opens to reveal Detective Inspector Holt.

'Come with me,' she says.

'Where to?' asks Adam.

'The Custody Sergeant.'

Angela

The wind and rain has been battering the front of Angela's shop all morning, keeping customers tucked up safe inside their houses. After catching up with her paperwork and placing orders for more scented candles and some small glass vases, which always sell well, she decides to close early. She is just pulling the blinds down when Helen pushes open the door, almost knocking Angela off her feet in the process.

Angela isn't in the mood to listen to Helen gossiping today. Now that she has decided to close the shop, she wants to get home as soon as possible. She wants to put her feet up and have a large glass of wine with Kamal.

'I'm just closing, Helen,' she says with a forced smile. 'The rain has kept everyone indoors today, so there's no point in staying open any longer.'

'They've charged him,' says Helen. Her eyes are wide and unblinking as she imparts this breaking news. She looks like she's about to cry.

'Charged who?' asks Angela. She knows who, but after what Jack had confessed to her yesterday, she has to be sure.

'Adam Hargreaves, the vicar,' says Helen. 'Who do you think? They've charged him with the murder of Miriam

Chadwick.'

'Are you sure? How do you know?'

'Mrs Hargreaves rang Claire and told her. That policewoman detective apparently called the vicarage and told her, the poor woman. She didn't even tell her in person. She rang her. How despicable is that?'

Are the wives of murderers usually given the courtesy of a personal visit by the police? Angela isn't sure. Then she remembers that Adam isn't a murderer, is he?

Jack is.

Jack

The police car pulls up outside number 8 Southgate Drive just as Jack sits down to have his snack of cheese and crackers. He has done what Angela told him and has been shopping. The larder and the fridge are both now stocked with plenty of tins, some fresh fruit, a bag of potatoes, and a pork chop. He doesn't know it is a police car at first. The shiny black Ford Granada with four doors looks the same as the car driven by the Gregsons over the road. He wonders whether it is them back from their holiday. But then he sees Detective Inspector Elena Holt getting out of the passenger side. The driver is the man who interviewed him with her last Thursday, the night his mother died. The younger man with the red and yellow tartan socks. He wonders whether he is wearing them again today, or something equally as gawdy.

He watches as they begin to saunter up his garden path. He puts his cheese and crackers onto the sofa and goes to open the door.

Hello Jack. Can we come in?

He holds the door open wide and asks them to wipe their feet on the mat. Mum didn't usually let people into the house with shoes on, he tells them. Elena looks down at her feet and seems to contemplate whether or not to remove her shoes, so he tells her it doesn't matter now, not after last week.

Elena leads the way into the living room at the front of the house. He forgets that there are many police officers who now know the layout of his house as well as he does.

We have some news for you, she says, as they all shuffle awkwardly around the coffee table in the middle of the room. He asks whether it is about Reverend Hargreaves, and she nods solemnly, as though she is about to tell him that the vicar has died, although he doubts that is the case. He is sure the police take good care of their prisoners at the police station. He has never heard of anyone being mistreated by them. Elena looks like the type of woman who has a caring side. She is smiling at him again, in the same way she smiled at him in the police car last week, when she turned around from her seat in the front and told him he would have to find somewhere else to sleep, as the forensic team had taken over his house. Every light was on and the front door was wide open. His mother would have had a hissy fit if she had seen the amount of people who traipsed through. None of them seemed to wipe their feet, despite the fact it was raining.

Would you like to sit down, Elena asks him. She gestures to the place at the end of the sofa where it is clear he was sitting before they arrived. The cushion is flattened and his cheese and crackers are waiting for him. He wants to tell her that he doesn't need her permission to sit down in his own house - the house he owns now that his mother is no longer here - but his mother taught him to be respectful of authority. He was always polite to doctors, teachers, and policemen as a child, and he will continue to be so.

Jack sits down and asks Elena and the other detective to sit down too. They both choose to sit in the armchairs, perched on the edge of the seats like a couple of budgies on a swing.

We have some news for you, Elena says. Jack wants to tell her she has already said that. But he sits patiently and waits for her to speak again. He looks across at the other detective. Do you remember DC Harry Beckford? Jack tells her that yes, he does. He remembers his socks. Harry laughs and lifts one leg of his trousers to reveal his socks. They are not tartan today, just a vivid red, the colour of his mother's blood. Jack laughs and tells him they are very nice and they complement his brown suit perfectly. He likes colourful socks. His mother always used to buy his socks for him, but they were always grey or black. From now on, he is going to buy himself some colourful ones. Harry tells him they are from Man About Town in Wellington, just off the high street. Jack nods as though he knows it, but he doesn't. He rarely goes to Wellington. It's too noisy and there are too many people.

Jack, says Elena, bringing a halt to the sartorial conversation, you remember we arrested Reverend Hargreaves yesterday?

How could he forget? Almost all the people in the church were crying, he tells her.

She agrees it was shocking, not least for his poor wife

and children. It is sad when they have to make an arrest of someone people look up to, a respected member of the community. But sometimes good people do bad things, and those people have to be arrested.

Has he done a bad thing? Jack wants to know.

Yes, Elena tells him. He killed your mother. She apologises over and over, as though she is the one who did the killing. He wants to tell her it's okay. She doesn't need to be upset. But he can't find the words. He swallows hard and blinks back tears.

Get him a tissue, Harry, commands Elena. Harry jumps up and looks around the room. Then Jack can hear him running up the stairs. Moments later, he returns with the toilet roll from the bathroom. Elena pulls a couple of sheets from it and hands them to Jack. As Jack wipes his face, she kneels in front of him, resting her hands on his knees, and asks him whether he will be okay. He doesn't know. How can he say whether he will be okay? He can't see into the future. He doesn't have a crystal ball. He doesn't say that, but he wonders why she has asked him such a daft question.

Elena gets to her feet and tells him there is one more thing he needs to know. Jack can't imagine what else Reverend Hargreaves might have done. Don't look so worried, Elena says. It's an update really. We want to keep you updated as we progress through the case and assess the evidence, she says. She asks him whether he would mind showing her the pan he used to cook the corned beef hash on Thursday. Then Harry tells him it might have been the murder weapon and that is why they wish to see it.

I knew that all along, says Jack.

You did? Elena creases up her face and two lines appear

on her forehead.

Yes, well you didn't find anything else, did you? The pan was right there next to the body, on the floor, and it was covered in blood, and I wondered why you didn't take it to examine it for fingerprints.

As soon as he says the word *body*, he feels odd. He shouldn't be talking about his mother in such cold terms. She was cruel and nasty sometimes and she spoke without thinking most of the time, but she was still his mother. He dabs at his eyes again with the sodden toilet roll.

Elena tells him she is sorry they didn't consider it beforehand. There is so much going on in the precious hours immediately following a murder, and things are sometimes missed in their fervour to solve the case quickly. She stands and Jack shows her the cupboard in the kitchen next to the oven where the pans are kept. She rummages through the cupboard and pulls out the biggest pan, a white one with a black lid. It used to have orange flowers painted around the side but the years of scrubbing at the enamel has washed most of them off. Now just flecks of orange paint appear here and there, as though the pan has been designed by a child who flicked paint at it from the other side of the room. A juvenile attempt at abstract art.

Is this the pan you used last Thursday? Elena wants to know. Jack nods and watches as she passes it to Harry. He puts it in a large brown paper bag marked 'Evidence' and tells Jack they need to take it to the police station for a while. They will need to test it to see if there are any traces of blood on it. There was blood everywhere, says Jack, but the cleaning company cleaned everything.

Elena nods and walks back into the living room, while Harry takes the pan to the car. Jack stands at the window as Harry unlocks the boot and carefully places the pan inside, handling it with the care of someone putting a sleeping baby to bed.

Elena tells him they don't know definitely that the pan was used to kill his mother. They will also be examining some items from the church and the vicarage. He asks them what, but she tells him she shouldn't say at the moment, not until they have proof.

Jack sits quietly for a moment and then asks Elena how they can be sure they have arrested the right man if they don't know what the murder weapon is. Having the murder weapon is just one piece of the jigsaw, she tells him. Lies and motives make up part of the case too. And the lack of an alibi. Again, she tells him she can't say too much until she has prepared the case properly for court and given her report to the superintendent.

Jack tries to think about what possible murder weapons could be hiding in a church. Carol is in there virtually every day, pottering around and polishing the brass. She will be shocked to see the police collecting this and that and searching the items for blood and bits of skin.

He wants to ask Elena whether she will have a giant magnifying glass to take to church, or will she just take things and then look at them under the magnifying glass at the police station. Yes, they will probably do that, he decides. Then they can take their time, without being interrupted by Carol, offering them endless cups of tea and biscuits; contaminating important evidence with crumbs from custard creams.

Elena asks him whether she should ring anyone for him. Who do you mean? Someone to come and sit with you, she says. He tells her he doesn't have a phone, but his friend

Angela down the road might call in later.

Is that Angela Bennett? asks Harry. He is back from his trip to the car and is standing in the doorway between the living room and the hall.

Yes, he says. She's been kind and calls in most days.

I thought you said you didn't know her, says Harry.

No, I didn't say that, says Jack. I know her very well. My mother cleans for her. She used to clean for her. Why would you say I didn't know her? She's a friend. I wouldn't lie about something like that.

Elena tells him to calm down. He hasn't done anything wrong.

Harry is pulling a notebook out of his jacket pocket and leafing through the pages. Last Thursday when you were interviewed at Wellington Police Station, you said you had never met Angela or Claire, but you knew the vicar. He turns the notepad around and holds it out at arm's length. Jack wouldn't be able to read the scribble, even if he saw it close up. I wrote it down as you said it, says Harry. It's called contemporaneous note taking. Taken at the time it was said.

Jack shakes his head. No, no, he didn't say that. The note is wrong.

He begins to hammer on the side of the sofa with his fist, slowly at first and then faster and faster, his fist clenched tightly. If these two weren't here, he would walk up and down the living room as Doctor McCarthy told him to do when he gets anxious. He wants them to leave now. He tells them to go and Elena says she is sorry for upsetting him. They will leave him alone now.

They go and he closes the front door behind them and then walks up and down the hallway for half an hour until he begins to feel better.

Elena

As she bounds up the stairs to Claire's office, Elena has already decided she isn't going to be so polite this time. She isn't going to wait outside in the dark and dusty stairwell for Claire to open the door. She will let herself in. She is propelled up the stairs, two at a time, by her rising anger. Having just left a tearful Jack with the news that they have charged his trusted vicar with his mother's murder, Elena isn't in the mood to take any crap from Claire. She is here to give her a piece of her mind. Harry is waiting outside in the car. She told him the conversation wouldn't be pleasant to witness.

Claire is on the phone when Elena pushes open the internal door to the office. If she had been speaking to Sophia, or her parents, Elena would have asked her to put the phone down and call them back later, but she appears to be speaking to a client. Claire is listening intently, the phone handle nestled between her head and her left shoulder, and she is frantically writing notes on a sheet of paper.

The anti-climax is difficult to digest, especially as Claire flashes her a welcome smile and points to the chair on the other side of the desk for her to take a seat. Claire raises her hand to indicate she will be another five minutes.

Elena wanders into the kitchen to get herself a glass of water. The draining board next to the sink is littered with dirty cups and plates. How could one person make such a mess? Elena couldn't work in a place like this. It's disgusting. She picks up one of the cups and examines a stain of dried coffee in the bottom. She contemplates giving it a wash, but can't see any dishcloth anywhere. She opens the door to the single wall cupboard, but there are no clean cups in there, just a half-empty jar of coffee and a small bag of sugar, left open. No doubt the mice have been helping themselves. Why doesn't Claire ever clean up? Surely she would work better in a clean environment.

Claire has finished her phone call now and joins Elena in the kitchen. 'Nice to see you,' she says. 'You've charged him then? Cheryl told me this morning. I was about to call you to see what you had on him. But you're here now. Have you got time for a coffee? I'll just give these cups a wash.'

'You were going to call me?' Elena shoves her hands into her trouser pockets, aware that she is clenching her fists and tightening her jaw.

'Yes.' Claire fills the kettle with water and switches it on. 'Cheryl's out of her mind, as you can imagine, and I thought I'd give her an update. She hasn't heard from Adam yet.'

'And you thought I'd discuss the case with you because…?'

'Well, because…? What? Why are you glaring at me like that?'

Elena leans close to Claire's face and speaks slowly, as though to a child who doesn't understand what she has done wrong. 'Because you're not on my team anymore, and I'm not obliged to discuss any of my cases with you. Do you understand me?'

Claire looks shocked for a second, and then her temper flares. Elena is expecting it and is prepared. Claire was always known as the feisty one, the one with the short fuse.

She should have been the one to have red hair. That's why she is here now, eking a living out of being a private detective, rather than still being a police detective. She could have been a sergeant by now, rather than that idiot Geoff Miller. A female inspector and a female sergeant in the same team are unheard of in any police force in the country, as far as Elena knows. They could have made history, the two of them. They were formidable together. When they attended crime scenes, Claire's sharp hazel eyes, always scanning, watching people, and taking in the surroundings, missed nothing. She used to pull her long hair into a practical bun or a ponytail, just as it is now, and get to work. Her air of calm confidence put witnesses at ease but also put suspects on edge. Claire's interview skills were second to none.

Elena thought about her many times yesterday as she was firing questions at Reverend Hargreaves. She wondered how quickly Claire would have been able to get a confession from him, with her uncanny instincts. She always knew when someone was pulling the wool over their eyes. Even some of the men at the station admired her. Despite being a woman and despite being relatively young, people like Geoff - the sexist dinosaur that he is - had to admit that she was the one who cracked the cases no one else could. How she did it, being so disorganised and untidy, nobody knew. Her desk had no semblance of order, just like the one she has now, but she never forgot important details of the cases she was working on.

'Who the hell do you think you are talking to?' Claire's face is pink and her eyes are hard. 'You're not my boss now, you know that, don't you?'

'I know that. You seem to be the one who's forgotten

that we don't work together. You seem to think you're entitled to privileged information on a case you're not connected to.'

'I was just trying to help Cheryl, that's all.' Claire pushes past Elena and storms back to her office. She grips onto the back of her chair but doesn't sit down.

Elena follows her. 'Trying to help Cheryl? How exactly are you doing that? By screwing her husband?'

Claire looks at her with shock. She deflates like sails on a yacht dropping after a tropical storm. She lowers her eyes and examines the multi-coloured pattern on the carpet. 'He told you then?'

'Yes. Apparently, you're his alibi. He was with you on the night of the murder, he said.'

'That's not true. He wasn't with me,' says Claire. 'I already told you I worked late and then went straight home from here. I don't know why he told you that.'

Both women are silent for a moment. Elena takes a cigarette packet from her trouser pocket, takes out a cigarette, and lights it with a flick of an elegant gold and black lighter. She doesn't offer one to Claire, knowing she doesn't smoke and never has done.

'You haven't given those up yet?' asks Claire.

Elena shakes her head as she takes a deep drag on the cigarette. 'I managed to go five days this time but this case necessitates a smoke. You know how it helps me to think.'

Claire pulls out the chair from behind her desk and sinks into it. She tugs at her ponytail, swirling her hair around the fingers of her left hand, as Elena has seen her do hundreds of times at the police station. Elena sits in the chair on the other side of the desk. It's easier to look Claire in the eyes if they are on the level. She disagrees with Geoff's policy of standing over suspects or witnesses. She would much rather be on eye level.

'I didn't expect you to say that,' says Elena.

'What?'

'That he wasn't with you. I thought you'd say he was.'

'You thought I'd lie for him? After all these years of knowing me, after being my best friend, you think I'd lie for someone who was being investigated for murder, even after I already told you where I was?'

Elena shrugs. 'I don't…'

Claire slams her hand onto the desk. 'Don't you dare say you don't know me anymore. You *do* know me, Elena. I am the same person I've always been. I've got integrity and honesty and…'

Elena is shaking her head. 'They're not the values of someone who sleeps with a married man, are they?' She doesn't ask the question with anger. She is merely putting the question as one with only one correct answer. It cannot be denied. 'A mistress of a married man with children cannot be said to have integrity and honesty. I'm sorry, but that's true and you know it.'

The high-pitched ring of Claire's phone interrupts their argument. They both stare at it on the corner of the desk.

'Are you going to get that?' asks Elena. 'It could be someone important, a new client or someone.'

Claire shakes her head and they sit listening to it until the ringing eventually stops. 'I don't want to argue with you,' says Claire with a sigh. 'I spent hours last night defending myself to Sophia. I'm not prepared to do it again. It's over between me and Adam anyway.'

'Well it will have to be over,' says Elena, taking another drag of her cigarette. 'He'll be spending the rest of his days behind bars.'

Claire leans forward, despite the cloud of smoke surrounding Claire. 'You don't seriously believe he did it, do you? Because I can tell you now, the Adam I know wouldn't hurt a fly.'

'I told you, I can't discuss the case.'

'Well, why are you here, then?' Claire's anger is building again.

'Because I'm leading a murder investigation.' Elena surprises herself by shouting. It isn't professional and if Claire were any other witness, she wouldn't raise her voice. She puffs on her cigarette again and tells herself to stay calm. 'I needed to check his alibi, and now I know he doesn't have one, so I'll be on my way.' She pushes back her chair and goes into the kitchen, where she extinguishes her cigarette under cold running water before dumping it in the bin. 'I'll let myself out,' she says, as she opens the door to the stairwell.

'Elena, wait. Someone must have seen him on Thursday night,' says Claire.

'He hasn't given me any names of people to ask. I'm not on his defence team. It's not my job to clear his name.'

'No, but it is your job to prove beyond a reasonable doubt that he did it.'

'Don't tell me what my job is.'

Claire raises her hands in surrender. 'I didn't mean it like that. Honestly, I didn't, but…' she pauses. 'Okay, let me ask the same question another way, is there someone who saw him at the murder scene?'

Elena sighs. 'You know I shouldn't be telling you any of this, but no, we don't have a witness to that effect.'

'What do you have?'

'A number of things: He lied about his alibi, he lied about seeing Miriam on Thursday morning...'

'For obvious reasons,' says Claire. 'The lie about Thursday morning, I mean. I presume he told you that Miriam walked in on him and me kissing?'

'Yes,' says Elena. 'Okay, I get that one, but what was he doing on Thursday night? He wasn't with you and he wasn't with this fictitious couple he said he was meeting. So where was he?'

'I don't know,' says Claire. She looks about to cry.

Once upon a time, Elena would have rushed over to her friend, pulled her into a hug, and told her everything would be all right. But now, she can't wait to leave. She longs for the comfort of her bright and modern office. She wants to be at her own desk under the expansive picture window that floods the room with light, the perfect place to watch the steady flow of passing traffic and the various people flitting between shops on the high street. The shine from the strip light in the ceiling and the wide radiator add warmth to the room, rather than this old-fashioned and dimly-lit space with its narrow window and trickle of natural light. She needs to get out of Eldenbridge. The quiet village green, the silent playground, and the empty streets sap her of energy. It is a lifeless place and holds too many painful memories. She can't wait to get back to Wellington, with its daily rhythm of town life.

'How on earth you can think in this dingy space, after working in the police station for so long, I've got no idea. The brown and orange swirls on this carpet are enough to give anyone a headache,' she says. The smile in her voice lets Claire know there is no malice.

'At least you can't see the coffee stains,' says Claire.

Elena says goodbye and trudges down the stairs. She wants to tell Claire about the handwritten note that fell out of Adam's pocket. She wants to ask her opinion about whether she thinks it was meant as a serious threat, some kind of blackmail, or is Adam simply a clumsy and inexperienced employer, begging his member of staff to keep a secret. But, like she said, Claire isn't on her team anymore.

Claire

'Has that copper gone?' asks Angela, as she pops her head around Claire's office door.

'Yes, she's gone,' says Claire. 'Come in, is everything okay?' Claire puts her pen down and pushes her notepad to the side of the desk. She might as well give up on her work. She isn't likely to be able to concentrate much today, after her visit to Cheryl, then the visit from Elena, and now Angela disturbing her afternoon.

'No, not at all okay,' says Angela. 'Helen told me about the vicar.'

'Yes, it's a shock, isn't it? Poor Cheryl. We've all been turned upside down today, but it must be a million times worse for her,' says Claire. And for me, she thinks. What about what I'm going through?

Claire is desperate to chat with Angela, to tell her what she is thinking, to get her opinion on whether she thinks Adam is guilty or innocent. Angela, despite her name, is far from angelic, but she is astute and an extremely good judge of character. Claire is desperate for assurance that she hasn't been sleeping with a killer.

Cheryl seemed sure of Adam's innocence, but she doesn't know him as well as she thinks she does. He has been lying to her for months and she has no idea. Elena seemed sure of Adam's guilt, but she is a police officer and her views could be tainted. All Claire wants is the truth. The elusive truth.

'Do you want a drink?' she says. 'I can put the kettle on?'

'Have you got anything stronger?' asks Angela 'I think I need a whiskey.'

Claire is expecting her to laugh, but Angela's face tells her she is serious. She and Angela have become unexpected work colleagues. They have never spent any time together outside of office and shop hours, but they have often had a coffee together, either in Claire's office or in the flower shop, where they have bonded over everyday frustrations. Angela has let off steam about Kamal a couple of times; how he can be lazy at home and lie on the sofa watching television for hours. He pulls his socks off and leaves them on the floor where they stay like abandoned kittens until Angela picks them up and puts them in the laundry basket. The only time he moves a muscle is when he wants to change the television channel, and he pushes himself up with a groan and ambles over to the box.

Before he moved in, Angela used to have a clean and tidy house where she could relax with a magazine while playing a record. She likes to listen to Tina Charles and Diana Ross. But now Kamal interrupts her peace by watching stupid game shows and programmes that profess to be funny, but never make her laugh. Tinny television voices fill her house every evening, apart from on a Thursday when he plays five-a-side football or on the odd occasion when she manages to drag him out to a restaurant or the theatre.

In return, Claire has moaned about Helen's cold porridge that she insists on making every weekday throughout the winter. 'Roll on the summer, when we can have something else,' said Claire. 'I love our weekend breakfasts when Helen isn't there.'

'Shall we go to the pub?' asks Claire. 'I wouldn't mind a vodka and tonic, and you can have that whiskey you're so badly craving.'

'Any other time, I would jump at the chance,' says Angela. 'But today, what I'm about to tell you is for your ears only. So, we have to stay here.'

Claire braces herself for what Angela is about to say, something about Adam, no doubt. Angela probably saw him coming out of Miriam's house on Thursday night. Even if he were covered in blood and still carrying the murder weapon, Angela wouldn't 'grass' to the police, but Claire would have to. She can't keep that kind of secret from Elena. She is beginning to sweat. She thinks of her and Adam in her bedroom on Friday afternoon when they had the house to themselves, when they lay in bed for hours, their bodies naked and tangled. She had trusted him. She had seen glimmers of his anger – when he became cross with his boys who were being boisterous and wouldn't listen to him; when he spoke sharply to Carol in church when she was particularly annoying, and on Sunday when he shouted at her down the phone from the police station – but she had no clue what he was truly capable of. How could she have been so stupid?

'Okay,' she says. 'Take a seat, you know you can trust me.'

'I know I can,' says Angela. She takes a deep breath and sits down. 'I should have told you this morning. But I wasn't sure whether to tell anyone or keep it to myself. Honestly, I've never been so conflicted in my life. I usually know what I'm doing, and bam, a decision is made and I stick to it. But this has got me in a tizzy.'

'I understand,' says Claire. 'Trust your gut. If you don't want to tell me, then that's fine. If you do, I'm all ears.' *Please don't tell me, please don't tell me.*

Angela nods. She turns around and checks that the internal door is firmly closed. 'I know about you and the vicar,' she says.

Claire feels her face burning hot for the third time that day. She hates that about herself, that her face has always shown her emotions when she often tries so hard to hide them. 'Have you told anyone?'

'No, and I wouldn't. Kamal was married when I met him. I'm not judging you for it. It happens all the time.'

Claire nods. 'Can I ask who told you?'

'Miriam,' says Angela. 'Last Thursday morning, just as I was opening the shop, she walked past. She was furious. She saw you snogging in church, didn't she?'

'Yes, she did, unfortunately.'

'At any other time, we could laugh about it, but not now.' Claire waits for Angela to continue. 'I don't know why she got so angry. It isn't as though she was the most virtuous person on the planet, was she? I'm sure she did plenty wrong in her time. Not a looker though, was she?'

Claire knows what Angela means; that Miriam wasn't

good-looking enough to attract a married man, in the same way Angela's blonde hair and powder blue eyes had attracted Kamal. The thought of how shallow her relationship with Adam is repulses her now. The thought that he only kissed her that first time because of her pretty face never occurred to her before. She thought he was being kind and he felt the connection between them, in the same way she did. But who was she kidding? From his side, the connection was purely physical, never emotional. Despite the fact they have been seeing each other for nine months, he hasn't yet told her he loves her. If he did, surely he would say it. What a fool she has been.

'It's over now, me and Adam,' she says. 'It was a huge mistake and it is never going to happen again.' Angela raises her eyebrows. 'I know what you're thinking, and no, it isn't just because he's banged up. I decided yesterday that it was over.'

'It's neither here nor there to me,' says Angela, 'but I wanted you to know that I know because it might colour your judgement about what I'm about to tell you, and I want us to have an honest chat about it.'

Angela tells her then about her conversation with Jack, when he leaned onto her shoulder and she put her arm around him last night, and then he told her he was the one who had killed his mother. It wasn't the vicar. She explains how Jack has been under his mother's tight control for years. She had been treating him like a child, making him believe he couldn't manage on his own just so he wouldn't leave her. Everything Miriam did was for her own benefit. She had no intention of ever setting her son free into the world, like normal parents do with their children. For years Jack had tolerated his mother because he had never known any different. She had been cruel to him from the moment he was born. But last Thursday, Jack lost his temper. Miriam had been particularly critical and telling him the corned beef hash had too much salt was the final straw that broke him. Claire listens intently as Angela tells her how Jack picked up the heavy pan, full to the brim of boiling stew, and hit his mother over the head with it.

'I don't believe it,' says Claire. 'That wouldn't have killed her, would it?'

Angela shrugs. 'I don't know. I'm just telling you what he told me.'

Before Adam was arrested, Claire believed, like most people in the village, that Miriam was probably killed by an intruder, someone who had tried the door handle and found it to be unlocked and had sneaked into the house in the hope of finding a stash of pound notes in an old woman's purse. That kind of opportune crime isn't unusual, in Claire's experience. She had seen the uniformed officers in a straight line, dozens of them, combing the ground for tiny clues and looking for the murder weapon. Nothing has been found, and here is Angela telling her it was in Jack's kitchen all this time, right under their noses.

'I want to believe it,' says Claire. 'Apart from anything, it would mean Adam is an innocent man, but the police don't arrest people without evidence.'

'Oh, come on,' says Angela, 'that's bollocks.'

Angela isn't going to agree with her, Claire knows that, but she knows how meticulous Elena is, and she wouldn't make a wrongful arrest. 'Oh God, I don't know what to think,' she says. 'I'd hate to think Adam did it, honestly, I would. More than anything. But I can't believe Jack killed his own mother in cold blood.'

'It wasn't like that,' says Angela, jumping to Jack's defence. '*He* isn't like that. He must have been pushed to his limit. You know in your job, your previous job I mean, how people lose their tempers and lash out.'

'Yes, it happens all the time, but Jack is such a gentle soul.'

'Exactly! I didn't know how to put it. You're so much better at words than me, but he *is* a gentle soul.'

'Well, thank you for telling me,' says Claire. 'I'll call Elena and tell her.'

'You can't do that,' screeches Angela. 'I didn't tell you so you could dob him in. He'll never cope in prison, you know that.'

'Angela, he's a murderer.'

'No. We can't tell anyone what he did. He'll never do it again. This was a one-off. He isn't a danger to anyone.'

Claire can see that Angela is on the edge of tears. 'No, no, no.' She pushes her chair back and paces up and down between her desk and the window. 'You can't drop this on me and expect me to keep it to myself. I have to act on the information.'

Angela presses her hands together in prayer. 'No! Please, Claire. Don't tell anyone. They will kill him in prison. He will be used as a daily punch bag.'

'So you want me to watch an innocent man go to prison? What planet are you on?'

'But don't you see? The vicar won't go to prison because he didn't do it. Surely there won't be any evidence against him?'

'I don't know. There was enough evidence to arrest

him,' says Claire.

'But is there enough to take the case to trial and get a conviction? I don't think so. Surely every man and his dog in the village will be a character witness for him. The jury won't have any choice. They will have to find him not guilty because he didn't do it.'

'You know the justice system doesn't work like that,' says Claire. 'There are dozens of innocent people in prison. Juries don't always get it right.'

Tuesday 11th October 1976

Claire

Claire can tell there is something different as she opens her eyes. It is much too early in the season for snow, yet she can feel the change in the temperature, just a degree or so colder than yesterday. Perhaps the storm clouds that have hung heavily over the village all week have finally moved on. The wind that was battering the house last night and whistling down the chimney as she went to bed seems to have settled. Perhaps today is the day they will be blessed with a bright blue sky.

She is thankful that the new central heating system they installed a few months ago has already burst into life and is gradually taking the chill from the room. A glance at the clock on her bedside cabinet confirms she still has a few minutes before the alarm goes off. It's funny how her body has become accustomed to waking at the same time each day.

She pushes the bed covers off and tiptoes to the window. She opens the curtains until, inch by inch, the world outside is revealed. She is right, there is no snow, but a delightful sunrise instead. She stays there for a moment, watching the black silhouette of the trees at the bottom of the garden slashing through a soft peach sky.

She can hear her niece, Wendy, gurgling in the room next door and Sophia's loving whispers of reply. She can picture the two of them; Sophia will be lifting Wendy from her cot and giving her a tight cuddle. Claire's heart is lifted a little.

Today is the 11th of October; the day that should have been her first wedding anniversary. A day she should have marked on the calendar, ringing the date with a red felt-tip pen in a great big heart shape. Not that she ever needed to, as this day will always be marked in her heart. It is tragic that Stephen isn't here with her, standing by her side as she watches the sunrise, but she smiles to herself as she remembers how much he loved her. He would be proud of her today, the way she has fought through the last twelve months, and the way she has built a business for herself. He would have loved to hear about her interesting clients as they chatted over dinner each evening.

For twelve months, she has been dreading today, a year since Stephen died. She was expecting to be an emotional mess, weeping and wailing all day and clinging to a photograph of Stephen in one hand and a sodden tissue in the other. But the burden of Stephen's grief seems lighter today, somehow. It is time, she thinks. It is time to let him go. She loved him, but she lost him, and now it is time to move on. She won't be moving on with Adam, but who knows, she could meet someone else who she will love equally as much as she loved Stephen.

She will telephone Elena later today and check she is okay. She will send her love to Elena's parents and wish them both well.

She puts on her dressing gown and greets Sophia on the landing outside their rooms. She takes Wendy in her arms and carries her downstairs while Sophia uses the bathroom.

Today will be a good day, she knows it will. She can feel

it. Adam is an innocent man and very soon he will be released and will be returned to his wife. All Claire needs to do is convince Elena of that.

Adam

Adam wakes to face his second morning in the police cell at Wellington Police Station. When the heavy fist hammers on the door and the custody sergeant tells him to stand back, he now knows what to expect. Cold, stewed tea and burnt toast. No surprises today. It is a small comfort, knowing what is going to happen. Fear lies in the unknown, and right now there is an ocean full of fear rushing around his body and his mind. There is so much that he doesn't know how to process it. He has never felt like this before. His life is out of control. Now he can appreciate what the young men about to march to war must have felt like. They must have been terrified, waking up each day not knowing what would happen and how the nightmare would end, or when it would end. As he chews on the cold toast, he tells himself that he is one of the lucky ones; things were much worse for the soldiers in the Second World War and for those poor young men sent to Vietnam. At least his life isn't at risk. He knows he will sleep tonight and he will still be alive. But he is experiencing a nightmare, nevertheless. Just because someone else's Hell is worse, doesn't lessen how bad this particular Hell is.

Tonight, when he puts his head down at the end of the day, his bed will be in a prison cell. Not a police cell, where there is relative comfort and civility, but an actual prison cell, and the thought of that terrifies him beyond belief.

Yesterday morning, he was taken to Wellington Magistrates Court in the back of a police van with three other criminals. He told himself he shouldn't think of them as criminals, not really. Everyone is innocent until they are proven guilty, aren't they? But they had a certain look about them that told Adam they had all been in this situation before. Veterans of the justice system. The quiet one, a tall thin man dressed in dark blue wide-legged jeans, a plain white t-shirt underneath a denim jacket, and dirty Adidas trainers kept his head down throughout the short journey, and avoided eye contact with anyone who looked his way. He didn't appear to be nervous, just resigned to his fate. World-weary. Adam wondered what he could possibly have done. He didn't have the aura of someone who was expecting to be released soon.

The other two men were those brought in together on Sunday night, the ones he presumed had been fighting, either with each other or with other people. They had sobered up somewhat, but the small environment of the police van was filled with alcoholic fumes and bad breath every time they opened their mouths. They appeared to be wearing the clothes they had worn on their evening out, patterned open-necked shirts, polyester trousers, and black leather shoes, although they now looked like they had been dragged through a hedge backwards. They both needed a good wash and a comb running through their messy hair and beards. The friends seemed to have forgotten their argument and were relaxed about their court appearance. They laughed about the situation they found themselves in and discussed whether they should plead guilty and 'get it over with'.

'No way, man. My wife will kill me if I go home with another fine,' one of them said.

His friend laughed. 'Yeah, and if she finds out what you were doing with Barbara, she'll cut your balls off, too. Either way, you're a dead man.'

'I'm going not guilty then. It's the only way I have a chance of living.' They both laughed and began to play fight, punching each other in the stomachs and knocking each other off the narrow bench. As the van lurched around a corner, one of them fell onto the hard floor.

'Behave yourselves back there! Sit back on the bench!' The policeman in the front passenger seat knocked on the glass partition between the front seats and the back of the van with his elbow. Order was restored.

Adam rubbed a hand over his chin and felt his stubble. He hadn't shaved since Sunday morning. That seemed so long ago he could hardly remember it. He envied his three companions for their beards. He had always fancied one but Cheryl didn't like them. She said it would give her a rash when they kissed. The bishop probably wouldn't like it either. He liked his clergy to be clean-shaven and well-presented. Cleanliness is next to Godliness. He could hear the bishop's voice in his head and wondered what he would have to say about all this.

Adam didn't feel clean, not in the slightest. He had been allowed to have a lukewarm shower in the police station and Cheryl had brought him some clean clothes, but ironically she had forgotten his razor. She had also forgotten the toothpaste, so he had scrubbed his teeth with a wet toothbrush. He didn't have the heart to ask her to go to the chemist and buy him some. She brought him the black suit and a clean black shirt he usually reserves for funerals, together with his dog collar. He didn't know what she was thinking by bringing that, and decided not to wear it.

He wasn't allowed to speak to her; he was simply given the bundle of clothes by the custody sergeant, who told him to strip off and hand his dirty clothes to him for Cheryl to take home. He imagined Cheryl waiting in the reception area of the police station, desperate to see her husband whilst at the same time embarrassed to be there, as it meant admitting her husband was in the cells.

'What are you here for, man?' one of the men in the van asked him.

'Murder,' he said. 'But I didn't do it,' he added when he saw how shocked they were.

'Naw man, I can tell that. You don't look the type.'

'Good luck, man,' said the other one.

After a short wait in a windowless communal cell underneath the magistrates court, he was introduced to Simon Beaumont, the man who was going to represent him. Mr Beaumont was smartly dressed in an expensive-looking pin-striped suit and pale blue shirt and tie, and he had an accent that suggested he was the recipient of a private education, but Adam immediately wanted to ask for someone else. He asked Mr Beaumont how long he had been qualified and was shocked when he said ten years. 'Don't let my boyish good looks fool you,' he had said. 'I'm very experienced and I'll make sure you have the best barrister.' He had put his hand on Adam's arm as he spoke and Adam felt his sincerity through the warmth of his touch and was somewhat reassured. He tried to listen to what he was being told about the court procedure, but by the time he was taken back to the cell from the small interview room, he had already forgotten most of what Mr Beaumont had said. Stress and worry are not conducive to learning.

Adam was taken into the dock of Court Number One. Three magistrates faced him behind the high bench on the opposite wall of the courtroom, looking down on him over their spectacles. Luckily, he didn't recognise any of them. He wondered whether they lived outside of the area, just for that reason. Standing in the dock in handcuffs was not how he wanted to be seen by anyone, but especially not Cheryl. Yet there she was, sitting in the courtroom on the back row, looking forlorn and tearful. He wanted to shout out to her and tell her he loved her and that he was okay, but he knew he couldn't. She flashed him a sad smile and then faced the front again.

The court clerk rose to his feet and asked him to confirm that he was Adam Jonathan Hargreaves, born on the 16th of September 1944. Adam confirmed he was.

'You are charged that on Thursday 7th October 1976 in Eldenbridge you did murder Miriam Jane Chadwick, contrary to common law. This is an indictable-only offence. Do you understand the charge?'

'Yes,' said Adam.

The prosecuting solicitor then stood up and outlined the evidence to the magistrates. Mr Beaumont had already told him that the evidence was 'flimsy' in his view. No witnesses to any altercation and no fingerprints found on any murder weapon did not add up to the strongest of cases. He confirmed that the saucepan had only one pair of fingerprints, which were not his. They were currently being compared to those of Jack Chadwick. Adam was about to ask whether that was a good thing, but Mr Beaumont preempted his question and explained that Mr Chadwick's fingerprints were expected to be on the saucepan, as he owned it, and the saucepan hadn't been confirmed as being the murder weapon in any event. So as Adam listened to the prosecutor telling the magistrates about the threatening note that was found in his cassock and the fact that he was unable to verify his whereabouts at the time of the murder, he told himself not to be unduly worried. He knew that the magistrates weren't the ones who were going to decide whether or not he was guilty. By the time of the trial, Mr Beaumont had said, the defence will be watertight. He would make sure of it.

Mr Beaumont then stood and addressed the magistrates. 'Your Worships, I have been instructed to represent the defendant. Whilst the defence acknowledges the gravity of the charge, we reserve our right to challenge the Crown's evidence at trial. The defendant will, in due course, enter a not-guilty plea. With that in mind, I would like to address the issue of bail.'

'The Crown objects to bail,' said the prosecutor, in a ridiculous half-stance with his hands on the bench in front of him and his bottom barely lifted from the seat, as though he didn't have the time to properly stand up straight. He sat back down and continued to flick through reams of paper on his desk; too busy and too important to properly listen to the proceedings.

'Your Worships, I submit that the defendant should be considered for bail. Mr Hargreaves is the vicar of St. Mary's Church in Eldenbridge and, as such, has strong ties to the community. He is a well-respected member of the community with no prior convictions. He is not a flight risk and is willing to comply with any conditions imposed by the court, including signing at the police station daily and surrendering his passport.'

Adam was horrified that Mr Beaumont had mentioned he was a vicar. He thought he was entitled to some kind of anonymity, but clearly not. The newspapers would have a field day with a scandal like this. His reputation would be ruined before the trial had even begun. As he looked at the back of Cheryl's head, at her beautiful chestnut hair that glimmers in the sun, he wanted to cry. He wanted to fall to his knees and sob and sob until he fell asleep. Maybe when he woke up, this nightmare would be over.

The magistrates whispered together for a couple of minutes and then delivered the news Adam had been dreading.

'We have considered the submissions from both sides, but in light of the seriousness of the charge, we are not minded to grant bail. The defendant will be remanded in custody until the committal hearing.'

Now as Adam waits to be transferred from the police station to the prison today, he doesn't know how he will endure a week of incarceration until the next court hearing. One day at a time, he tells himself. Just endure one day at a time. Sweet Jesus.

Jack

There have been no visitors to number 8 Southgate Drive for twenty-four hours, not since Elena and her brightly-coloured sock-wearing colleague popped in yesterday to tell Jack about the vicar being charged with the murder of his mother.

Jack had expected Angela to call in and see him last night on her way home after she had closed the shop, but she didn't arrive. He wanted to show her the food he had bought, so she could tell him how well he was doing. He isn't as stupid as his mother made him out to be. He is quite capable of cooking himself a good meal without having to be told what to make and what ingredients to buy. After all, he did all the cooking when his mother was alive anyway.

At around four o'clock, Jack had wrapped himself up in his anorak and had braved the wind and rain to walk the short distance to Angela's shop, but when he arrived, he saw that the blinds were down and the sign said *Closed*. He searched his pockets for change and found a couple of two pence pieces for the phone, but when he was inside the phone box, with the receiver in his hand, he remembered that he didn't know Angela's telephone number. It would be written down at home somewhere, in his mother's address book that is still in the top drawer of the sideboard. But by the time he arrived home, he had lost the urge to speak to her. He took off his coat and hung it on the hook at the bottom of the stairs next to his mother's.

Angela said she would help him to clear out his mother's clothes when he was ready. After the funeral, she said. When the dust has settled.

Now, Jack sees Claire walking down the cul-de-sac, seemingly making a beeline for his house. He watches her open the garden gate and then seconds later, he hears her knock on the front door. She is calling Jack! Jack! through the letterbox, as though he hadn't heard her three knocks that were loud enough to wake the dead.

He hasn't spoken to Claire before, apart from saying

hello in church and on the odd occasion when they bumped into each other in the shop, but she seems like a nice person. His mother told him, when she first began cleaning for her, that Claire and Sophia were a couple of spoilt princesses. She said they came from a rich family and had been handed that grand three-storey house 'on a plate'. Their grandmother had left them a tonne of money when she died, so neither had to work for it.

'Some people have all the luck,' she said. 'I've got to stand on my own two feet, scrubbing other people's houses, while they get given a luxury house for nowt.'

Jack had listened to conversations between the Simons sisters and various people in church and from what he had heard, their house was far from luxurious when they first moved in. It was cold and damp and the windows were draughty. The kitchen was made up of little more than an old gas oven which was 'a death-trap' and something called a Belfast sink. They had workmen in for months ripping out the kitchen and bathroom and doing some painting and decorating. He would have liked to see it, but he was too nervous to speak to the sisters and make friends with them. Neither of them had boyfriends and being a similar age to him, he didn't want them to think he was chatting them up. He didn't want to be laughed at. His mother had made it clear that they wouldn't be interested in someone like him.

'Don't even think about it,' she said one Sunday as they sat in church waiting for the service to begin. 'I can see you looking at them. You've not got a cat in hell's chance of getting to know someone like them. Look at you. You need a good wash first and your teeth would benefit from a bit of toothpaste every now and then.'

Jack had had a good wash that day, and he had cleaned

his teeth, as he does every day. His clothes were all clean and he had sprayed under his arms with deodorant. He knew his mother was wrong. He knew she was just being mean, but she was that way out and he didn't want to create a scene. So he hid his head behind his hymn book and kept himself to himself.

Hello Jack. Claire is standing on his doorstep now, smiling at him. She wants to know if she can come in and speak to him for a moment. He would rather she didn't. It's nearly tea-time and in half an hour it will be time to close the curtains and settle down for the evening, but he steps to one side and allows her to come in. His mother had many faults but one of the things she did well was to teach her son good manners.

He asks her if she would like a cup of tea and is thankful that she says no, as he hates that time between waiting for the kettle to boil and finishing the tea when he isn't sure whether to start a conversation, or wait until they are seated in the living room.

Claire tells him she doesn't want to sit down. She is comfortable standing, if that's okay with him. She keeps looking towards the door and Jack wants to ask her if she is expecting someone else to arrive. He wonders whether she can see his mother. He wouldn't be surprised. Her ghost is all over the place, mainly in the kitchen, where Jack sees her standing over him when he's cooking, peering over his shoulder, criticism dripping onto his food.

I don't want you to be angry, Claire says. But Angela told me something very important that you told her on Sunday night.

Jack knows what she is going to say. Angela has told Claire his secret, hasn't she? Even though she said she wouldn't tell anyone and he trusted her to keep it to herself. He wonders whether Angela knows that Claire used to be a police lady. She obviously doesn't, which explains her mistake. If she'd known, she would never have told a secret like that to the police. Angela doesn't do that kind of thing. She won't tell the police anything.

Claire is talking to him as though he is stupid. He doesn't know why people do that. He is more intelligent than most people he meets.

You know during a police investigation, when the detectives are trying to solve the case and they piece together all the bits of evidence?

Yes, says Jack.

Well it's really important to let the police have *all* the information so they can make the right decision about the case, isn't it? They can't solve it properly if they don't know everything, can they? Every little bit. You have to tell the truth. You know that don't you?

Claire is talking too much and too quickly. She isn't giving him time to reply. One question quickly follows another, without leaving a gap for him to fill.

I'm not a child! And I'm not stupid!

Claire flinches slightly when he shouts. He remembers how his mother shouted at him and he didn't like it, so he says sorry, sorry. He didn't mean to shout. Claire takes a step back and looks towards the door again. He wants to ask her what she can see.

She says sorry, too. She knows he isn't a child and she doesn't mean to treat him like one. She says sorry again. You know you need to tell the truth though, don't you?

He tells her he told the truth to Angela. He shrugs and puts his hands into his trouser pockets. He doesn't know what else he needs to do.

Claire wants to know if it is true. Is it true that he told Angela he had killed Miriam?

Jack nods.

Good. That's good, says Claire.

He isn't sure what's good about it. My mum being dead is good? he asks.

Claire tells him she didn't mean that. She means that it is good he is now telling the truth. It's good to tell the truth, she repeats.

He doesn't say anything. What else is there to say?

Then she wants to know why he didn't tell the police what he had done when he was first interviewed.

Jack shrugs. How can he explain what happened that night when he doesn't understand it himself? He needs some time to process his thoughts and put them into an order he can understand. The events of the evening are jumbled and blurred in his mind. When his mother came home and they argued; when she blamed him for overfilling her cup with tea; when he went to the shop; when his mother tried a mouthful of the hash and said it had too much salt; when she shouted and threw the spoon across the kitchen. All of those events are jumbled. He can remember seeing his mother on the floor and he can remember the look on her face when she stared up at him in disbelief. She had been an angry person his whole life, but he had never seen her so angry as in that moment. He knew he had to hit her again, otherwise she would have found the strength to get up and he would have ended up being the one lying on the floor surrounded by pools of his own blood. He doesn't tell Claire any of this. She won't understand.

It's okay, Claire tells him. Can we go to the police station now? Would you be willing to tell the detectives what you told Angela?

Jack tells her he doesn't want to get into trouble.

It was an accident though, surely? If it was an accident, nobody gets into trouble for that, says Claire. You didn't mean to kill her, did you?

She wasn't nice to me, Jack tells her. She wouldn't let me speak to you and your sister in church.

Claire seems to look sad when he says that and Jack wonders whether she would have liked to speak to him, given the chance. Well, we're speaking now, aren't we? She looks at the clock on the mantelpiece. Jack explains that isn't the correct time. The clock is set ten minutes fast as his mother didn't like to be late for anything.

'It's best to be early,' she told him. 'Only selfish people are late; people who think they are so important that others should stand around and wait for them.'

Nobody ever stood around and waited for him, as he never went anywhere to meet anyone, except for the lady detective at the police station when he went to collect the keys to his house, but that's not the same, as she was there anyway. If she had planned to go out and had waited for him, well it was her own fault for not giving him a specific time to be there. He got to the police station as quickly as he could.

Claire says she thinks her friend Elena will still be working now. They should go and see her before it's too late. Before she finishes her shift. Will you come and see her?

What about? he asks.

Claire explains how telling Angela what happened to his mother isn't enough. He will need to go and see Elena at the police station and she will write everything down and he can sign it. It's called a Section Nine Statement. It's nothing to worry about, it just refers to Section Nine of the Criminal Justice Act, and it means it is an official statement where he tells the truth and signs his name to confirm that the statement is true.

Criminal Justice Act? I'm not a criminal. I'm not.

No, no, no, Claire is saying. Don't worry about that bit. It's about justice. That's the word you need to concentrate on. Justice. Because if the statement is true, justice is carried out, do you see?

She looks at the clock again and tells him she needs to ring the police station to check whether Elena is still there. She tells him she will run to the telephone box at the bottom of the road and will come straight back.

Then she is gone, telling him to wait there for her. Don't go anywhere, please don't go anywhere. Jack waits for her while he watches out of the window and listens to the ticking of the mantelpiece clock.

Did you hear that, Mum? Claire Simons has asked me to wait here. She wants to speak to me. You can't believe it, can you? Maybe I'm not stupid-as-dog-shit after all.

Elena

It has been a long day and Elena is ready to go home, but when the phone call arrives from Claire telling her Jack has confessed to killing his mother and she will bring him to the police station in her car, she has no choice but to stay and interview him.

Elena gestures to Harry through the glass partition separating her office from the open-plan CID room for him to come and speak to her.

'Yes, boss,' he says.

'I've just had Claire on the phone,' she says. 'I don't know what to make of what she's just told me. I need a fag.'

'What did she say, boss?' asks Harry.

Elena searches the top drawer of her desk, and then the second one down. 'Where the bloody hell did I put them?'

'Your coat pocket, boss?' He gestures to the hook behind the door where her raincoat is hanging. He knows Elena never carries a handbag.

'Yes, thank you, Harry. My head's all over the place.' She finds her cigarettes in one of the pockets. She lights one quickly and takes a drag. 'I thought this case was done,' she says. 'Give the room a spray with that, will you? You know how I hate my office to stink.'

Harry picks up the bottle of Shalimar perfume and sprays it around the room. 'My girlfriend will think I've been with someone else now.'

'Keep her on her toes then, won't it?' Elena takes another drag on the cigarette and opens the office window an inch to let in some fresh air.

'Boss? You were saying you spoke to Claire. What did she say?'

'Apparently, Jack Chadwick has coughed to Angela Bennett that he killed his mother.'

'I knew it.' Harry punches the air. 'I knew it was him.'

'Steady on, we don't have any other evidence yet and

Angela Bennett is highly unlikely to want to stand in a witness box and do us all a favour, is she?'

'Not likely, no, boss. So what's your plan.'

'Claire is bringing Jack in to speak to us. She'll be here in half an hour.'

'And you're going to interview him? Can I sit in with you?'

'Yes, and yes, but keep it to yourself, will you? Don't let on to DS Miller.' She looks out into the open-plan office. Rahul has his head down, concentrating on a pile of papers, tapping his pen intermittently on his bottom lip. Geoff is in the process of tidying his desk for the evening, which means he will be leaving soon. He puts his pen next to his notebook in the top drawer every night, so he knows where to find them in the morning. The wire tray marked In-Box is pushed to the edge of the desk and all the papers are gathered and shuffled until they are lined up neatly. The desk phone is straightened and placed next to the in-tray. When his desk is tidy, Geoff is happy to go home. He has worked in the same way ever since he became a detective. 'I might look like a slob sometimes, but I like to start the day with a tidy desk,' he told Elena when she asked him why he was so fastidious.

'I won't say a word to him,' says Harry.

'If he asks you why you're here late, just fob him off and tell him you're waiting for a lift home from your girlfriend or something. Tell him anything. I don't want him to be in this interview. He will go in with all guns blazing and will ruin it. Jack needs to be treated very carefully.'

'Do you think he did it, boss?'

'I honestly don't know. I know you have always thought he was the one, but I had my eyes on the vicar. I thought we had the case wrapped up. Let's see what he has to say for himself, shall we?'

*

Half an hour later, Elena and Harry are sitting across the table from Jack in the Victim Suite. She has thanked Claire for bringing him, but told her not to wait. She told her the interview might take a while, so she should go home. She knows Claire will understand that there is a high likelihood that Jack will be kept in custody, although right now, it's too early to say. Before she went, Claire asked Elena if she could let her know what happens. Elena wanted to remind her about the conversation they had in her office, about the fact she isn't a detective anymore and she doesn't have the right to privileged information. But to keep the peace, Elena simply smiled and said she would speak to her soon. She didn't want to upset her any more than necessary today. She hasn't forgotten that today would have been Claire and Stephen's first wedding anniversary; the anniversary of Stephen's death.

Elena wants Jack to be comfortable. She asks him whether he is warm enough and whether he would like a cup of tea before they begin their chat. She is reluctant to call it an interview, as she doesn't want it to sound too formal. Harry asked her before they came downstairs whether she planned to arrest him. She told him they didn't have enough evidence yet, as she wouldn't trust Angela as far as she could throw her. 'Let's just take it one step at a time and as soon as he tells us what he did, I'll let you arrest him.' Harry grinned and told her it would be a pleasure.

'Jack, I'd like to thank you for coming to see me. Do

you understand why you're here?'

'Yes,' he says. 'Claire Simons said I should speak to you about what happened to my mother.'

'Yes, that's right. My colleague, DC Harry Beckford, will write down everything you say and at the end of this interview, you can sign the witness statement to say the contents are a true record of what you have just said, is that okay?'

Jack nods. 'Have you got red socks on today, Harry?' he says.

Elena has already warned Harry to be polite and gentle with Jack and she is pleased to see him lift his trouser leg and give it a shake so Jack can see his socks. Today they are navy blue with narrow yellow stripes. Jack smiles and says he likes them.

'In your own words, Jack,' says Elena, 'slowly if you can so that Harry has a chance to write everything down, can you tell me exactly what happened from around four o'clock on Thursday the 7th of October, up to the time you found your mother on the floor of the kitchen.'

'Do you want me to begin from the time she came in from work?'

'Yes please.'

'She came home about ten minutes past four, something like that. The clock on the mantelpiece in the living room is always ten minutes fast, so I never know what the real time is exactly. But I was watching out for her through the window in the living room, and I spotted her walking down the road. Usually, when I see her, I run into the kitchen and bring the kettle to the boil again. You should always make tea with freshly boiled water.'

'So you made her a cup of tea, like you normally did?

Then what happened?'

'We stood in the kitchen for a minute, talking. She liked to put her own milk in. I had made the corned beef hash and it was ready in the pan. It was simmering, keeping warm for her.' Jack takes a deep breath. 'I didn't want to tell you the last time we spoke about it, but we started to argue, and there was some shouting. I didn't want you to think badly of my mum, so I didn't mention it.'

Elena sits forward in her chair. 'What did you argue about, Jack?'

'About the potato hash mainly, but other things as well. She was angry that I had used all the corned beef, and she was angry that her cup had too much tea in it. A bit spilled over into the saucer and she blamed me for filling it to the top, even though she was the one who put the milk in. She shouted at me and told me to tip a bit down the sink so she could drink it.'

'Is that what the shouting was? Your neighbour, Eve Hardy, said she could hear shouting through the wall.'

Jack nods. 'Mum was angry with me, but she was also angry with Angela, which didn't help. Angela was planning a trip to Spain and Mum said she was boasting about it and reading a catalogue and getting in the way while she was trying to clean the house.'

'Was that on Thursday?'

'No, she cleaned for Angela on Wednesday but she was still seething about it. So, I told her we could go on holiday one day and she shouted at me because I don't have a job. She said nobody would give me a job because I didn't have a clean shirt on. I told her it was a clean shirt and she shouted at me again and told me I was a liar. But I wasn't lying to her. It was a clean shirt.' Jack stops talking and looks down at his shirt. He licks his finger and rubs at an imaginary stain on the front pocket.

'What happened then, after your mother said your shirt wasn't clean?'

'I went into the kitchen because she said I was burning the hash. That was another lie, it wasn't burning, it was keeping warm on a low light, but I wanted to get out of her way. But she followed me.' Jack leans forward, with his elbows on his knees and rests his head in his hands. He runs his hands over his hair backwards and forwards.

'Jack?'

'Yes?' He looks up, as though he has just remembered he is not alone and that Elena is still here in the room. 'Can you tell me happened in the kitchen?'

'She said the potato hash was too thick, that there wasn't enough stock in it. I told her it was all right. I had been cooking it for hours and there was nothing wrong with it. But Mum didn't like me to give her back chat, so she punched me on my arm and she threw the wooden spoon across the room. There was gravy everywhere.'

'Did you get angry then?'

'Why would I get angry?'

'Weren't you the one who would have to mop up the gravy?'

'Yes, but I always clean the kitchen anyway.'

'What happened then, Jack?'

'I can't remember.'

Elena looks at Harry who has stopped writing. His pen is poised over the lined paper. He is desperate to hear the words of confession from Jack. 'Try and remember what happened. I know it is upsetting, but we need to know the truth of what happened that night.'

'I am telling you the truth.'

'Oh, I know that.' Elena smiles. 'But we need *all* the truth, do you understand?' Jack nods. 'So tell me what happened. Your mum has just punched your arm and thrown the wooden spoon on the floor. What happened then?'

'She asked me to go to the shop for some cigarettes. She only had a couple left in her packet, so I took a pound note from her purse and went to Robertsons. She doesn't like me to take her purse in case I lose it, so I just took a pound note.'

'And you went to the shop and bought the packet of cigarettes at around twenty to five, so you must have left your house at around half past four, is that right? About half an hour after your mum got home from work?'

'I can't remember,' says Jack.

'The lady in the shop remembers you being there at twenty to five. She remembers the time because she said it had been a long day and she kept looking at the clock because she wanted to go home.' Jack nods and Elena waits for him to continue. After a moment, it is clear he isn't going to say anything else without a prompt. 'Is it true that you walked around the village for more than an hour?'

Jack shrugs his shoulders. 'I can't remember exactly.'

'The village is quite small, isn't it?' Jack nods. 'So I presume you had walked around the green, and up to the church, around by the school and past that new estate of houses. How long would you think that took you?'

'I don't know.' Jack is keeping his head down, avoiding eye contact with Elena or Harry.

Elena can see that Harry is anxious to jump in and

challenge Jack, but she doesn't want Jack to shut down and stop talking. She gives Harry a look that tells him to keep a back seat, for now.

'Can you tell me what happened when you went back home, after you had been to the shop?'

'Mum's handbag was in the hall, so I put the change back into her purse and went into the kitchen.'

'And?'

'She was on the floor.'

'Are you sure?'

'Yes, she was on the floor in the kitchen, and I wasn't sure if she was dead or not, so I picked her up and she didn't move, so I hugged her and hugged her.'

'Are you telling us that your mother was already dead when you came back from the shop?' says Harry. Jack nods. 'That isn't what you told Angela Bennett is it, Jack? So who's telling lies here, you or Angela?'

'I'm not telling lies.' He looks up, with an earnest expression on his face that urges Elena to challenge him.

Elena can't believe what she is hearing. Jack hasn't changed his story at all. She shouldn't have expected to come into the interview room and walk out with a confession to murder. Who is she kidding? It never happens. She is annoyed with herself for being so stupid, for being so gullible, but what was she expected to do? She would have been hauled over the coals if she hadn't interviewed him again after what Claire told her, despite the fact he is clearly attention-seeking and just wasting their time.

'It must be Angela who is telling lies then, because she says you told her that you killed your mother,' says Harry.

'Jack, listen to me, Jack,' says Elena. 'Was it an accident?

Did your mum fall and hit her head and die accidentally?'

Elena can see Jack's mind working and he appears to be about to tell her that, yes, it was an accident, and that he didn't mean to do it. She gives him a moment to think.

'I'm not telling lies,' he says. 'She was dead when I came back from the shop. So I ran to the telephone box and called 999.'

'You killed her, didn't you, Jack?' says Harry.

'No, I didn't,' he shouts. His cheeks are pink, his knuckles are white. 'Can I go home now? It's getting late.'

Elena opens the door of the Victim Suite and watches as Jack walks down the corridor and out of the police station.

Wednesday 12th October 1976

Elena

After Jack left the police station yesterday, Elena collected her coat from her office and drove home. She left his unsigned witness statement in her in-tray. She will deal with it on Friday when the team returns to work. Right now, she desperately needs a couple of days' rest. Her Teasmade machine provided a hot cup of tea at eight o'clock this morning without the need to venture into the kitchen and she has no plans to get out of bed for another hour, maybe more. She picks up a book that has been abandoned for too long and tries to put any thoughts of Jack Chadwick and Adam Hargreaves out of her mind. She has never been so glad that she isn't a resident of Eldenbridge. That village is beginning to give her the creeps.

She has only managed to read a few pages of her book when the telephone rings. She picks up the extension sitting on her bedside cabinet. It will be her mum. Elena should have called her last night when she got home from work, but exhaustion took over and all she wanted to do was relax in the bath and get an early night. She hasn't spoken to her for a few days. She feels guilty that her mum worries about her safety, even though she regularly tries to reassure her she is perfectly safe in Wellington where, on the whole, she deals with petty criminals who are not very adept at their job and are certainly not dangerous.

'I know what it's like being on the frontline,' her mum said the last time they spoke. 'You're doing an extremely dangerous job.'

'Mum, I'm not on the frontline, and it's not like in Starsky and Hutch. Nobody has guns.'

'Someone has just been murdered in Eldenbridge, haven't they? It can happen anywhere these days.'

'I suppose it can, but try not to worry about me. I'm absolutely fine.'

She picks up the phone. 'Hello, is that you, Mum?' she says.

'No, Elena, it's me, Claire.'

'Sorry, I thought it would be my mum. I should have called her last night, but I was too tired to talk by the time I got home.'

'I know how you feel. I hope I'm not ringing too early, but I wondered if you got anywhere with Jack?'

'No. I appreciate you trying to help, honestly I do, but it was a complete waste of time. He didn't tell me anything other than what he said when I first spoke to him last week.'

'Honestly? But…'

'Yes, honestly. He said he went to the shop, had a walk around the village and when he went back into the house, his mother was already dead.'

'But he told Angela Bennett that he killed her. Why would he say that if it wasn't true?'

Elena sighs. She is too tired for this conversation right now. 'I don't know,' she says. 'But whatever his motivation, he is clearly lying. Maybe he wanted some attention from Angela, or maybe he is a fantasist who wanted to believe he had done something out of the ordinary. I have no idea how his mind works, but I'm afraid, as far as the police are concerned, the murderer is already locked up. I'm sorry it's not the news you wanted to hear.'

Claire

'So what is your plan of action?' asks Trevor. Claire and Trevor are at the kitchen table and Helen is kneading bread dough at the flour-covered worktop. They are talking about the murder of Miriam Chadwick, which seems to be the only topic of conversation around the village. Claire is courageously ploughing her way through a bowl of Helen's thick porridge.

'I don't know,' says Claire. 'I don't know what to think. I have gone from being shocked that Adam was arrested, then resigning myself to the fact that he must be guilty because Elena rarely makes his mistakes, then being overjoyed that Jack said he did it, and now I don't know what to think.'

'You think Elena was right when she called Jack a fantasist?' asks Trevor.

'Maybe, but I don't know him very well,' says Claire. She shovels a spoonful of porridge into her mouth and bravely swallows it.

'If you'd like my view,' says Trevor. 'I believe it's entirely possible that Jack committed the murder, told Angela in order to unburden himself, but then changed his mind when he sat in the police station, when the reality of possibly going to prison made him panic.'

'I think you might be right, but that doesn't help Adam.

Elena has got something on him, but I don't know what it is. She won't speak to me about it.'

'If you believe Adam to be an innocent man, it is your civil duty to do everything you can to ensure he is released.'

Claire nodded. 'I should help him, shouldn't I? So you don't think I'm a mad woman for trying?'

'No, who else can help him, if not you? I would imagine his wife is too traumatised to be of much help, and you're an ex-detective. You know the legal system better than anyone else in this village.'

'Yes, and the system relies on witness evidence, but finding witnesses to a murder that happened in the privacy of someone's home will be impossible. The only person who heard anything is Eve, but the police have spoken to her already. All she can say is that she heard some shouting, which wasn't unusual.'

Sophia enters the room carrying Wendy, who is freshly washed and dressed in a purple knitted dress and matching tights. 'I thought you were trying to prove Adam is innocent, rather than proving Jack is guilty. Wouldn't that be easier?' she says.

Claire nods. 'I was thinking I could prove Adam didn't do it by focusing on how I could prove that Jack did. But yes, you're right, I just need to find a way of proving Adam wasn't in Eldenbridge last Thursday. Any ideas?

'I know this is stating the obvious,' says Sophia, 'but why don't you start by finding someone who saw him that night? You know where he went, don't you? Someone must have seen him.'

On Saturday afternoon just after Elena had visited him at the rectory, Adam telephoned Claire and told her he had been out at the time of Miriam's murder because he needed to 'clear his head'. He drove to the countryside north of Wellington and pulled into a layby where he sat in the car and prayed for guidance. After a few minutes, he decided to go for a short walk, but it had started to rain, so he hadn't gone far before he returned to the car, where he had listened to Radio Four for a while. Before he knew it, it was ten o'clock and he panicked that he had been out so long. He turned the car around and made his way home, where he told his wife that he was late because the young couple he had been to see had kept him talking for hours about various different subjects.

Claire was annoyed with him for lying to the police. She told him it was unnecessary and when the truth came out, they wouldn't trust anything he said. At that time, she had no idea what serious trouble his lie would get him into. She had told him to go and spend time with his wife and children, and had ended the call abruptly. She didn't want to listen to his reasons for clearing his head. He was being self-indulgent, in her view. Looking back, that was the beginning of the end for Claire. The beginning of her being fed up with all the lies. Cheryl and Sophia, and even Trevor and Helen were all being lied to and she didn't want to be complicit any longer.

'He told me he went for a long drive and then had a walk to clear his head. He didn't speak to anyone,' says Claire. She knows Adam's feelings for her have been growing lately and he was probably frightened of what that might mean. Maybe he loves her, but he doesn't want to leave his wife. He wants the excitement that an extra-marital affair brings, without having to give up his family. It is the age-old predicament of the married man.

'Eve said something interesting yesterday,' says Helen.

'On Saturday afternoon, Jack arrived back home after staying in the hotel down the road. You know he had to stay there for a couple of days while his house was being cleaned?'

'I didn't think about it, but yes I'd imagine there would have been blood everywhere,' says Claire.

'Well, when the cleaning team finished, they gave the keys to Eve. She told me that when Jack came home and she gave the keys to him, he lost his temper and shouted at her. He said she was the one who had ruined his mother's reputation by telling the police she could hear shouting through the dividing wall, like she was somehow responsible for making Miriam look bad.'

'Poor Eve,' says Sophia.

'Yes, she was in tears,' says Helen. 'She was a bit scared too, if I'm honest. She thinks Jack can be unpredictable and she was glad when Angela arrived and took Jack inside. She thought he was going to hit her. He was very angry with her.'

'I know what she means about him being unpredictable,' says Claire. 'I didn't feel entirely safe when I was with him yesterday, but I just put that down to my copper's intuition running on overtime, after what Angela told me. But I don't think that's really enough to prove a murder.'

'Maybe not,' says Helen. 'But the point I'm getting at is that all little bits add up to a whole, don't they? I'm thinking about all the people Jack comes across in his day-to-day life, if you could get statements from them all about his bad temper and aggressive outbursts, then maybe it would help to paint a picture of who he truly is.'

If Jack were the one on trial, character witnesses would

be extremely important, but it isn't enough to have him arrested and Claire knows it won't help Adam. 'Thanks, Helen,' she says. 'You have given me an idea. The people who would be interesting to speak to are those who work in the hotel where Jack stayed. Maybe he said something to them about why he was there and what happened.'

'It's a long shot, isn't it?' asks Sophia. 'But worth a try. Do you know which hotel he stayed in?'

'It was the Eldenbridge Hotel,' says Helen. 'It isn't far away, just on the main A6.'

'I agree, it is a long shot,' says Claire, 'but it's better than nothing. I need to make a start. Who knows what will come up when you start to talk to people.'

'Are you going to write your own statement, Claire?' asks Trevor. 'You could tell the court directly that you know Jack killed his mother.'

Claire shakes her head. 'I can't, unfortunately. He didn't tell me, he told Angela. My evidence won't count because I didn't hear it directly from the horse's mouth. It's hearsay.'

'That's a shame. What about Angela's statement then?' asks Trevor. 'She can tell the police what Jack told her, can't she?'

'She can, but whether she will or not are two different things. Lancashire Police Force isn't on her Christmas card list, but I'm certainly going to try and persuade her.'

'Are you going to tell Cheryl what you're trying to do to help Adam?' asks Trevor.

'Not yet,' says Claire. 'I don't want to raise her hopes and then dash them against the wall if I can't help her. She's pretty fragile at the moment.'

*

Claire arrives at the Eldenbridge Hotel shortly after nine o'clock. The reception area is quiet, except for a woman reading a newspaper in a chair underneath the window. A pot of tea sits on the table in front of her and a small suitcase rests at her feet. The young woman behind the counter is typing something with the forefingers of each hand. Claire notices long red nails on delicate fingers.

She looks up as Claire approaches the counter. 'Good morning, welcome to the Eldenbridge Hotel, how can I help you?' She smiles and leans her head to one side. Her name badge says Alison.

Claire wonders how many times she has to say that throughout the day. 'Good morning, my name's Claire Simons, I'm a private detective from Eldenbridge. Have you got time to answer a few questions about a guest who stayed here a few nights ago?'

'Wow, a private detective. Like Columbo?'

'Well, he's not a private detective, he's a real detective, with the police force. Well, not real, because he's fiction, but you know what I mean.'

'Oh yes, he keeps telling everyone he works for the LAPD, doesn't he? Los Angeles Police Department. I like him. He always cracks the case in the end, doesn't he?'

'Yes he does…'

'That cigar though, annoying isn't it? They stink, those things.'

'Yes, they do. I don't think our police would allow a detective to scatter cigar ash at a crime scene in the way he does.'

The young woman laughs, then apologises when the telephone rings and she has to break off their chat to answer it. 'Good morning, welcome to the Eldenbridge Hotel, how can I help you?' she says to the person on the other end of the phone. Claire waits while Alison flicks through the huge diary on the desk. 'Yes, we have a double room available on Saturday. Would you like me to book you in?' She scribbles the name of the guest in the book. 'Thank you very much. I'll look forward to seeing you on Saturday.'

Claire is pleased that she is friendly and outgoing. She is exactly the type of person Jack may have opened up to. Surely she would have asked him the purpose of his stay. He would have been traumatised by the events of Thursday, and probably told her he was there on the recommendation of the police after the unfortunate and tragic murder of his mother. But would he have gone on to tell a complete stranger that he was the one who had killed her? Extremely unlikely. Before the investigation has started, Claire is beginning to think she is wasting her time. She should go back to her office now and tackle the pile of unopened post that grows and grows every day, instead of wasting her time looking for people Jack confessed to.

'Sorry about that,' says Alison. 'How can I help you?'

'I'm here to ask some questions about a man called Jack Chadwick who stayed with you last week…'

'Yes,

I remember him. What a creep,' says Alison. She visibly shudders. 'I didn't like him at all. He kept looking at my chest when I was talking to him.' She looks down at her name badge which is positioned directly over her right breast.

'I'm not defending him, not one little bit, but is it possible he was looking at your name badge, rather than your chest?' asks Claire.

Alison laughs and begins to unfasten the badge. 'Yeah, maybe I'll move it a bit higher up.' She unpins the badge and positions it just under the neck seam of her t-shirt. 'There, that's better,' she says. 'Although I'd rather not have to wear one at all. It makes holes in all my best stuff.'

'Can you tell me about Jack? Did you talk to him much?'

'No, I avoided him wherever possible, to be honest. I had to knock on his door to tell him the cleaning company had phoned and left a message for him, but other than that, I didn't talk to him.'

'What was the message from the cleaning company?'

'That they had finished cleaning his house and he could go home. I thought he'd be pleased. I thought I was knocking on his door with good news, but he had a face like thunder and started going on about how he didn't want to go home.'

'Did he say why?'

'Just that he wasn't ready. To be honest, I came back to reception pretty sharpish. I didn't want to be alone with him in a hotel corridor, you know what I mean? I didn't feel safe, and there was nobody else about.'

'Yes, I do know what you mean. So, did he tell you why he was here?'

'No, I wasn't on duty when he checked in. I knew it was something to do with a crime. I presumed he had been the victim of a burglary or something. They trash the place sometimes, don't they? I thought that was why his house had to be cleaned.'

'So you didn't know that his mother had been murdered?'

'No! Oh my God, that's awful.' She puts her hands over her mouth and Claire can see the beginnings of tears in her eyes. 'I had no idea. Well, it's no wonder he was acting a bit odd. He must have been in shock or something. The poor bloke. I feel sorry for him now. I should have been a bit more kind.'

'Yes, it isn't easy for him. His mother was killed on Thursday evening. It was a shock to him. I wondered if he said anything to anyone about it.'

'He didn't say anything to me. I didn't know anything like that had happened. I don't read the papers – they annoy me. I don't want to look at other women's tits on page three, thank you very much.'

'I'm with you on that,' says Claire. 'Is there anyone else here who had contact with Jack? I need to ask whether he mentioned anything of significance to anyone, you know, anything that will help the police investigation.'

'Of course, of course, I'll get Bill for you. He's in the back office.'

But Bill is of no further help than Alison. He can remember Jack being in the hotel; he was on duty when Jack asked whether he could have his room for another night. He remembers him being perfectly polite, but they didn't engage in any conversation.

Claire leaves the hotel no further towards helping Adam than when she went in.

Angela

Angela bangs on Claire's front door persistently with her fist. Even when she sees the light go on in the hall and she sees an outline of a woman walking towards the front door, she doesn't stop. Even when she hears someone shout, 'Hold on! Hold on! I'm coming!' she continues to hammer.

The door is opened by Sophia. Angela barges past her and marches into the living room. 'Where is she?' she says, when she sees the room is empty.

Sophia closes the living room door behind her, keeping Angela and her barely disguised temper contained. 'Don't you dare come into my house shouting and screaming like this,' she says. She points a finger at Angela's chest. 'This is my house and I have a baby asleep upstairs, so calm yourself down, or piss off.'

'Quite the little tiger protecting your cub, aren't you? Get out of my way and tell me where she is.'

'No, I will not tell you where she is. What do you want, anyway?' says Sophia.

Angela ignores the question, grabs Sophia by her upper arms, and pushes her out of the way. She is easy to move. She weighs next to nothing. 'Is she in the kitchen, or upstairs? You might as well tell me because I'll find her.'

Angela pulls the living room door open and is about to storm into the kitchen, but Trevor blocks her way. The narrow hall is the perfect width for one person. 'Don't think I won't pick you up and move you, old man, because I will if I have to,' she snarls.

'I might not be as young as I once was, but I've spent time in the Royal Tank Regiment and I have come across many more frightening adversaries than you. I suggest you calm down and speak to us in a proper manner, or else you will find yourself on your backside on the pavement outside in the cold.'

Angela takes a deep breath and tries to keep her anger at a manageable level. 'I need to speak to Claire. That bitch has told the coppers something that Jack told me in confidence. I need a word with her.'

'Get a grip of yourself, Angela. You can't bully Claire, or any of us for that matter,' says Sophia. 'What's done is done. Claire isn't here anyway, so you'd better leave.'

'She didn't have any right to go shouting her mouth off to the police,' says Angela. Her face is inches away from Sophia's. Trevor steps between them. He reaches across and places his left hand on Angela's right shoulder and gently pushes her backwards. It has the desired effect and she takes a step back.

The front door is still open and everyone turns when they hear the metal gate being pushed open. Claire is running up the garden path towards the house, her face red, her eyes wide with horror.

'There's a fire! There's a fire!' she shouts. 'Jack's house is on fire. The police and fire brigade are there.'

'Is he okay?' asks Angela, running down the hall towards Claire. 'Did you see him?'

'No, I didn't. Some of the neighbours are outside, being kept back by the police. They're still trying to get the fire under control. The flames are sky-high though. If he was in there, he won't be getting out alive.'

Thursday 13th October 1976

Cheryl

Cheryl stands outside Lancashire Prison, her heart pounding hard and her stomach churning with anxiety. She had forced herself to eat some toast with the children before she took them to school this morning, and she had made herself a milky coffee but she is now regretting her decision. She feels sick.

She has only ever seen a prison on the television and is surprised by how striking it is. She feels tiny standing in front of the red brick building, with its barred windows and huge double doors, painted the colour of a raven's feathers. The wall around the prison is taller than a house and stretches down the road as far as she can see. On either side of the double doors stands two imposing towers, with three floors of narrow windows, each one topped with a pointed grey slate roof. It looks like a city centre castle. An image of the Tower of London flashes into her mind, and she forces herself to dismiss it.

On any other day, she would have been impressed by the building's architecture and taken an interest in its Victorian history. But now, she just wants to get inside, get the visit over with, and get back home. She can't bear to think of her poor husband being held inside and she knows she will break down in tears the moment she sees him, despite her willingness to stay strong.

She walks to a door at the side of the left-hand tower and rings the bell. After a moment, it is opened by a surly prison guard, dressed in a black overcoat and a peaked cap with the words *Her Majesty's Prison* on the front, as though there can be any confusion as to where they are. He takes the folded Visiting Order from her and ushers her towards another member of staff waiting at a locked gate. He doesn't say hello, goodbye, please or thank you, or acknowledge her in any way. Customer service and politeness are obviously not a part of his job training.

Feeling like a prisoner herself, Cheryl is led to a locker room, where she is ordered to put all her belongings, including her coat and scarf, into a locker. She is then led to another locked steel gate where she is told to stand with her legs apart and her arms outstretched while a young female officer, who appears to be as proficient in hostility as her colleagues, carries out a brief body search. Cheryl closes her eyes, fighting back tears, and tries to imagine she is at the airport, on her way to Spain for their holidays. The children are behind her, laughing with Adam because she is the one to have been chosen by the security staff who are carrying out random searches.

In the visitors' waiting room, she scans the space for a seat. Two long rows of grey chairs, all bolted to the floor by their metal legs, face another two rows. Their hard wooden seats, worn by years of visitors, gleam under the harsh fluorescent lights. Between the rows, an assortment of plastic toys and broken pieces of Lego are scattered about the floor. Most of the seats are already occupied by other female visitors, some with children and some with small babies. Cheryl finds an empty chair at the end of one of the front rows. She looks at her watch. There are only five minutes before the start of visiting time. She can't bear to be in this place much longer, even though she has only just arrived.

She seems to be the only visitor who is traumatised by this experience. Is this because it is her first time? Surely the next visit will be easier. Some of these women could have been here dozens of times, if not hundreds of times. They must get hardened to it.

She tries not to, but she can't help judging the other women, as she looks around. Nobody had made an effort to dress up, from what she could see. Some of them are wearing makeup, but most of them are not. She tries not to stare at the woman sitting directly opposite. Her greasy hair is pulled back from her face and tied in a high ponytail. Her deep-set eyes are staring, unblinking, at the floor; the grey circles beneath them failing to hide the fact that she isn't sleeping well or eating enough vegetables. Her jeans are dirty and threadbare at one of the knees, and a small hole has started to appear at the big toe of her once-white pumps. She could have been pretty, in another life. A few good meals, some sun on her face, and a shower would transform her.

I am not like these people, Cheryl tells herself. I shouldn't be here. This shouldn't be my life. My husband isn't like their husbands. He shouldn't be here either.

She begins to cry again and wipes at her running mascara with her finger. This is why the other women aren't wearing makeup, she thinks. She doesn't want Adam to see her looking like this. He will be upset. She is about to tell the guard she wants to leave, that she has changed her mind and doesn't want to be here, when a bell sounds to indicate the start of visiting time. A door at the opposite end of the room is opened by another guard and the visitors surge forwards, emptying out into a much larger visiting room, which is furnished with dozens of small tables, with one wooden chair on one side of the table, and two identical chairs on the other.

She follows the crowd into the room and searches for table number nine, which is thankfully at the side of the room, up against the wall. She is suddenly hot and claustrophobic, the polo-neck sweater she is wearing isn't helping, and she is thankful for the position of the table. She could not have coped with being in the middle of the room.

Suddenly the prisoners are filing in, one after another, searching for their girlfriends, wives, and children. She sees him, her handsome, charming, and wonderful husband, dragging his feet towards her. He is dressed in cheap blue cotton trousers and a blue ill-fitting shirt, identical to the other prisoners.

'You're so pale and thin,' she says as he reaches her and sits at the table. 'Is that a bruise under your right eye?'

He touches the delicate skin under his eye which met with someone's fist in the canteen yesterday. 'No, I'm fine, stop worrying. I can't have got any thinner, all I seem to be eating is bread and potatoes.' He lets out a hollow laugh heavy with sadness.

Cheryl wants to run from the room, down the narrow corridors, and escape into the fresh air. There is no oxygen in this room. It smells of disinfectant, stained clothes, and unwashed men. It smells of lies, deceit, greed, and dishonesty. It smells of murder. Neither she nor Adam should be here.

'How have you been, darling? I have missed you,' says Adam. 'How are the boys?'

'I'm fine,' she says. 'The boys are fine too. I haven't told them where you are. I've said you're away with the bishop doing some work.'

'That's probably wise,' he says. 'For now, at least.'

She feels as though she hasn't heard his voice for months. She has almost forgotten what he sounds like. He reaches across the table and stills her nervous hands with his. They feel dry, like crumbling autumn leaves, and his fingernails are bitten short.

'No touching!' barks a guard as he paces the gaps between the tables.

Cheryl snatches her hands away.

'I don't know how you're coping,' she whispers. 'How can people shout at us like that when we've done nothing wrong?'

They sit for a moment in silence. So much to say to each other, but nothing comes to mind.

'My solicitor is good,' says Adam eventually. 'He came to see me yesterday morning. He said the case against me isn't strong at all, but the main thing stumbling block is that I can't prove my alibi.'

'We need to trace that couple,' says Cheryl. 'I looked in your diary and there was nothing written there for Thursday night. I searched in the bin and everywhere I could think of for a note you may have screwed up and put in the bin. Can you remember where you wrote their names and addresses down? I'll go and see them. They will confirm where you were, won't they?'

Adam blinks rapidly but he can't stop the tears as they

fall down his cheeks. 'I don't know how…'

She interrupts him. 'Please don't cry, darling. Don't worry about anything now. I hate to see you upset. I'll have another search of the vestry and I won't stop searching until I've been over every inch of it. It has got to be there somewhere.'

'But I didn't…'

'Oh, I almost forgot to tell you,' she says. She always talks too much when she's nervous. She is aware she is doing it and she doesn't mean to keep interrupting Adam, but she won't be able to listen to him and concentrate on his words until her own have all tumbled out. 'There has been a fire in the village. Jack's house has burned down. There's nothing left of it, it is practically a shell.'

'What do you mean? Completely burned down?'

'Yes, and Eve Hardy's house has lots of smoke damage, too. She has moved in with her sister temporarily.'

'Is everyone safe?'

'No,' she says. 'I'm sorry to be the bearer of bad news, but Jack Chadwick died in the fire.'

Adam allows his tears to fall freely. He is crying for himself, for his wife and children, and for Jack who lost his life less than a week after he lost his mother. 'I'll pray for him,' he says. 'That's terrible news. Was it caused by a chip pan?'

Cheryl shakes her head. 'No, as far as they can tell, the fire was started on purpose. I spoke to Claire Simons this morning, and she told me the accelerant was petrol. Apparently, they can tell from the way the fire burns, and from the smell it leaves behind, or something like that.'

'You spoke to Claire?'

'Yes, she's been really kind. She has been to see me a

couple of times since you got arrested. I told her I was coming to see you today. Adam? Are you listening?'

'Yes, yes, you absolute beauty.' He begins to laugh. 'I have remembered something. I don't know why I didn't think of it before.'

'What is it?'

'I put petrol in the car on Thursday night. It was running on empty and I put two pounds in at a petrol station on the other side of Wellington. It was a BP garage. This is the proof I need that I wasn't in Eldenbridge when Miriam died, isn't it? I can't be in two places at once.'

Cheryl wants to smile. She wants to hope that all their troubles are over, but it can't be this easy. 'I wonder if the man will remember you?' she says. 'What if he doesn't?'

'I think he will,' says Adam, 'because he made a joke about having to go to confession. I was still wearing my dog collar.'

Cheryl can smile now. 'That's wonderful,' she says. 'I'll tell Claire and ask her to go and speak to him, shall I?'

Adam shakes his head. 'I think you should ring Elena Holt at the police station and ask her to do it. Then she can't accuse us of interfering with a witness or anything.'

'Will she do it, do you think? What if she says it is too late, that the case against you is already being prepared?'

'All you can do is ask her and if she says no, then ask Claire to go. But this might be my only chance to prove where I was on Thursday night.'

Friday 14th October 1976

Elena

'Good morning team. I hope you have all had a good rest. Back to work and raring to go, eh?' Elena is standing in front of the blackboard in the incident room. Geoff, Harry, and Rahul are perched on various tables. Imogen has reluctantly been sent back to uniform patrol now that an arrest has been made. 'Operation Bulldog is far from over. We need to make sure we have a watertight case for court.'

'Agreed,' says Geoff. 'We don't want our inspector having egg on her face, do we lads? You know what it's like having a female in charge. Most of the men at the top are waiting for her to fall, so let's make sure she doesn't.'

'Here, here,' says Harry.

'Geoff, I'm not sure if you're being chivalrous or you're taking the piss,' says Elena.

'Just telling it as it is,' says Geoff. 'I'm not allowed to be chivalrous these days. Women Libbers don't like it. Seriously though, we're all behind you, boss.'

'Thank you, Geoff.' Elena is genuinely touched by his show of support. 'Okay, let's go through the evidence we have so far. We have an unsigned Section Nine statement from Adam Hargreaves following his interviews. We need to change that situation. We can't rock up at court with an unsigned statement. Harry, can you re-word it and get it to a satisfactory state where he's happy to sign it?'

'Yes, boss,' says Harry.

'Take out the sentences about him telling lies to the police. I can't see him admitting to that in a month of Sundays. Write that he was mistaken. But make sure your own statement uses the word 'lies', as I will, too. Because he did lie, there's no doubt about it.' Harry nods and makes a note in his notepad. 'We've got the pathology report confirming the victim died from two blows to the head with a blunt instrument and I'm going to speak to the pathologist and ask him, in his view, could the victim have died if she was hit with any of the heavy objects in the church, given the fact that Adam Hargreaves' fingerprints were not found on the saucepan. Regarding the statements from all the neighbours, I know they were asked if they saw anybody hanging around the cul-de-sac that they didn't know, any suspicious activity that they noticed, but I want them to think about the times that Reverend Hargreaves visited the house. He reckons he was a regular visitor, which would explain his fingerprints about the place, but I'm not so sure about that. Why would he visit Miriam at home if he saw her twice a week at church? It doesn't make sense. Rahul, can you attend to that?'

'Yes, boss.'

'Okay, so that brings me to the threatening note that Hargreaves wrote to Miriam Chadwick. I am the one who picked it up from the floor in the church, so my statement will cover that but Geoff, when you do yours, can you include a paragraph about the vicar's demeanour? He didn't want us to read it, did he?'

'No, he didn't. And now we know why. If it wasn't for that note, he wouldn't have had to confess to his little love affair with Claire, would he? I'm telling you, you can't trust anyone these days. Even vicars are playing away.'

'Does that mean you are, Sergeant? Is there something you want to get off your chest?' asks Harry.

Geoff laughs. 'Absolutely not. I wouldn't cheat on my beautiful wife. Why go out for a burger when you've got a steak at home?'

'You're disgusting, all of you,' says Elena. 'Now then, settle down, we've got lots more work to do before we can relax. I've got some news that some of you may not be aware of yet. Jack Chadwick died on Wednesday night in a house fire at 8 Southgate Drive. The preliminary report from the Fire Brigade suggests the fire was caused by petrol being thrown around the downstairs rooms.' Elena reads from the report. 'I quote "It seems that carpets in the living room and the hallway were liberally doused with Four Star petrol. The remains of a metal container were discovered on the first step of the staircase to the upper floor. The container was placed neatly, next to the wall and it did not appear to have been discarded."'

'Bloody hell,' says Geoff. 'Where was Jack when this happened?'

'He was found upstairs in his bed,' says Elena.

'What's odd about this,' says Harry, 'is that the fire started in the middle of the afternoon. My parents still live in Eldenbridge, so I found out about it from them. What I can't understand is why he was in bed at that time of the day. I mean, if he hadn't been, maybe he would have stood a chance of escaping out the back door.'

Elena shakes her head. 'I don't think he wanted to escape. The house was locked up. Both the front and back doors were locked and bolted from the inside. This isn't a case of arson, if that's what you are thinking. Jack did this to his own house. This is a case of suicide.'

'Now it makes sense,' says Harry. 'Considering what he told Angela Bennett.'

'What do you mean?' asks Geoff.

'I was about to tell you,' says Elena. 'Jack Chadwick was brought to the police station on Wednesday by Claire Simons. Apparently, he had spoken to Angela Bennett the day before and had confessed that he was the one to have killed his mother. Angela Bennett told Claire, who persuaded him to come to the station to make a statement. However, before you all want to rush to the prison and set the vicar free, by the time Jack got here, he had clearly changed his mind and told us exactly the same story that he told us on the day of the murder.'

'I asked him outright to confirm he had killed her, and he said no,' says Harry.

'You were in the interview room?' asks Geoff.

'You had already gone home,' says Elena. 'He didn't arrive here until late, so I asked Harry to help me out.'

'You should have called me at home, boss. I would have come back and beaten a confession out of him,' says Geoff.

Elena doesn't reply, but a small part of her regrets not asking Geoff to be part of the interview team. He might be heavy-handed and aggressive, but he generally gets the job done. Now they have nothing, except a potentially innocent man languishing in a prison cell awaiting a trial that could take nine months to be listed in court. 'Yes, I probably should,' she says. 'That was an error on my part. I thought his confession would be easy. I've now got the unenviable job of explaining this fiasco to the superintendent this morning.'

'So to sum it up, without Angela Bennett's evidence, we are up Shit Creek without a paddle,' says Geoff.

'Exactly,' says Elena. 'How do you feel about going to see her Geoff? If your relationship, if I can call it that, has completely broken down, then I'll send someone else.'

'I hate to admit defeat, but I don't think she will talk to me. Probably best if you get someone else to do it. I know I can usually charm the birds out of the trees, but Angela Bennett is the toughest bird I've ever come across.'

'I'll speak to her myself,' says Elena. 'I've got some time this afternoon.'

A knock on the door interrupts their meeting. It is Brian from the front desk. 'Sorry to interrupt, ma'am, but there's a Mrs Cheryl Hargreaves to see you. The vicar's wife from Eldenbridge. I've put her in the interview room on the ground floor.'

'Thank you, Brian. I'll come down in a moment. Okay, team, we'll meet here again at four-thirty. It's my turn to get the treats in, so I'll take a detour to the cake shop. See you all later.'

*

Initially, Elena wasn't sure whether to believe Cheryl Hargreaves or not when she told her about the mysterious witness who could now support the vicar's alibi. After all, she would probably do anything for her husband and it is not unheard of for wives to tell lies to get their husbands his Get Out of Jail Free card. But there was something about Cheryl's persona that made her change her mind. Not just because she is the vicar's wife, but because she seems to be a genuinely nice person, whose world has been turned upside down through no fault of her own.

Cheryl told Elena she could have driven to the petrol station herself, or asked Claire to go on her behalf, to speak to anyone there who remembers putting petrol in a vicar's car on Thursday night, but she said she would rather the police go instead. When she explained that it was Adam's suggestion, so neither of them could be accused of interfering with a witness, Elena began to question whether he had been telling the truth all along. A tiny nagging voice in her head was telling her that Adam and Cheryl Hargreaves were both decent people. Yes, Adam was having an illicit affair, but that didn't mean he was a cold-blooded murderer.

Geoff was the one who had jumped in and arrested Adam, but Elena could have released him after the interview. She should have released him. She didn't need to charge him. She knew he wouldn't abscond. She should have taken her time, gathered some more evidence, and made a more informed decision. Maybe if Jack had confessed to the killing in an interview, with a little persuasion from Geoff, things would be different.

There was no doubt about it, she had been pressured to get an early result, partly because the case had made it into a national newspaper - First Murder in English Village in Two Hundred Years - and partly because she was so anxious to make a good impression with her superior officers.

Now, she has a chance of putting it right. If she can get a signed statement from someone at the petrol station, and she can persuade Angela Bennett to give a statement about what Jack told her, she stands a chance of getting the case against the vicar discontinued.

She parks her car at the side of the petrol station, out of the way of the two pumps, and goes into the small shop, which is little more than a concrete shed. A middle-aged man in greasy overalls is stacking shelves with tins of engine oil. She shows him her warrant card. 'My name is Detective Inspector Elena Holt. I wonder if I could ask you and anyone else who works here a couple of questions.'

The man straightens up and rubs his right hand on the leg of his overalls. He holds it out and Elena shakes it. 'Pleased to help the strong arm of the law whenever I can,' he says. 'I've got a nephew in the force, down in London. What can I do for you, detective?'

'Can you tell me whether you were working last Thursday, the 7th of October?'

The man nods. 'Aye, I work Monday to Friday.'

'Can you tell me what time you work, when you start and when you finish?'

'I'm not in trouble, am I?' The man laughs.

'No, not at all. Someone has given us an alibi and I need to check it out. You may or may not be able to remember him coming to get some petrol.'

'Rightie oh, well I usually start at eight in the morning and close around six in the evening.'

'Can you remember seeing this man?' Elena shows him the photograph of Adam brought to the station by Cheryl. It is a photograph of him in church wearing his dog collar and cassock. 'He may not have been wearing the full uniform, but I'm led to believe he was wearing the dog collar at the time he spoke to someone from this garage.'

The man nods enthusiastically. 'Aye, I remember him. We had a joke while I was putting the petrol in for him. I told him I had sinned and hadn't been to confession for a while. He laughed and said he wasn't a Catholic priest, but if I was truly sorry, God would still love me. Nice bloke he was. Very pleasant. I told him I wasn't bothered about whether God loved me or not, I just didn't want to end up in Hell's fiery furnace.' The man laughs at his joke.

'I know it might be difficult, but can you remember what time he was here?'

'It's not difficult at all, I can tell you exactly what time he was here. I have everything written down in my ledger. Follow me.' With a practiced motion, he unhooks a latch on the counter and swings the counter flap upward to allow access behind it. Stepping aside, he gestures for Elena to follow him into the narrow space of neatly stacked stock and piles of paperwork. A sales ledger lies open on a grimy shelf attached to the wall. The paper reeks of oil and petrol. The man flicks the pages back to the 7th of October. 'Here you go,' he says. 'Five-forty. He had two pounds worth of petrol and paid with a cheque. He said he had rushed out of the house and had forgotten to bring any cash.'

'I don't suppose you can remember the name of the bank, so we could trace the cheque?' asks Elena. 'Not that I don't trust your ledger, but we like to take a belts and braces approach where possible.'

'I don't remember the name, but it will still be here. I haven't had time to go to the bank yet.' The man opens a drawer underneath the till, takes out a handful of cheques, and sifts through them. 'Here it is. The Trustee Savings Bank, two pounds only.'

Elena looks at the cheque which is clearly signed *Rev A Hargreaves* and dated 7th of October 1976. It appears that the vicar has an alibi after all.

Cheryl

For the first time in a week, Cheryl is beginning to feel optimistic. Adam was quietly confident that the man at the petrol station would remember him, as they laughed about the man not wanting to end up in Hell because he hadn't been to confession for a while. 'I know there aren't many vicars in the area,' Adam had said. 'He's got to remember me.' Also, the fact that Adam had paid for the petrol with a cheque was extremely fortuitous. Tomorrow, she can go to the bank and ask them to send her an up-to-date statement. The cheque will show on there, clear as day.

She is looking forward to a nice cup of tea and a sit down with a magazine before she has to collect the boys from school. As she waits for the kettle to boil, she picks up the post from behind the front door. A handwritten letter addressed to *The Vicar, Adam Hargreaves* has the postmark from Eldenbridge Post Office, dated 12th October. Who on earth would post a letter at the Post Office and bother to buy a first-class stamp when they could have walked five minutes and hand-delivered the letter themselves? She won't see Adam for another week, and she is sure he won't mind if she opens it. She goes into his office and finds the letter-opener on his desk. She slips it underneath the paper and rips the envelope open. The letter is written on good quality cream-coloured Basildon Bond notepaper. Wednesday 12th October is written in the top left-hand corner of the page.

> *Dear Reverend Hargreaves,*
> *If I was in church I would go onto my knees and confess to you and God about what I have done. I never meant for you to be arrested for murder. You should not be in prison. I should be.*
> *I am the killer, not you.*
> *I ask for God's forgiveness for what I have done.*
> *I also ask for your forgiveness for what I have done.*
> *On Thursday last week I killed my mum in our kitchen. She was angry and was shouting at me and I became as angry as her. I picked up the pan of potato hash and I smashed her on the head with it. I didn't mean to kill her at first. But something made me do it. I just wanted her to shut up going on and on and on at me.*
> *But when she was on the floor, she looked at me with so much anger. If I didn't kill her she would have killed me. So I hit her again and then she died.*
> *I don't want to go to prison. I told the police I was out at the shop and a burglar must done it. This was not true. When I came back from the shop she was still alive but then I killed her.*
> *I am now going to kill myself and I hope you can get out of prison.*
> *I am sorry I did it and I confess to God,*
> *Signed Jack Chadwick*

Cheryl reads the letter again to make sure she has understood it. The lack of commas and poor grammar don't make it easy to read, but the message is clear. This is the evidence she needs to get Adam's name cleared. It has arrived at just the right time, like manna from Heaven.

Angela

Angela is serving a customer when the postman arrives. He waves the letter in the air by way of a greeting and leaves it on the corner of the counter.

She takes the cash from the customer, hands her the bouquet of flowers, and waits for her to leave before she opens the letter. She is just about to take the letter from the envelope when she rushes to the door and locks it. She needs to be uninterrupted. She has a feeling that the letter is from Jack.

A lump forms in her throat as she sees the content of the letter and the cream-coloured paper she could imagine Jack buying from the Post Office especially for this task.

Dear Angela,

I am sorry I told you what I did the other night. I am not sorry because you told Claire. I forgive you for telling Claire. But I am sorry you had to know. I think you liked my mum even though you said you didn't. I know you have been upset about her being killed.

I did not mean to kill her but when I had hit her once I knew I had to hit her again. She would have killed me. You know that. She was mean to me all the time and I am not sorry she is dead but I am sorry the vicar has been put in jail. He has not done anything wrong. This is not JUSTICE.

I have written a letter to him telling him I am sorry and I hope he gets out of jail soon.

I don't want to go to prison. I would rather die so I can go to

Heaven and be with Mum.
You are a good friend and I love you.
Love from Jack

Angela manages to hold back the tears until she reads the last line. She did love Jack and she would have taken care of him. Now it is too late to tell him. The thought of him setting fire to his own house so that he could die is so dreadful, she doesn't want to contemplate it. She can only hope that he died of smoke inhalation before the flames got to him.

Elena

Elena can see Angela inside the shop leaning on the counter, reading a letter. She rattles the door, but it doesn't open.

'I'm closed,' shouts Angela. Her eyes look red and swollen and she has streaks of mascara down her cheeks.

'I need to talk to you about Jack,' says Elena through the door. 'Please let me in.'

Elena can see Angela contemplating what to do. She has had enough dealings with the police for her to know she won't be left alone until she co-operates. Angela wipes her face with the back of her hand, pulls back the bolt from the top of the door, and opens it. 'What do you want?' she says. 'Now's not a good time.'

'I won't keep you long,' says Elena. 'But I need to speak to you about Jack. I need a witness statement about what he told you. I know he confessed to killing Miriam, but at the police station, he denied it. He must have got scared.' Angela is looking at Elena as though she is a piece of dirt on her shoe.

Angela walks to the counter and hands the letter to Elena. 'I don't need to give you a statement. Everything you need is right here.' She taps on the paper. 'He says he also wrote to the vicar, so you might want to call round there and see if it has arrived.' Angela swipes at more tears. 'He was a good person, you know. He didn't deserve the treatment that bitch of a mother gave him, and he certainly didn't deserve to die so young. He wasn't yet thirty years old.'

Elena reads the letter twice, unable to believe what she is seeing. The poor man. So frightened of prison that he died the most horrible death imaginable. 'I'll need to take this back to the station,' she says. She folds it quickly and puts it back in the envelope before Angela has a chance to grab it out of her hand. But Angela seems too upset and deflated to put up a fight.

She thanks her for her time and makes her way across to the vicarage to see Cheryl.

EPILOGUE
Friday 31st December 1976

Adam

Adam and Cheryl haven't been out for a drink on New Year's Eve since before the boys were born, but the invitation to the private party at the Dog and Duck in the village was too difficult for them to resist. Carol is babysitting and when they left her a couple of hours ago, she was happy and comfortable on the sofa reading Peter Pan aloud to the boys. She will be spending the night with them at the vicarage, so she can go to bed when she is tired.

'You two stay out as late as you want,' she said. 'There's no need for you to run back home as soon as midnight strikes. I'll be in bed an hour before then, so don't worry about me.'

Now as he sips his gin and tonic, Adam can see Claire across the other side of the pub. He said hello to her, like he would say hello to any other member of his congregation, but he hasn't spoken to her privately since he was released from prison. She hasn't asked to speak to him and he hasn't approached her. Both of them seem to be happy with that arrangement. Their affair was nice while it lasted, but he is glad it is over. He struggled to cope with the guilt. He will never be unfaithful again.

He is pleased to see Claire looking happy. She is with her sister, Sophia, and Detective Inspector Holt. 'Call me

Elena,' she said earlier when she saw him. He shook her hand and wished her a Happy New Year. He offered to buy her a drink and she said thank you, she would have a glass of red wine.

He is pleased that Claire has made it up with her. She told him about how she had lost touch with Stephen's sister after he died, and it seemed sad that she would lose her fiancé and her best friend at the same time.

He turns to his wife and kisses her forehead tenderly. Cheryl clinks her wine glass on the side of his glass of gin. 'Happy New Year, darling,' she says.

THE END

Author's Note

I hope you enjoyed this murder mystery and the fact that it is set in the 1970s. For those of you – like me – who are old enough to remember the era, I hope it gave you an element of nostalgia. For those younger ones, you can only imagine what life was like without mobile phones and the internet, and when most homes didn't have a telephone or a car. Can you imagine having to report a violent crime and having to leave your home and run down the street to the phone box to ring 999?

I was ten in 1976 and remember there being a phone box at the end of our street, close to the corner shop. I was regularly sent to the shop for bits and bobs and often, the phone would be ringing as I passed it. When I answered it, it would invariably be a young woman asking to speak to Carl Barrowclough. Carl was a handsome twenty-year-old – think Barry Gibb – who wore his shirt unbuttoned to his waist, with wide trousers and platform shoes. He was the older brother of my best friend, Linda, who lived around the corner.

I don't know how many people left the phone dangling to go and knock on Carl's door to tell him he was wanted, but I certainly did. Carl had his pick of dates, and I don't remember him rushing to get to the phone.

Ten years later, I joined the police force in Lancashire and was stationed at Lancaster. Although times had moved on from the seventies, the organization was still very old-fashioned and set in its ways, and many of my male colleagues were very sexist. They didn't see anything wrong in their behaviour – that's just how it was back then. I, as a young female, was protected by them and was shielded from the more violent criminals. On a nightshift, I was asked to work in 'comms' which meant that I answered the phone rather than walking the street on my own. I was happy to do it, but I knew that my long term career would suffer if I wasn't treated as an equal.

In the book, when Mrs Chadwick is murdered and Elena needs an extra pair of hands to help her with the investigation, I gave her a female officer, although back in my police station, I doubt that would have happened. The CID room was filled with men, and you had to be 'one of the boys' in order to climb the career ladder. This meant joining in with their banter and rude jokes and going for a drink in the pub at the end of every shift.

I wanted to be a detective – I was pretty good at interviewing people, I thought, and I was a methodical worker, although I wasn't keen on the drinking culture that accompanied the role. I told my sergeant, who practically laughed in my face and told me that they already had a woman in CID. They didn't need another.

It never occurred to me to fight him. The organization was too big, so I left and went off to study law instead.

I know that Elena would have been a special person and would have had to work extremely hard to be a detective inspector in 1976. I was only aware of one female officer of that rank when I worked there. She was in the Family Liaison Unit. Even then, I remember thinking that it was a cop out (pardon the pun), and that she was the token woman who had been promoted, and that she was given the female role of working mainly with families and children.

But the joy of writing fiction is that I now have the ability to change things. I can have women in seats of power, although I had to create Geoff, a man who is clearly uncomfortable with Elena's position.

Now, I am in the wonderful position of beginning to plan my next novel. Should I remain in the past, or write something contemporary? If you have a view, please let me know via my social media.

If you have enjoyed this book, I would greatly appreciate it if you would write a review on Amazon. It really helps with future sales.

Thank you so much.

Now, if you'd like to sample another of my books, continue reading Chapter One of my historical novel, An Unfortunate Situation, which is set in 1908. Violet, a housemaid, is pregnant by Ernest Compton, the son of her employers. She hopes to marry him, but instead, Mrs Compton makes her a cruel offer – sell the baby to them, to be brought up by a childless family member, or be cast out with no money and no reference.

Chapter One
September 1908 - Violet

I am standing in front of the mistress in the drawing room, with a racing heart and sweaty palms, while she sips her tea. I can sense that within the next few minutes, I am going to be dismissed, sent away from Compton Hall in disgrace.

'Sit down, Violet,' she says.

I perch on the edge of the opposite sofa, thankful for the barrier of the low table between us. I put my hands underneath my thighs for a moment, but withdraw them quickly and place them on my lap. My right hand clings onto my left thumb, as I learned to do in school when Sister Beatrice would walk slowly between the small wooden desks and rap any child sharply on the knuckles if they were judged to be fidgeting.

Mrs Compton raises her eyes from her cup and stares into the fire. The black hearth that I had scrubbed on my hands and knees at six o'clock this morning gleams like polished obsidian and the fire is perfectly lit. Not too many logs have been used. I know that the mistress doesn't like the room to be too hot during the day, September being such an unpredictable month.

'Something has come to my attention,' she says. She hasn't yet looked me in the eyes and continues to examine the dancing flames in the grate. I follow her gaze and wait for her to continue. 'I understand that you are in an unfortunate situation…'

We are interrupted by the intrusion of Mr Compton. I shouldn't call it an intrusion; in all fairness, this is his house. But he is so seldom around that when he is, it feels alien. When he is at home, he moves about the house in a cloud of cigar smoke, which follows him to his study, where he shuts himself in for long periods of time. Often he is alone, but sometimes male visitors in black suits and bowler hats accompany him. Raised voices can be heard through the door and whichever maid delivers their refreshments, does so cautiously and with anticipation.

I jump up as soon as he appears, as though my legs are burnt by the rich velvet fabric of the sofa.

'Where are we up to?' barks Mr Compton.

He reaches the fireplace in a few long strides and stands with his back to it. The cigar smoke swirls behind him before it finally catches him up. He blows it away and Mrs Compton coughs gently. He rolls his eyes and waves his hand in front of him until the smoke dissipates. I watch as a slurry of ash falls from his cigar and lands on the rug. It isn't my rug. What do I care if it's ruined? But the careless act, the act of a privileged man who has never had to count his pennies, or watch his tired wife beating the dust from the rug, annoys me and I concentrate hard to keep a neutral countenance.

'We haven't yet started,' says Mrs Compton. 'Sit down, Violet, please.' She finally looks at me.

I look over to Mr Compton, who is examining the burning end of his cigar, concentrating on blowing onto it to fuel the ember. As he shows no objection, I sit down again and wait for my employers to decide my fate.

'I was just explaining to Violet that we are aware of her unfortunate situation,' says Mrs Compton.

Mr Compton doesn't look at me but nods and takes another puff of his cigar. 'Has the girl seen a doctor yet?'

'I don't know, dear, I haven't had the chance to ask her yet,' answers Mrs Compton. 'Well?'

'No, ma'am,' I reply. I can feel a blush rising from my neck into my cheeks. I'm not sure what I was expecting, but I certainly wasn't expecting the conversation to begin in such a personal manner.

'So you might be wrong then?' asks Mr Compton. He lifts his chin and peers down his nose at me as he awaits the reply, willing me to defy him. But defy him I must.

'No, sir, there's no mistake.' I have missed four of my monthlies, but I keep this private information to myself.

'I would call it a huge mistake,' he bellows. 'And are you sure that the baby is Ernest's?'

I have heard Mr Compton's loud voice many times reverberating through the walls of the house but I have never personally been on the receiving end, and the shock of his accusation brings tears to my eyes. I assure him that the baby may be a mistake, in that it was unintended, but there is no mistake as to the father. It most definitely belongs to his son. I want to tell him that Ernest is happy, that he loves me, and that I love him, but I bite my tongue.

Mr Compton storms over to the window and looks out onto the garden. He straightens the long curtain and I wait for another outburst in which he tells me that my work is shoddy. He has been known to walk into a room that has just been cleaned and run his fingers along the woodwork and the mantelpiece, searching for dust.

'Darling, I'm sure you have better things to do,' says Mrs Compton. 'Why don't you finish your work in your study and I shall speak to Violet. I'll ring for Cook to bring you some tea and cake, shall I?'

Mr Compton hovers on the edge of acquiescence before he finally agrees and leaves the room.

'Now then,' says Mrs Compton. 'Shall we begin again?'

'Yes, ma'am,' I manage to say between sobs that have suddenly overtaken my capacity to speak.

'Now, now, Violet,' says Mrs Compton. 'You must dry your eyes.'

I take out a clean handkerchief from my pocket and wipe my eyes and my nose. I take deep breaths and ready myself, for by now I am pretty sure that Mr and Mrs Compton are not going to welcome me into the bosom of their family as their future daughter-in-law. I wait for Mrs Compton to dismiss me and wonder whether it would be impertinent to ask her for a reference. I look towards the window and thank the Lord that the threatening clouds haven't yet dropped any rain. I might be able to make it to the train station before the storm which is inevitably coming.

'Violet, we need to have a serious conversation,' says Mrs Compton.

'Yes, ma'am,' I reply.

Since that evening in early Spring when Philip caught me and Ernest in the downstairs kitchen together, I have been anxiously waiting for this moment. Philip had seen Ernest's lips on my neck and his hands on my breasts as he pushed me up against the wall. He may have been forgiven for thinking that Master Compton was taking advantage of a young housemaid - as I'm sure in some houses such instances are not unknown - were it not for the giggle that escaped my lips and the fact that my fingers were wrapped around Ernest's hair as I pulled him closer towards me.

I didn't hear the kitchen door open, but I heard Philip's sharp intake of breath and I heard him slam the door shut behind him. I pushed Ernest away and rushed across the kitchen to open it, to call out to Philip, to plead with him for his discretion. But all I saw was the retreating back of the chauffeur as he scuttled down the narrow corridor, his tailcoat swishing angrily, a lamp held aloft in front of him.

'Father must be home,' said Ernest calmly, peering over my shoulder.

I turned and looked up at his face and couldn't see any traces of concern. But then again, he wouldn't be the one who would be punished for fraternising with one of the servants. He wouldn't be the one who would be dismissed from the house with no reference. I burst into tears, closed the kitchen door, and sank in despair onto one of the wooden dining chairs around the old kitchen table.

'Don't cry,' said Ernest, sitting down next to me and stroking my hand. 'You're not worried, are you? Philip won't say anything. I'll have a word with him and make sure of it.'

I couldn't speak for a moment. The thought of Ernest taking Philip to one side and pleading for his silence was abhorrent. Philip's allegiance was to Mr Compton and he alone. Everyone knew that. I snatched my hand away, lifted my apron to my face, and wiped my eyes. 'You shouldn't be down here,' I said. 'Your father will be looking for you.'

'I doubt it,' said Ernest. 'He will be drunk and he will fall into his bed within a few minutes.'

'That's where I need to be,' I said. 'I have to be up early and it's almost midnight already.'

'Then I shall accompany you,' Ernest whispered.

His words were followed by a gentle kiss on my hand. I rose to my feet and we tiptoed up the servants' stairs together, hand in hand, and silently into my bedroom at the top of the house.

Neither of us had much sleep that night, but as he curled around me in my tiny single bed, I must have drifted off to sleep at some point because I remember waking to the sound of the cockerel; a sound which ordinarily I would have cursed for waking me too early, but for which sound that day I was extremely grateful. I nudged Ernest awake and urged him to dress quickly and go back to his own room before anyone saw him.

I remember that I went about that day in a daze, daydreaming of what might be, had I been born into a different family; had I been destined to be a lady, instead of a lady's maid, or had Ernest been destined to be a gentleman's valet, instead of a gentleman. I dreamed that Ernest would tell his parents of our blossoming romance and that his parents, being the modern liberal thinkers that they were, would tell him that they could not have chosen anyone better for him. Mr Compton in an avuncular manner would say that I was intelligent and kind and pretty, and I would make the perfect wife for his young son. My years in service would not count against me, Mrs Compton would add. Quite the contrary, in fact; my skills would no doubt be useful, as I could teach my own servants how things should be done. My experience would be invaluable to the running of a household.

In reality, I know it will never be so and I constantly tell myself that, despite my intelligence and good education, I need to look for my husband elsewhere. Ernest isn't the one for me and wishing will never make it so. I need to choose someone else. Philip will make someone a fine husband one day. Being a chauffeur is a good job. He isn't much older than me and he isn't bad looking. He can be surly and grumpy, but we all have our faults. Arthur, the butcher's apprentice, who delivers fresh meat twice a week, wouldn't be a bad choice for me either. He has had an eye on me for a long time. I can tell by the way he winks at me and lingers by the door if I happen to be in the kitchen at the time of the deliveries. Cook had to shoo him away last week, telling him that he would be missed very soon by his boss if he didn't get a move on and she had lunch to make.

'Get out of the road, lad,' she had said, wafting her tea towel at him until he retreated out of the kitchen and into the yard.

But I don't want Philip or Arthur. I want Ernest.

The morning after that first night, I should have told myself that it was a once-in-a-lifetime circumstance and I should forget that it had ever happened. I had been foolish and reckless and should never have allowed a man to spend the night in my bed. I should have told myself that Ernest would undoubtedly forget it and he would move on to his next conquest, as sure as eggs are eggs. But that choice wasn't mine to make, it seemed. Ernest made sure that I didn't forget it, by seeking me out the next night after dinner and kissing me again, this time in the yard by the kitchen door. And the night after that, and the night after that.

As I sit here now, I wonder how much Mrs Compton knows about what has happened between me and her son. She knows that I am carrying his child – I told Ernest a few days ago – but does she know that we are in love? He must have told her. He must have explained that when I told him the news, he was overjoyed.

Mrs Compton had sent me to Skipton to collect a pair of her shoes from the cobblers that day, and I was prepared to walk, it being a beautiful and dry Autumn day, but Ernest had offered to drive me, telling his mother about some non-existent errand that he also had in the town. She was distracted by her letter writing and didn't pay either of us too much notice. If she had, she would have seen the conspiratorial wink he gave me and my uncontrollable blushes.

Once I had collected the mistress's shoes, Ernest persuaded me to take a walk with him in the Castle Woods, and for an hour or so, I forgot that our relationship was doomed, so wrapped up was I in the moment. We held hands and I pretended that this could last forever. When finally I had to face the truth, I stopped under an old oak tree and told him that I had some important news to tell him. The leaves on the trees were the colour of dying embers. The late afternoon sun struggled bravely through the canopy but, despite its efforts, it failed to warm me and I shivered as I leaned against the trunk, despite the fact that I was wearing my overcoat.

'There's no easy way to break this news,' I said. 'So, I'll just come out and say it.'

'What is it?' said Ernest. 'You're not leaving Compton Hall, are you?'

'I'm having a baby.' I blurted out the words like a bomb and waited for the explosion. I touched my expanding tummy. 'Surely you must have noticed?'

Ernest stepped away initially. He turned his back on me and held his face in his hands. Then he sprinted back to me and swung me around in his arms, so high that my feet lifted off the ground. He laughed into my ear and told me that he loved me and that everything was going to be fine. He promised that he would speak to his parents. They would be over the moon, he said. 'There's nothing more important than family,' he said.

I hoped he was right, but am I being naive by thinking that a relationship between a working-class housemaid - albeit an educated one - the daughter of a factory worker, would ever be accepted by upper-class people such as the Comptons? Yes, maybe. Probably. But optimism combined with young love is an extremely strong force.

Now, as I try to decipher the look on Mrs Compton's face, my optimism is shrinking. I am struggling to decide whether she is angry, disappointed, and appalled, or whether she is in fact over the moon. She does not have the look of an ecstatic expectant grandmother. The chasm between us could not be greater. My plain black dress is littered with dust after a morning's work, my clogs are scuffed, my fingernails need a scrub, and the skin on my hands is dry and chapped. Mrs Compton in her high-necked blouse, decorated with delicate embroidered lace the colour of whipped cream, and her elegant cloud-grey skirt which skims black leather boots is spotlessly clean.

'Ernest told me and his father that you think the baby might be due in February, is that correct?' she says. I nod. 'It will be here before we know it. And are you well? Or are you sickly?'

'I'm quite well, thank you, ma'am. Although I tire easily.'

'Yes, that's to be expected,' she says. 'Do your parents know of your condition?'

'No, ma'am, although I expect they will do before long.'

'No, no,' says Mrs Compton with a sudden shake of her head and a wag of her index finger. 'They do not need to know.'

'I don't understand, ma'am.'

Mrs Compton puts her cup and saucer onto the table and shuffles forward in her chair. For a moment, I think that she is going to grasp my hand, but she doesn't. I still can't fathom what she's thinking. She smiles at me but her eyes are as cold as flint.

'I would like to discuss something with you, Violet,' she says. 'We have a plan and I think you will agree that it is something that will benefit both of us.'

Printed in Great Britain
by Amazon